MW01107618

**Other Books by this Author**
See Right Through Me
Puppy Love

# Hearts AND Flowers BORDER

### REVISED SECOND EDITION

L.T. Smith

# Acknowledgements

Once again, without Astrid Ohletz's dedication to the publishing profession, I doubt I would have ever seen this book published again. *Hearts and Flowers Border* was the very first story I'd ever written, and, considering we are talking a fair few years since this happened, I still worry about how she will fare in this big old world we live in. Astrid has helped to calm those fears through gentle suggestions and guidance.

Next on my "hit" list is Day Petersen. Thank you, Day. You have worked diligently—again—to make *Hearts* the best she could possibly be, and all done with an eagle eye and a ready smile. Considering editing is probably the worst part of writing, you make it seem so much better.

Now on to the front cover. Wow. And definitely WOW again. Amanda Chron—you are a genius. I absolutely love what you have done with my baby. You have made her look like she is a million dollars. I still can't believe what you managed to accomplish with my mumbled suggestions of "Erm…a flower? And erm…words?"

Finally. Thank you, reader. You have made me want to keep writing, and considering *Hearts* was my first story, through you and your support, I am hoping she won't be my last.

# Dedication

Ann and Ju. To the maddest, kindest, funniest, most supportive, wittiest sisters a girl could have. I am truly blessed to have you two watching my back.

*Part One*

## PRESENT DAY

Life, my life, was being turned upside down and inside out. For a second time.

Yesterday, I was just me—marking, planning, teaching, and bawling at kids who jacked around in class. It was all I had, all I needed. Until today.

It had been an ordinary day. I had forgotten I even had a conference scheduled until just before the tap on the door of my classroom. Still, in that split second it was as if I knew, deep down, that this disremembered appointment would hold something for me.

I think the giveaway was the way that time slowed down as the door opened. The groaning of the hinges announced the arrival of a hand, a firm, grasping hand that clutched the poor defenceless handle. The hand was at the end of a toned, tanned arm. The arm, as arms tend to be, was attached to a broad shoulder, which pinned itself to a body.

I scanned the rest of the visitor, noting the long legs and the ender hips, but it was the ice blue eyes that captured me.

Have you ever experienced the sensation of your stomach dropping into your shoes only to shoot back up into your mouth? That's what it felt like. It felt as if I had been transported back thirteen years to a time when those blue eyes became the centre of my world.

Fear gripped me. Honestly. It gripped me right around the heart, as if to squeeze the life out of it.

The room seemed to shrink; I seemed to expand. Not good.

That's all I remember.

In the blackness filling my head, I could hear a concerned voice whispering my name, but it seemed too distant to be talking to me. The voice was familiar, too familiar. Remembering what destruction it had wrought, I wanted to shut it out.

Slender, strong fingers gently stroked my face, and I knew I had to open my eyes to see whether it was all a dream.

I forced my eyes to open, then blinked away the startling light. Blurry images danced in front of me until anxious blue eyes became the focus of my attention, the centre of my world once again.

It had been ten years since I had last looked into her eyes. Ten long years of not seeing her.

With that realisation, I fainted for the second time.

## THIRTEEN YEARS PREVIOUSLY

"Fuck off, dyke!" I'd always had a way with words. "Clam smacking arse licker!"

I should warn you now—I tend to swear when I'm distressed, nervous, happy, sad, melancholy, watching telly, drunk, sober... I could go on, but I guess you get the picture.

I was sixteen years old and already had the mouth of a sailor. My vitriolic display was aimed at Justine Russell. She got on my tits. She always sucked up to the teachers, but was a complete bitch to everyone else. Finding out she had been caught with her pants down, literally, in the changing rooms with Ms "Bulldyke" Wilkins had been a serendipity. I vowed to put a "SPECIAL" in the school magazine. I even made myself a mental note to not forget the hearts and flowers border, which would attract attention.

I hated school. School was filled with two classes of people: popular and unpopular. Guess which class I fitted into. I had the dress sense of a kebab, the social skills of an amoeba, and the

nce of a dog busting for a pee. I definitely did not belong
ie prominent social circle, aka, the popular group. But then,
iidn't matter. I didn't feel I deserved to be in that group, and,
ore importantly, I didn't *want* to be.

You see, I don't think things through before I speak my mind.
My mouth had gotten me into far too many scrapes and scraps.
Consequently, I'd had more black eyes and fat lips than Mike
Tyson. This is the way of the typical Mancunian. Honestly, if
I had behaved any other way, my family would have disowned
me.

In retrospect, it's a pity they didn't.

I think I was repressed. Oppressed? Suppressed? Depressed?
One of them. Delete as applicable.

You see, I wanted to be the one in the changing rooms with...
Well, not with Bulldyke. She was—fuck—a bloke with tits and
a mullet. No. I went more for the dark haired beauties with classic features—straight nose, long black hair, tanned, lithe body,
tall. In two words—Emma Jenkins. She was hot. And she didn't
even know I existed.

It seemed as if she'd just suddenly appeared at the end of
Year 10. Where she had been until then, only God knew. Probably avoiding me, if she had any sense.

You know when time slows down and everything moves in
slow motion, like in the films? That's how it was when I first
saw her.

I was rushing to Maths...

Does that makes sense? Does anyone really rush to Maths?
But I digress.

I was walking to Maths rather quickly—that sounds better—
and she was coming down the hall toward me with the Bitches
of Eastwick, laughing, head back and laughing.

Things began to move in slow motion from that moment on.

My legs felt as if they were controlled by a puppet master.

4

They lifted slowly and then noiselessly placed themselves on the ground. I took in the whole scene. Her head was back and she was laughing, but I couldn't hear anything. Her mouth was open, displaying beautiful straight teeth encased by lips that had been formed from red velvet. Perfection. Her head slowly came forward, her closed eyes began to bud open. Fluttering black eyelashes blinked open, like she was taking in the world at that moment, to reveal blue eyes...blue, blue eyes.

I was transfixed, rooted to the spot. My breathing became erratic; my heart was pumping so hard, it bruised the inside of my chest. Numbness engulfed me. My mouth was dry, like cardboard, and I thought I was going to keel over.

Long hair fanned behind her as she flicked her raven locks over her shoulder. It appeared to stop in mid-air, like in cheesy movies, and then fall behind her. A long sleek arm raised to finger stray locks into place. She had grace of a ballerina, and the poise—strong, sure of herself.

The total opposite of me.

My eyes drifted down her body, etching every minute detail into my memory. Her skirt stopped a few inches from her knees. Tanned legs went on for miles, and my eyes thoroughly enjoyed the ride, although my stomach decided it didn't like long journeys.

My gaze seemed to focus in on something, something that seemed so out of place, so unexpected.

Doc Martens!

I shook my head to clear it. But... Doc Martens! A revelation, a complete contrast to what I was expecting. Did ballerinas wear Doc Martens? Well, they did now.

I looked back to her face and was captured by blue eyes. Her expression was hard to read, but she looked kind of startled.

Then the group was gone.

And summer arrived.

Six weeks of slob time. Perfect. And if hadn't been for spotting "the Girl in the Docs" just before school went out, I would have loved every minute of it. The image of her in the corridor replayed in my mind like a BBC rerun. I guiltily embraced every visual—hands stroking her hair, the crooked smile, the parted, glistening lips. Every time I thought of "the incident," it became a little more interesting.

The Bitches weren't there, obviously, just her and me. The school was empty...

No. I wasn't going there. Not then. Not ever.

I found that out the hard way.

# Chapter Three

I finished all my coursework in the first week, leaving time to watch total khak on the telly for the remainder of the holidays.

I did enjoy outdoor activities, like hanging around the park drinking cider and smoking roll-ups. I was rather partial to the occasional drunken fumble with some unidentified person near the golf course, usually female, but I didn't leave out the lads. Everyday activities for the slovenly girl. Hey, I was a teenager. I had no morals.

Summer wheezed its way through July and August, and plunged me back into school before I was ready for it. Classes were the same. Teachers droned on about exams and expectations, all of them wanting you to do well so it would look good in the league tables. I spent most of my time staring blankly out of the window. And that's when I saw her again.

She was on the all-weather pitch with a bunch of other girls. Her short gym skirt reached up to her panty line exhibiting long legs—sleek, tanned, and muscular. I could feel myself salivating. Her breasts were bobbing as she was explaining and demonstrating to some dip-shit how to perform the shot put. She looked so serious, so sexy, so hot.

"Miss Stewart!"

My green eyes blinked, dismissing the image that I had conjured up, and then turned to face the History teacher who had called my name.

"Yes, Miss?" I said coyly.

"Is there something more interesting out there than learning about the Second World War?"

"God no, Miss. I thought I saw a peeper watching the girls on the pitch. I was concerned for their safety, Miss." I thought that was a pretty good save.

Miss came over and assessed the scene. "I can't see anyone. Whereabouts?"

"Near the tall girl with black hair, Miss, just behind the bushes..." I drifted off for effect.

"What? Near Emma Jenkins?"

So that was her name. I held it in my arms, hugging it to my chest with the primness of a Jane Austen character. *"Oh, Mr Darcy... I shouldn't...really..."*

I later found out she was the captain of the athletics team, and really popular.

Shit.

Every time I saw her, my stomach would put on a performance—dancing and spinning, how novel. She was perfect. Her eyes were the colour of summer. Her voice— God, her voice was like angels' wings brushing tenderly against a harp.

Mushy enough? Sometimes I even surprise myself.

I was truly a goner. She probably thought I had a stutter and a skin complaint, as I used to sputter "excuse me" whilst reddening like a bolisha beacon every time I saw her. And that was as often as I could muster.

I guess I was what you could call a semi-stalker. Wherever she was, I happened to be just casually walking past at the same time. I don't know why I did that. I didn't have the guts to talk to her, so why bother stalking her? And me, gob shite extraordinaire, was at a loss for words for a change.

I became her shadow. Always hanging back, a face in the crowd, a nobody. She, on the other hand, was a social butterfly. She fluttered her wings, and landed effortlessly in any situation. Wherever she went, people smiled, joked, came to life. Emma had that effect on people—made them forget their troubles, made them feel special. She was loved by all, but especially by me.

The words to the old Police song came to mind, about watching the girl of his dreams. He must have been a stalker too.

The first time she spoke to me, I was totally unprepared for it.

Lined up in the dinner queue, waiting to get Listeria or something just as unappetising, I felt something, someone, behind me. I was in mid rant at the dinner lady, the thin one with the moustache and an uncanny resemblance to Fred Astaire if he had sported facial hair.

I know this is off topic, but did you ever notice there are always two kinds of dinner ladies: a fat, short one who everyone loves and thinks of as a surrogate mum, and a thin evil one—the spawn of Satan—who you would avoid like school gravy.

"Call that a portion? You couldn't feed a gnat on that!" I was on a roll, in my prime. "Don't be so tight. Put another scoop on!"

"Sorry, luv."

She didn't look sorry. Smug was the word I'd have used to describe her. I was getting fired up now, skinny little fuc—

"Is there a problem?" I could almost hear her angel wings. "Are you okay?"

I turned around to greet blue eyes looking at me with concern. "Yeah. Sorry," I mumbled, embarrassed. 'Did my heart love till now? Foreswear it sight, for I never saw true beauty till this night' was accompanied by the "baboom, baboom, ba boooom!" of my heart and an ache so strong it almost winded me.

God. I was standing next to Emma Jenkins. She was talking to me. I was inches away from her, and she had noticed me. Noticed me! I could smell her scent—spicy, exotic, yet so familiar.

"Hurry up, Stewart." Piss off! One of the Bitches had decided to speed us along. "We only get fifty minutes for lunch."

"Hey...isn't that the stalker?" Chief Bitch chimed in. "I thought you'd be somewhere following someone."

How did they know?

Once again, my ability to keep my mouth shut was on holiday for the duration. "Why don't you just go fuck yourself? 'Cos with a face like yours—"

"Stewart! My office. One o'clock!"

Shit. The Head.

I was humiliated, again.

Emma looked at me with embarrassment. I don't know what she was embarrassed about. Maybe my way with words.

I grabbed my tray and skulked off down the line, only to leave the lot at the end of the counter. How could I sit in the canteen knowing that she had witnessed me making a total dick out of myself? I did the only thing possible. I left.

How could I stalk her now? I felt like a fool, saying stuff like that in front of her. Everyone knew I had been internally excluded for "using profanity" on school premises. Fuck 'em. I didn't care about them. But she knew. Emma *knew* I had been stalking her. I was well and truly mortified.

Nearly a month went by, and I avoided Emma Jenkins like the plague. Yes, the plague. She was the plague. Emma plagued every thought I had...awake or asleep; she plagued my conscience and my heart. She was a disease; a disease I wouldn't mind dying from. What an agonisingly beautiful way to die that would be.

Trying to get back in the Head's good books, I signed up for mentoring duties. I was an excellent student, although that might be difficult to believe, and it was likely that I would get nearly all A's or A*'s. In other words—bloody good grades. My mentoring duties were to help other students who were struggling with certain subjects "attain a better understanding, thus a better grade" to quote the Head himself, who, in my opinion, was a bit up his own arse.

I was in charge of English Language and Literature revision. God, how I loved those subjects, loved them. El oh vee ee dee them. I loved the creativity, the logic, the rationality, the uncertainty, the certainty, the ability to take an idea and go with it. Everything.

I love the written word, you see. Grammar, too, believe it or not—verbs, adverbs, abstract nouns, everything that made up language, even down to punctuation. I loved the way we begin to understand how we are influenced every second of every day, how writers affect us, sculpt us into what they want us to be, want us to think.

I'm rambling. Trying to put off the inevitable, I suppose.

Mock exams were winging their merry way towards us like winged demons, preventing us from having any life apart from studying. I was lucky. I didn't need to study as hard as the other kids. It kind of came natural to me. I'm not being arrogant. There's no need to issue a "Big Head alert" just yet. I was just fortunate, I guess.

Anyway.

School was in panic mode, as everyone thought the end of the world was upon us. It was only the mocks, but everyone thought they were the "be all and end all," that our whole futures were linked to this set of tests. Mocks were there to show us how little we had actually learned in our time at school. Honestly, that's the easy explanation for them.

Well, I had been assigned four students who needed extra coaching. One lad, Peter Levens, and three girls, Phoebe Dixon, Justine Russell—yes, Justine, bugger—and, yep, as you might guess, Emma Jenkins. Obviously, I went straight to the Head of Year 11 and told him I couldn't take four students, as it was too much. Thankfully, he agreed, and took Phoebe Dixon off the list. What could I do? Grin and bear it, that was all.

Through messages in the registers and all that, I arranged for us all to meet in the library at lunch time the following Monday. Then I spent the weekend trying to catch a life threatening illness, get hit by a car, contract alcohol poisoning—anything that might get me out of tutoring. All I ended up doing was copping off up the golf course with a girl with a bad case of acne, the tongue of a serpent, and the sucking capabilities of a Dyson cleaner. My neck looked like it'd had a close encounter with the Boston Strangler. Come to think of it, she did bear an uncanny resemblance to Tony Curtis.

Monday arrived, and I felt sick to the pit of my stomach. Lessons dragged along, all the teachers sounding as tired as the students. Double Science kicked off my week with the most evil teacher in the school, Mr Mackenzie. Twat, for short.

He was rake thin and looked like he lived in the prep room at the back of the Science Labs. You know—plugged himself in at night to recharge his "evilness" batteries. To this day, I can't stand science teachers; they make my skin crawl. I know it's unreasonable, and I also know they are not all like Mackenzie, but...

I'm rambling again.

He was malevolence personified, and Monday was not his day, or mine, for that matter.

It started out wrong. I'd gotten up late and spent ages trying to cover the bite marks, opting for a polo neck jumper underneath my regulation school shirt. That was my downfall.

Mackenzie liked uniformity. He liked the fact that we lost our individuality every day and became as much an automaton as he was.

"Is that school uniform, Stewart?"

I feigned innocence. "What, Sir? My tie?"

"No, girl, that rolled up bandage around your neck."

I was sure his lips didn't move.

"You know the policy on uniform—nothing underneath your shirt."

"Not even a bra, Sir?"

"Don't get smart with me, girl. Go and remove the offending item, now."

"But, Sir, my Nan said I must keep it on. It's on account of my condition."

"Which is?"

"I'd rather not say in front of everyone else, Sir." I couldn't think of anything else to say.

"Well, let's talk about it in the back, then."

After a lot of pleading and lying, I ended up in the girls' toilets removing the "offending" item of clothing, even though I'd told him about my consumptive tendencies. I do have rather an overactive imagination, especially with teachers. They are usually quite gullible.

You should have seen Mackenzie's face when I returned to class. There was nothing gullible about his expression.

"What is that around your neck, Stewart?"

"What? My tie, Sir?" I knew I was pissing him off, but what the heck.

"No, stupid girl, the bruising."

"Got my head stuck in a door, Sir."

That excuse was so old, it was a cliché.

The class erupted in cheers and wolf whistles. Me being me,

I decided that a curtsey was in order. After all, I was the star of the show.

That did it—two after school detentions and a letter home. Fuck. Forgery time.

Geography was just as bad. One would think that they had never seen a love bite before. I swore I was going to kill the bint who had given them to me, vowing that she wouldn't be able to suck the froth off her coffee when I'd done with her.

One o'clock saw me sitting in the library with a stack of books, the distinct smell of foundation make-up in the air. Every time the door opened, my heart shot into my mouth, probably to have a squint at who was coming in.

Peter Levens was the first to turn up, sweaty and smelling of stagnant water. He had tried to cover this up with a liberal spraying of Lynx, or some other prepubescent deodoriser that promised gorgeous women would fall at his feet. Not a good combination. Overall, he had an aroma faintly resembling stale cat piss.

Then came the clam-smacking arse-licker, Justine Russell, in all her glory. Granted, she wasn't bad looking. It was...oh, I don't know, her fake-ness, I think.

"Hi," she purred. "You're sooo sweet doing this."

She placed her hand on my shoulder and rubbed in a slow circular motion. She mustn't have known it was me who put the article in the school magazine. Lovely border it was, too.

I looked expectantly over her shoulder at the door of the library. No one else was behind her. My stomach was in knots. "There should be someone else. Shall we wait?" Was that panic in my voice? No. Concern, I think.

Liar.

"We haven't got much time. Lunch is over soon, and mocks are just around the corner," Justine said in a little girl kind of way. Not innocently, but like you would expect prostitutes to talk to kinky clients.

Shuddering, I agreed to begin.

Emma didn't show up. Our first date—I mean meeting—and she didn't show up. Shit. Wasn't I even good enough to help her with her work? Was it the fact that I used to stalk her that had put her off?

No. I wasn't going to think about that now.

Surprisingly, we all worked hard and achieved quite a lot in the thirty minutes. At the end of the session, Peter grabbed his stuff, shoved it in his bag, and left with a "thanks" tossed over his shoulder. His smell lingered a little longer than he did.

Justine was another matter.

"Are you free later?" Her hand was on my forearm, stopping me packing my things away. "It would be nice if we could, you know, get together apart from studying." She gave me a half smile, more like a leer, and winked saucily.

She reminded me of Moll Flanders. You know, Defoe's slutty heroine.

"No can do, Justine. I'm so busy at the moment. I..." I was beginning to get flustered.

She went for the jugular. "But I thought you were like me, into girls."

Fuck. I nearly choked. Yes, I had the odd fumble, but nothing...nothing... I actually gulped. Nothing like that.

I had to get out of this, and fast. I could feel the rod shoving itself up my backside as it tried to give support to my flaccid spine.

My green eyes looked squarely into her brown ones. My expression was cold, steely. "Well, you thought wrong, didn't you?"

She shrank back. She probably thought I was going to smack her.

"And even if I was into sex with girls, do you honestly believe I'd screw one of Bulldyke's conquests?"

Talk about a change in a person. One minute she was asking me out, the next, knocking me out. Her hand came out so fast I didn't have time to block it. Smack. Right in the eye. She turned about and stomped out of the library, looking like she was the victim.

Jesus. I'd never understand women.

Later that evening I was sprawled on my back in my bedroom, gazing at the ceiling, which was covered in little lights organized into constellations. I was in pain—spiritual, emotional, and physical pain, thanks to fucking Justine Russell. Emma had rejected me. Before even knowing me, she had rejected me.

A sob worked its way up my throat. I covered my eyes with the backs of my forearms, trying to block out the world and how I had been cast aside, unwanted yet again.

The sob left my mouth in a rush, breaking apart in a staccato rhythm reserved for grief. I was grieving, grieving for the chance to be someone else, to show someone else who I could be—someone different who wanted to be different.

The backs of my arms were getting wet. Salty tears smeared themselves along the flesh, burning like acid, intensifying the anguish and despair that was running full pelt through every molecule. Every inch of me felt it, every hair and fibre that made up this degenerate, this waste of space that was me.

I turned awkwardly onto my side and let the tears flow, accompanying them with a low keening, a breaking deep within.

Eventually I fell into a fitful sleep.

# Chapter Four

Tuesday greeted me in its usual pleasant way, sunshine bursting through the window in a radiant shower. I felt like shit. My eyes ached, as did my chest, from the previous night's exertions, and I wanted to curl up and die. Eventually I got my sorry carcass out of bed, got dressed, and headed downstairs.

"Morning," Mum's voice greeted me from the front room where she was attempting the Cindy Crawford workout.

Doesn't really have the same effect, seeing a woman in her late forties with a beer belly and a half smoked fag hanging out of her mouth. Was she trying to kill herself? Not quickly enough, by all accounts, as she was still here. A sigh escaped me.

Standing straight, wheezing followed by a hacking cough, she turned to face me. "What's the matter with your face? You been gobbing off again?"

Loads of sympathy there. Thanks, Mum.

"You'd better put a spark to it. You'll be late for school." A cough gripped her, and she doubled over, nearly bringing up her lungs. In between bursts of smoke-induced coughing, she spluttered, "Don't…think…you're staying off…nursing a hangover…'cos you're not."

I could hear the phlegm rattling around in her chest. She staggered forward and put out her cigarette, only to reach for her packet and light a fresh one. One more cough and a swallow, and she was a good as new. She turned to face me, wrinkles standing out around her mouth, the tell-tale sign of an inveterate smoker.

"Did you hear me, lady? You're not staying off nursing a hangover."

"No. Only Dad does that," I shot back, totally pissed off.

"We're not going into that again, are we? He's having a few problems. You know that."

"So are we all, but I don't take it out on the rest of you. One of these days, I'll hit the fucker back." I turned my back on her, snatched my schoolbag, and did a prima donna out the front door. Let her take my little brother Harry to school. It was about time she started behaving like his mother and stopped relying on me to fill in as a surrogate mum. I wasn't going to hang about waiting for her to make any more excuses for her husband, my father, the pitiful excuse himself.

I nearly escaped, too. If it hadn't been for that perverted postman trying to cop a feel, I'd have been clear away.

"You'd better watch that attitude, lady!" her gravelly voice bawled behind me. "You should show us some respect."

"Kiss my arse!" I shouted back, slapping the body part in question with the flat of my hand.

I turned to the postman and gave him one of my best smiles. I had him hook, line, and sinker. "And you," the grin was making my face ache, "can go and fuck yourself. Paedophile. Touch me again, and your tonsils will have the company of your nuts. Capiche?" Too many Robert De Nero films, I think.

Then I was gone, like a bat out of hell, scurrying up the road. Sniggering.

I felt better, believe it or not.

# Chapter Five

The week flew by with no sight of Emma Jenkins. I met the other two in the library the following Monday. Peter was, well, Peter...cat pee Pete. He got on with things, then went on his merry little way. Justine was another matter.

At first she was...um...a twat, for want of a better word. She constantly questioned what I was doing, knocking my confidence in the only thing that I loved. Then, a complete turn-around.

Peter had gone, and Justine was slowly packing her things away.

"Sorry about last week," she mumbled. She looked sorry, too, which was a surprise. "I didn't mean to, you know, and...to hit you."

Yeah, hit versus hit on—subtle difference there.

"I'd like to make it up to you. How about a coffee after school?"

I was on the verge of letting her down, gently this time for obvious reasons. Then I thought, fuck it, what could go wrong? It was only a coffee, right?

Wrong.

I know we said after school, but Justine said it would be better if we met later for some reason or another. I didn't care either way; I just wanted to get away from the arguments at home. Things there were starting to get pretty ugly—Dad drinking too much, and Mum not really caring that Harry and I seemed to cop the brunt of it all. It seemed that as long as she could do what she wanted, could ignore the times he hit us, then all was well and dandy in her world.

We met outside Café Rouge at six-thirty. So there we were, having a half decent conversation, drinking lattes accompanied by little caramel biscuits and putting the world to rights. I eventually let down my defences enough to agree to go for a stroll up by the canal.

Big… Did I say big? Yes. Big mistake. I think you get the message.

It was secluded up near the canal. A number of reasons brought that about. Firstly, the canal path is where the winos, druggies, and homeless people go to escape the coppers. Secondly, it was a little off the beaten track, and you feared for your safety. Finally, and this is the biggy, the thing I forgot when I agreed to go there with her, this was where people went to get it on, or off. Swingers and doggers were regulars up there, but it really appealed to gays—especially those who were that far in the closet they couldn't see past last year's clothes.

We were chatting amiably about school, Justine lulling me into a false sense of security by asking about Ted Hughes, and I didn't see it coming. I swear. Not swearing in the sailor way… Aw, you know.

Anyway, halfway under the bridge, she stopped, turned, and looked me squarely in the eyes. "Do you know how much I like you?" Her hand came out as she spoke.

I didn't move away, which apparently bolstered her courage.

She stepped closer, and her fingers touched my cheek. The touch changed into a gentle caress. I swallowed. Hard.

"I've liked you for such a long time."

Her face was coming closer to mine. She was taller than me, but then again, most people were taller than me... And, I'm going off the point.

"You don't have to do anything. I'll just please you. I've wanted you for so, so long." Her voice was gentle, massaging my broken ego, pandering to my longing for a connection with someone. She leaned closer. Her breath was uneven, ragged. I could hear it catching at the back of her throat as her fingers trailed down my face, across my jaw, and then slowly down my neck.

My stomach began to perform a little jig. A tiny flame lit in my pants, a tiny flame of expectation. "Justine, I—"

"Shush, baby."

She was smooth, I'll give her that.

Her hand slid lower until it was cupping my breast.

A sigh escaped from deep within me, and she took that as a green light and leaned in for the kill.

The kiss was soft against my mouth. She gently circled my lips with the tip of her tongue, an unspoken question hanging between us. The opening of my mouth gave her the answer she wanted, and it slipped inside like a weary traveller looking for a place to rest.

I sucked at it delicately, enjoying the texture.

She increased the pressure of her tongue, long languid strokes that stoked the fire building in me. Her hand was rubbing my breast, tenderly at first, but with a building pressure that incensed my nipple and made it spring to life under her touch. Wetness was building between my legs, my hips undulating against her thigh trying, longing to ease the ache.

Her mouth moved to my ear, and she flicked her tongue over

the earlobe, her soft breath seeping in to enflame my already burning need. My eyes fluttered closed. I inhaled deeply and absorbed the moment.

She moved down to my throat, licking, sucking, claiming me. Her body pressed into mine, pushing me gently against the wall. Her body weight pinned me there, not that I was complaining. I had too many things going on to think about anything but her tongue, her mouth, her exploring hands that were playing with the hem of my top.

Her cool hand pushed back the material and then ventured toward its goal, teasing the nipples back to life. My hips were grinding into her; I was beginning to pant.

A soft moan escaped her lips, and I captured it with my mouth, moaning in response as she pinched and rolled each nipple in turn.

Fuck. I was going to cum at this rate. I wanted her inside me, pumping her fingers deep, deep inside. Oh God, I needed release. I needed to taste her, to take her, to fuck her.

I released my hold on her soft brown hair so that I could grasp her breast. Playtime was over; the big girls were out. I ground the palm of my hand against her, sucking the place where her neck met her jaw. She was humping me, grunting and murmuring in my over-sensitive ears.

"Ohh, baby…fuck me…make…me…cum…please…oh God…angel…fuck me, fuck me."

What was a girl supposed to do? She offered it to me on a plate.

Never losing connection with her throat, I roughly turned her around so I was the dominant one, and I slammed her against the wall. My hands were manic, everywhere at once. I hoisted her skirt up to her waist and shoved my hand between her parted thighs. Her panties were soaked through; I had done that. I smiled smugly.

She leaned heavily against the wall, her legs becoming weaker by the second.

I began my exploration. My hand slipped around the edge of her panties, eliciting a guttural moan from her.

"What do you want me to do, eh? Fingers or tongue?" I licked her ear for effect, pretending to know what I was supposed to do.

"Fingers. God, yes…fingers."

I slithered my fingers into her pants, past soft pubic hair, and delved into a scorching pot of want. So wet. My fingers pushed past the lips and hovered near her opening, teasing. I pulled back to concentrate on her clit. The small hard nub was screaming for attention.

She went rigid, then began to crush herself onto my upturned hand—groaning, moaning, whimpering, climbing up to the place where the world disappears into flashing, blinking lights. A world where nothing else matters. A world where you love and are loved in return. A world where it didn't matter if you were different.

I opened my eyes and stared at her pleasure filled face.

She was on the verge of cumming hard. Her moans were disjointed, breaking apart, waiting for the big one. I stared. My hips stopped, and then my hand. She clung to me, trying to get the rhythm flowing again.

No. Not this time.

"Don't stop, baby, I'm nearly there."

I had to see her eyes. Had to know.

Her eyelids pulled back slowly to reveal uncertain brown eyes. Not blue…brown.

'I'm sorry. I can't…'

She looked confused. "Come on, don't worry," she cooed, and grabbed my arse, pulled it towards her and began to pound herself into me. "I don't have to… Let me taste you…just one taste," she murmured. She began to lower herself, grabbing for my zip at the same time.

I stepped back. "Sorry, Justine. Look, you're really nice and all, but I can't. I just can't, okay?"

Confused eyes changed to angry slits. "What the fuck! What's your game? You were well into this too, and you know it. What's the problem? Is it me?" The anger changed to hurt.

"No…no, it's me. I…" I didn't the get chance to finish.

Wham. Smack. Straight in the eye. Again.

Then she was gone.

The next morning I was toying with the idea of skiving off school. The last thing I needed was a confrontation with Justine Russell. I couldn't deal with her anger at the moment. I felt too fragile, and my face hurt like buggery.

I could hear them downstairs, a growing rumble highlighting the storm that was on its way. That decided it—school it was. Anything was better than a beating.

Half dressed, I stumbled out of my bedroom and found Harry cowering in the corner of the landing.

"What's up, squirt?" I knelt next to him and tried to smooth his ruffled hair, to no avail. "What are you doing there?"

"Hiding," he whispered.

He began to shake, holding back the sobs that were rattling around his chest. Like me, he had learned the hard way—crying was not how you got them to notice you. The only notice they would take of you was at the end of their fists.

"Come on, pipsqueak. Let's get you ready for school."

I don't know what little boys do in the bathroom, but I *do* know what they don't do. Wash. He was my brother and I loved him dearly, but the distinct smell of pee that followed him around like a puppy was sometimes overwhelming. "Back in. And this time *wash*—with soap," I chided.

Five minutes passed and out he trotted with an almost angelic glow about him, the smell of soap and toothpaste girding him in a shield of cleanliness…at least as much cleanliness as Harry could cope with.

He finished getting dressed while I rummaged through Mum's purse for dinner money for the both of us, keeping one eye on the door and an ear to the ground, so to speak.

As we were leaving the house, I heard the smack. He was hitting her again, and although I didn't see eye to eye with her on just about anything, that's one thing I didn't condone. Still, part of me was relieved Harry and I were out of punching distance.

A short stop at the phone box, my impression of a concerned neighbour, and we were on our way again.

*That should sort him out for a while. They'll hold him until he sobers up enough to be let out. Bastard.*

At the school gates, I gave Harry a hug and a quick ruffle of his hair, and he was gone. He bounded up to his mates, the morning distress almost erased from his mind.

Almost.

I arrived at school twenty minutes late. Shit. I'd missed the beginning of Geography. No, I'm not a Geography lover, but we were sorting out places for the field trip the following Monday. It was a two-day sleepover at Whitby. Classy, in a "kipping in a tiny room with probably someone you couldn't stand and probably bedbugs" kind of classy. But at least I could get away from home for a while. We had to be in the lesson because we were being assigned our sleeping quarters, and if we had any "issues" with whomever our bunkmate was, we had to sort it out then rather than later.

It didn't really matter to me, as long as I didn't have to bunk with Justine.

"Nice of you to show up, Stewart."

Some teachers really had a chip on their shoulder. They should get laid more often. It might dislodge the stick that was rammed firmly up their—

"Are you with us? Hello?"

I'd blanked out a little, probably because I could see Justine Russell glaring at me from the back of the room.

Without warning, the scene cued in my mind: I *slithered my fingers into her pants, past soft pubic hair, and delved into a scorching pot of want. So wet. My fingers pushed past the lips and hovered near her opening, teasing. I pulled back to concentrate on her clit. The small hard nub was screaming for attention.*

I swallowed audibly, feeling a tingle in my pants. *Don't go there*, I scolded myself. *You couldn't even pull it off the first time.*

"Are you going to stand there all day, Stewart? Or are you going to sit down so we can carry on with the lesson?"

I stumbled to my seat, blushing furiously.

The teacher seemed smug, likely thinking *she* had embarrassed me. *If she only knew.*

"As I was saying," she glared in my direction "…if you want to find out more about the accommodation, come and see me at break time. And for the people who couldn't be bothered to turn up on time…" Another pointed glare.

Fuck off. I looked out of the window.

"…check the notice boards at lunch. And please, please don't come to me with stupid reasons why you can't bunk with someone, or else you'll find yourself bunking with me and Ms Wilkins."

*Fuck that.* I turned and shot Justine a knowing look, then winked.

She stuck two fingers up at me whilst mouthing "Fuck you."

Charming words from such a delicate flower. I giggled to myself. I felt a little better now.

Lunchtime had me feeling completely different. I'd had my lunch, the Kamikaze Special, then went behind the gym for a quick fag with the rest of the miscreants. And then my day was shoved down the toilet again. Yes, you guessed it—the Geography field trip.

I stood in front of the notice board to check out the names, laughing when I saw Justine's name next to Debbie Mitchell's. Even I knew they absolutely hated each other. *Thank you, God.*

Still chuckling, I hunted out my name. I blinked, blinked again. Rubbed my eyes, shook my head to clear it, but it stayed the same. I was bunking with Emma Jenkins. *No. It must be a mistake. She's not in my class, she can't be... I can't share with her. She thinks I'm a stalker. She hates me.* Thoughts of laughing at Justine's and Debbie's situation flashed through my mind. *That's different. But why? Because it was happening to Justine, evidently. I can't sleep in the same room...get undressed...her get undressed.*

That stopped me cold. Emma Jenkins, naked, in a room with me. *But she hates me. She didn't show up for mentoring, so I doubt she'll strip off and flash those fabulous...assets.*

"What's the matter, Stewart? Deciding who else to fuck about?"

Justine. Obviously. "Just leave it out, Justine." I turned, dismissing her with my back.

She grabbed my arm, pulling me round to face her.

"Get your hands off me," I hissed.

"You didn't say that last night, did you? I thought you were quite partial to me grabbing your tits. You were moaning enough then. What changed?"

"I didn't like the view," I spat.

"Really?" Her tone became almost playful, in a spiteful way. By this time a crowd was gathering, but I didn't give a shit.

"Was that before or after you shoved your hand between my

legs?" She smiled. She knew I was dying here. "Didn't you like finger fucking me, eh?"

My face was burning. The anger I was holding inside was bursting to lash out, so, I let it go. "Actually, no. It was like shagging a corpse." I lied, I know. "You should practice kissing the back of your hand more, Russell, you might pick up a few tips. And for fuck sake," I paused for effect, "...trim your quim."

A chuckle went through the gathering.

Her face paled for a moment, and then flooded with blood as her anger returned with a vengeance.

I turned to go before she kicked off again, and slammed straight into Emma Jenkins, who staggered backwards, taking me with her. We fell into a heap on the floor, me on top, my hands on her tits, my face inches away from hers. Blue eyes looked into mine.

Click. There was a connection. A connection that felt so real, so familiar—like we had looked into each other's eyes thousands of times before.

It seemed like an age before I realised where my hands were. I tore my eyes from hers, swallowed, and began to struggle to my feet. I felt exposed, cornered in some strange way, and I didn't know how to react.

She held her hand out for me to help her up. Cool, elegant fingers wrapped themselves around my clammy hand, and I eased her to her feet. I must have brought her up a little more forcefully than I realised, as she tipped forward and landed in my arms.

Bliss.

It felt like I moulded into her, her scent inviting my senses to wake up and smell paradise.

"Are you alright?"

Her soft, gentle voice caressed my ear and established a place for itself in my soul.

I looked up, quite a way up. Six foot of pure sex appeal encased me in strong arms, staving off the world, and Justine Russell. Nothing existed around me apart from her body and those eyes.

I had come home.

"Yes, I—"

"Stewart. Russell. My office, now!"

Shit.

A faltering smile flickered over my lips, and I became aware that I was still in her arms. "Sorry."

She let me go, a shy crooked smile hovering over her perfect face.

"Don't touch her, Jenkins. She's a clit tease."

Fucking Russell. So, I did the only thing I could do in that situation. I smacked Justine Russell right between the eyes.

It felt great.

# Chapter Six

Three days suspension, to take effect immediately.

I'd expected worse, but I'd explained, in detail, to the utterly homophobic "but trying to understand" Head, about how we had nearly had unprotected sex the previous night, but I'd stopped because I'd realised it was wrong. I'd even put in details about how wet she was, that she wanted me to fuck her and then lick her out.

He softened a little, probably because he became flustered, and was easy on both of us.

I was even allowed to go on the Geography field trip, and so was Justine, but we had to stay away from each other. As if I'd be going anywhere near that psycho.

It wasn't too bad being home for three days. The police had carted Dad off to the police station, kept him in overnight, and then released him. God only knew when he'd be back. Usually he was at least a week away from home after his incarcerations. Mum had liberally applied a ton of make-up and swanned off to bingo. We didn't expect her back anytime soon, either, which was fine by me.

Three days filled with fun and games—just me and Harry. I kept him off school for company. Not good, I know, but it was an opportunity to lavish him with as much love and attention as he could handle. His eyes began to sparkle again; fear was replaced by peace. It was the happiest I think either of us had been in a long time, until The Bastard came home.

We'd been asleep for a couple of hours, curled up on the settee, hugging each other, totally content and relaxed. The telly was on low and the gas fire lit the room—really homey.

The front door opened with such force, it cracked the plaster wall behind it.

"What the fuck!" I shot up, pulling Harry protectively behind me.

"Where's that bitch?"

Pissed. How unusual. "We don't know." My voice was calm, but I was scared.

He didn't look as if he had his senses about him. His eyes were vacant, cold.

Slap. My face stung.

He grabbed for the front of my pyjamas, and I heard the rip. His nails dug into my flesh.

"Run, Harry!" I shoved The Bastard away and aimed a kick at his crotch.

He caught my foot and shoved me back onto the couch. "Fiery little fucker, aren't you? I like that in a woman." He leered at my exposed breasts and licked his lips. "It's about time I showed you what your old man can do. I think you'll like it."

Then he was on top of me.

His drunken breath was turning my stomach, but not as much as the impotent thrusting of his flaccid dick.

"You need to be taught a lesson, bitch, and I can make it last all night." He began to push my pyjama bottoms down, scratching the inside of my thighs in the process. A long, thick tongue slapped itself on the side of my face and trailed down towards my mouth.

I couldn't move. Fear gripped me and pinned me down as surely as he had.

He leaned back, one hand around my throat, the other clumsily undoing his pants. His eyes were on me, his tongue, full of spit, licked his chapped lips. "You're gonna love this." A short laugh shot out of his mouth, and he smiled, but it didn't reach his eyes. They stayed dull and emotionless.

Thud. I saw the glint of the ashtray as the light from the gas fire caught it.

He fell, unmoving, on top of me, a slow trickle of blood slithering down his temple.

Harry stood behind him, holding the large glass ashtray high in the air, ready to strike again.

"It's all right, sweetheart. It's okay. He can't hurt us now," I soothed, but the panic was still in my voice.

Harry stood like a statue, frozen in time in an almost comical pose.

I gripped The Bastard's shoulders and shoved him off me. He was a dead weight, but I had the momentum and the motivation. No way was either of us going to be there when he came around.

"Come on, squirt, let's get out of here." I grabbed at Harry's hand, and I heard the thump of the ashtray hitting the carpet. I had to nearly drag my brother to the stairs, as he kept looking back at the freakish tableau laid out in the front room. "Come on, honey. Up." I pulled at his arm again, and it was as if he came to life. "We need to get ready, love."

"Do I have to wash again?"

I choked out a laugh that was immediately replaced by torturous tears crawling down my face. "Don't worry about that, babe. Just get some warm clothes on, okay?"

In less than five minutes, we were free, making our way to

Sarah's. She was Mum's sister, who lived a good walk away. It would seem even further with us toting two holdalls, but we didn't have anywhere else to go.

Mum and Sarah did not see eye to eye, probably because Sarah lived with her partner Elaine and had a much better life than Mum did. Therefore, we were banned from ever going there, especially since the showdown in the high street two years before, where Mum had called Sarah a "fucking dyke." Now you know who I get my extensive vocabulary from.

Sarah hadn't flinched, though. She stared Mum squarely in the eyes, hatred oozing out, and spat, "Well, at least I didn't plump for second best." With that, she had turned and blended into the gathering crowd, never to be seen by us again.

Until this night.

I quite liked Aunty Sarah. She was very much on my wavelength, and knew what a pair of bastards my parents were. Also, she had always tried to stick up for me and Harry, and I had missed her since she had been banished. And now, it was the only place we could go where we might be taken in.

Shocked green eyes greeted us when Sarah opened the door. I think seeing two obviously distressed relatives, wearing a mishmash of clothing and carrying bags, nearly gave her a turn. She shook her head, and it was as a fog lifted and she suddenly realised that her nephew and niece were actually standing on her doorstep.

"Come in. Come in. *God*."

In some inexplicable way, the panic in her voice calmed me. Sarah grabbed our holdalls and dumped them on the floor before turning and drawing us into a tight, welcoming embrace. She seemed atilt as she tried to hug both me and Harry at the same time.

She pulled away, then looked firstly at me and then Harry, then back at me. "What's she done now?"

My resolve cracked, and tears appeared as Harry gripped my leg and pulled himself closer to me. I tried to swallow down the emotions roiling within me, but I couldn't speak.

"Let's get you settled, and then you can tell me, okay?" Sarah's voice was soothing. "Come."

When at last we were sitting on her sofa, I felt safe. I felt that if I could tell Sarah what had happened, things wouldn't go back to how they always ended up...wouldn't go back to waiting for the next time he wanted to...wanted to...

I shuddered, then turned to look at Harry. A nod from me to him, followed by an acknowledging nod of response from him. We needed to tell Sarah everything, but for now we needed to focus on what had just happened.

Elaine, Sarah's partner, didn't say a word whilst we were talking. She perched on the arm of the sofa next to Sarah, her face expressionless, until I got to the part where my father had tried to have sex with me.

I saw her jaw clench, and a flash of anger swept across her face before she stood and turned away from us.

I paused in my retelling.

"Go on, love." Elaine was livid, but her voice was exceptionally soft. "I'm listening."

Sarah patted my knee and smiled in reassurance. Harry moved closer to her, his head trying to burrow into her comforting presence. Without batting an eyelid, she lifted her arm and put it around him, then drew him closer.

Speaking of the repulsive events of the evening, although difficult, performed a cleansing. Once all the years of verbal, physical, and emotional abuse began to flow out of my mouth, I couldn't stop. It was as if the top had been removed from the bottle of pent up despair I had been holding inside, and by exposing the disturbing secrets of my life to someone who cared, I might be able to begin to put them behind me.

When we had finished telling them of the night's events, and those that we had been subjected to for so many days and nights before, Sarah was immediately on the phone to the police. It seemed like they were there in no time. Elaine sat on the floor next to Harry and stroked his back whilst giving me reassuring looks.

Two hours, three hot chocolates, and a plate of biscuits later, the police had been given all the information they needed. They picked The Bastard up halfway down the road where we lived, bawling at the top of his voice for me to "come back and get some."

Someone who specialised in rape cases attempted to counsel me, but I stressed that I hadn't been raped, just assaulted, and that was bad enough.

I could still feel his weight...smell his breath...feel his hands...

The police left with reassurances that we wouldn't be seeing that bastard—their words, although I would have to agree—again for a long time.

We could only hope that was true.

Mum had been located. Aunty Sarah knew that Mum would be at her "fancy man's" in Stalybridge. Trussed up like a school-girl, Mum was shagging him when the police turned up. Fucking slut. Not surprisingly, she didn't seem to give a fuck about Harry or me. She said we should be safe at Sarah's. She'd sure changed her bloody tune. She hated Sarah, except when it was convenient.

The police told Sarah, with Harry and my ears wiggling, that reports on both our parents had been filed with the courts and the Social Services.

About bloody time. Only time would tell if anything would come of it, time being the great healer and all.

Watching Sarah and Elaine with Harry made my heart ache.

Curled on Elaine's knee, he sat with his thumb pressed into his mouth. The fear on his features had eased, but it was still there behind his eyes. Elaine stroked his hair, painting him with soothing words, gently rocking him in a maternal rhythm. His eyes were drooping, and when sleep finally came for him like a welcome friend, she still held him, caressing him, keeping him safe in her arms. Something his mother should have done.

"You both can stay here as long as you want, you know. There's plenty of room. It would be a chance for us to, you know, get to know each other." Elaine spoke softly, her eyes shifting from me to Sarah, who nodded her approval.

Suddenly tired from the exploits of the evening, I nodded feebly. I felt secure here, safe. It seemed as if I was home at last.

After taking a hot shower and attending to my cuts and bruises, I snuggled underneath a thick duvet that smelled of springtime. I was exhausted—physically, spiritually, and emotionally spent.

The constellations were absent, of course. Funny, but I missed them twinkling and comforting me from above. I missed the Great Bear and the Plough that I traced nightly with my finger with half closed eyes. Well, I could always get another one to lie underneath.

I closed my swollen eyes and drifted into sleep.

We went back home on the Saturday to collect all our things, and I mean all. Sarah and Elaine were perfect. Their constant attention to Harry and me made us feel like we had died and gone to heaven. They had discussed it with one another, and said that living with them could be a permanent thing if we wanted. All it needed was a court order and the permission of one of our parents.

I froze when I heard that. No way would either of them give up their meal tickets. But Elaine didn't see a problem. She was a solicitor, a partner, to be exact. Both she and Sarah were financially secure, and more than prepared to take on a ready-made family. I didn't want to build my hopes up. It seemed too good to be true, like a fairy tale.

Harry was slowly coming out of his shell, like a hermit crab at last facing life out of the pod. Sarah and Elaine showered him with love and attention, and it was a joy to watch. His arms raised aloft every time one of them passed, asking for a hug, a hug that was never denied. It was a metamorphosis—the ugly duckling turning into a swan. He no longer smelled of pee, and he took special care of his hair, which he combed lovingly with only the tiniest amount of spit, and he smiled easily, displaying a gap where his front tooth should be.

Do you know what is truly heart breaking, though? I still heard him crying out for his mum in the night. Her—the one who didn't give two shits about either of us. Harry's nightmares were still coming thick and fast, and he needed more than me to help him. Remember, I was a teenager, barely out of childhood myself. I felt impotent, useless.

But when I saw Sarah and Elaine in his room, holding him, calming him down, I knew he—we—could get through this. Fingers crossed and God willing.

# Chapter Seven

Monday came quickly. I had forgotten about the field trip, even forgotten about Emma Jenkins for a few minutes, until I suddenly remembered late on the Sunday evening. With Sarah's help, I managed to get together everything I needed. I lugged my over-full holdall through the school gates and skulked about the coach park, waiting for the stragglers to arrive. I could see Justine in the corner talking to a bunch of girls whilst shooting sly glances in my direction. Like the drama queen I am, I kissed the back of my hand, and mouthed "kiss my arse." I'm such a lady.

Ms Davies strolled up, chatting intently with Ms Wilkins. They became quite heated at one point, with Ms Davies grabbing the gym teacher's arm and stopping her in her tracks. More heated words, sly glances, a cupped cheek. What the…? A cupped cheek?

It was so quick, I think only Justine and I spotted it. We looked at each other in amazement, shrugged our shoulders, and then shook our heads. What business was it of ours? Maybe the teachers were taking my advice at last—getting laid and getting rid of that stick up their—

"Help me with this, Stewart."

I turned to see the frosty expression of the Geography teacher humping...no, not the PE teacher...her holdall and two rucksacks that looked to be full of worksheets.

"Can I help?"

Cue angel's wings.

I turned, slowly. My senses were in overdrive. My heart was thudding in my chest, and my clothes seemed restrictive to the point of being unbearable.

"Hi," I squeaked out, the pitch alarming even myself.

"Do you need a hand?" Emma's eyes met mine.

Click. There it was again.

"No...yes...whatever." God, I felt like a jerk.

She smiled sympathetically at me and reached for the holdall at the same time that I did. Our hands grabbed one another's, and electricity sparked all the way up my arm and then down my chest, settling somewhere in my lower region.

*Jesus. I could get electrocuted—you should never mix electricity with water.*

She seemed stunned.

I hadn't electrocuted her, had I?

Our hands flew apart, and the holdall fell to the ground with a thump.

"Watch what you're doing, girls!" Ms Davies shouted.

I laughed—the nervous kind that always get you into trouble—and that broke the tension. Although Ms Davies didn't see the funny side to it. Do teachers ever?

Coach loaded, names taken, and everyone on the bus—and we were off. It was going to take at least four hours to get there, so I opted for a double seat of my own and a good book. I put my headphones on and listened to the radio. "Sinead O'Connor. What a load of sh—" I stopped in mid-word.

The words to the song hit me right in the chest and then

bounced around. The mourning tone of the singer mixed with words of loss. God. I could empathise with the loneliness...the tears...the feeling of guilt. But still, why was that affecting me now?

I turned in my seat to look at Emma Jenkins who was two rows behind, chatting with a group of girls.

*Why do you affect me so? I don't even know you, but you make me feel lonely. It seems like years have gone by, and I have finally found you again.*

How stupid. I shook my head and began to turn back to the front, glimpsing very interested brown eyes watching my every move as I did so. I think that unnerved me the most, you know— Justine witnessing my sudden vulnerability.

The guesthouse we were staying in was quite nice, not brilliant or lush, but nice; homey in a Seventies kind of way.

"Get into your pairs!" shouted Bulldyke.

I felt a hand on my arm.

"I think I'm with you."

Such blue eyes. *I wish you were with me.* I swallowed, trying to get some moisture into my mouth so I could speak. "Are you Emma Jenkins?" Smooth operator.

She nodded and stuck out her hand. "It's a pleasure to meet you, Laura." She gripped my hand and pumped it up and down in a comical way.

We both laughed, a genuine laugh this time, almost relaxed.

"Oi! You two!" Bulldyke again. "You've got the attic room next to Ms Davies and me. Serves you right for not paying attention."

I found out what she meant by that soon enough. The attic up was eight flights of stairs. The last two staircases were designed for hump backed dwarfs with extremely small feet. Did I mention nerves of steel, too? By the time we got to our room, we were knackered and collapsed on candlewick-covered beds.

Emma panted, "I feel like I've stepped back in time."

So did I, but for completely different reasons. This was becoming creepy, but in a good way. "Yeah. Very quaint," I answered.

"Beds are comfy, though. How's yours?"

Blue eyes caught mine, and I smiled at her. I couldn't help it. I was in a room with Emma Jenkins and, as well as being really hot and drop dead gorgeous, she had a great personality, too. And she hadn't mentioned the stalking incident, which obviously was a bonus.

"I've been meaning to grab you for ages now."

That captured my full attention.

"You've been running the mentoring club, right? For English?"

*Here it comes. This is when she goes off at me.*

"I'm so sorry I didn't turn up."

*Wait a minute. She's sorry?*

"I was on holiday with my parents. I didn't get your message until I got back to school."

I was still stuck on the apology part.

"They're separated, but were trying again for my benefit. Waste of time, that was."

I could feel a sweat moustache beginning to form, so I swiped at it and tried to look relaxed. "God, don't worry about that. I didn't notice you weren't there." *Liar.*

She looked a little upset at my words.

"Well... I did notice." *Did she brighten up then?* "But...well... it doesn't matter...if you're free—"

"I'd love to," she interrupted, leaning over and patting my arm. "Come on. We have to meet the others."

This was becoming a good day.

The first two days were hectic. Death by worksheet, believe me. I'd only spoken to Justine once, and that was under duress. She had collared me as I was making my way to bed on the first night.

"If you want a little company later..."

Did the girl have no self-respect?

"...you are more than welcome to come to my room. Debbie is shacking up with Jason after lights out, and..." She trailed her finger down my arm.

I shuddered and glared at her, trying to ignore the interested looks we were getting from Emma.

"For any reason...you're more than welcome."

I brushed her off. Naturally. That girl was a psycho. After all that had happened, she still wanted to shag me. The hairs on my arms stood to attention, and my skin felt as if it had thousands of miniscule insects crawling over it. This was a good indication I wouldn't be taking her up on her offer.

The last night was a real laugh. We were leaving after lunch the next day, and the teachers allowed us to have wine with our meal, a little too much for some. We ended up singing and pratting about until Ms Davies decided that we needed our sleep, all the while looking at Ms Wilkins.

Emma and I went up to bed at the same time. When we reached our door, I was surprised to see it was open. I pushed tentatively and peeked inside.

*No one. Must have left it unlocked, or, the chambermaid could have done it.*

Emma used the bathroom first whilst I sorted out my bag for the next day. When I rested my hand on the bed as I leaned over to reach my kit, my hand felt wet. "What the..." I pulled the covers back and revealed a big wet patch on the mattress.

Emma chuckled. "You could have gone first if you wanted."

Where did she come from?

"I don't understand..." But I did. Fucking Russell had done this. Payback, or she wanted me in her room. "It's Justine. Got to be."

"Tell the teachers."

"That's what she wants me to do. She knows I know it's her, but if I blame her... Shit, the Head'll have my balls."

Emma looked surprised.

"Don't worry about it, I'll kip on the floor."

"You'll do no such thing. You can bunk with me."

Those five little words. Bugger. All the moisture disappeared from my mouth disappeared, and however hard I tried to convince her that sleeping on the floor was no hardship, she wouldn't take no for an answer. I had to agree. Honestly, there was no other option.

I spent ages in the bathroom, mainly out of nerves. I was going to be sleeping in the same bed as Emma Jenkins—shit, like real close, full body contact. I didn't trust myself to keep my hands off her, and I really didn't know if I wanted to.

After we sorted the mattress out into prime drying position, we got into bed. We looked like sardines in that small single bed, and I was clinging to the side like a drowning woman. I was stiff, afraid to move in case I might accidentally touch her, in case I couldn't stop touching her.

"You'll fall out like that. Scoot over here a bit. Turn this way. It'll be more comfortable. Trust me."

I trusted her, it was myself I had doubts about.

She was on her back, the lights from outside lighting up the side of her face, making her profile seem almost majestic. Blue eyes looked grey; her lips looked dark, inviting. She must have been able to hear my heartbeat, or even feel it for that matter.

"Night, Laura."

She closed those perfect eyes, and fell asleep almost instantly. Her breathing was soft, even. Her chest kept the same rhythm, and I was transfixed. I took it all in, etching it to memory to devour later in bite sized morsels. This was the closest I had been to her without an audience. I loved it, although I was still slightly panicked and a little turned on. Her full body length was running down next to mine. I could feel the heat of it, the softness.

Thud thud thud thud.

*What on earth?* It was coming from next door. But that was... Shit. The teachers were shagging.

"God yes...just there...*fuck*...yes."

Bloody hell—Wilkins and Davies were at it. I sniggered.

Emma turned on her side to face me, still asleep.

"Faster...um yeah... I need more..."

The headboard was thudding faster now, a manic rhythm taking up.

"Fuck me... God yes...yes...yesss...oh fuck...make me cum... harder...please... Mariel..."

Mariel? I sniggered again.

Emma snuggled closer.

I was beginning to get hornier. I was in bed with the woman of my dreams, listening to two women fuck each other's brains out not ten feet away. I was in deep shit.

The moisture was building up between my legs, and I had an ache there that was steadily becoming unbearable. God. I needed to just slip my fingers...

Emma's arm snaked across my stomach, so slowly, and it felt as if she had stroked my skin along the way.

Shit shit shit. How could I sneak out of bed and manually get rid of this throbbing that was building, when she had me pinned there with her strong, muscular, tanned, toned... Fuck it! Describing her was not going to stop me getting more turned on, was it?

The two next door were going at it hammer and tongs. The

headboard would definitely need replacing in the morning.

"Fuuuuuuuccccccckkkkk yesyesyesyes yesssssssss...baby... YES!"

And there it was. One, maybe two satisfied women. I was clasping and unclasping the muscles to my anguish. What I wouldn't have done for a little pressure.

Sighing in her sleep, Emma's leg came up between my thighs and pushed itself into my need.

I gasped out loud, the pleasure resulting from that movement nearly my undoing.

"Ssshhhh, honey," she murmured, pulling me to her until my head was underneath her chin and her face was buried in my hair. "Sleep now. It will be better in the morning."

*What did she mean by that?*

I didn't care, couldn't think, and didn't care that I couldn't think. I was in heaven.

After about thirty minutes and loads of mental cold showers, I drifted off, totally content to be in her arms again.

Again?

Oh, it doesn't matter.

Sunlight trickled through the window and illuminated the bed where we were wrapped around each other. I had spent a while guiltily watching her sleep, smelling her scent, feeling her soft breasts nestling into my shoulder.

Slam. The door burst open to reveal Justine Russell and her cronies.

"No wonder you didn't take me up on the offer, Stewart. New conquest, is it?"

I was like a rabbit caught in the headlights. I couldn't move. I looked guilty: I knew that. So when my gaze met Emma's confused expression, I nearly died of embarrassment. I did the only thing I could think of—I shot up, pushed past the sniggering bunch of twats in the doorway, ran down the corridor, and locked myself in the bathroom.

# Chapter Eight

The journey back to school seemed to take an age. I sat on my own, headphones on, blocking everything out. Emma had tried to talk to me, but I just turned away from her and stared out of the window, my hands cupping the headphones to drown out her voice. I felt her move away, down to her friends at the back of the coach.

To be honest, I was disappointed that she hadn't tried harder. But it wasn't her fault that she was in the middle of the war between Justine and me.

Countryside flitted past me, but I wasn't really paying much attention to it. My mind kept sneaking back to images of Emma nestled beside me—the softness of her hair, the rhythm of her breathing, her scent. Then the image of Justine standing in the doorway would break through, and I was filled with abhorrence for myself, and that bitch, Russell.

Immediately upon our arrival, I jumped down off the coach and then stalked off. I could hear Emma shouting for me from behind, but I kept on going. As I turned the corner, I could see her towering over Justine Russell, shouting something in her face, but I was too far away to hear the words.

Home at last, I threw my bag in the hallway and stomped into the lounge. I was greeted by a picturesque scene: Harry on Sarah's knee, reading a book aloud to her. All past events forgotten, my heart filled with love.

"Laurie!" Harry bounded up to me, arms outstretched, a glow about him – just the thing to lift my spirits.

"Hey, squirt." I scooped him up into a giant hug. "How's the main man?"

"Mum came today. She's not happy, Laurie."

I didn't have to look at his face to know he was worried. I looked at Sarah, who shrugged and sighed.

"She's upset because they have stopped her income support and the family allowance. She should have thought of that when she let *him* keep coming back," Sarah said.

She stood and walked over to me, holding out her arms for a hug.

I fell into her embrace, and the dam broke. A sob that I had been keeping buried for God knows how long broke free. Tears worked their way from behind painfully closed eyes and tracked thickly down my cheeks.

"Hey, don't worry. You won't be going back there again."

Her soothing voice made things worse. I started shaking, coughing out cries and gripping her all the harder.

She stroked my back, shushing me, caressing me with words. "Come on. There now…get it all out."

"You…you…dddon't un-der-stand. It's not that…I'm…cry-ing…a…bout," I panted out between sobs.

Sarah led me to the sofa, sat me down, and then went to the drinks cabinet. "Not that I agree with drinking, but I think I'll make an exception." She gave me a brandy and ordered me to sip it and calm myself so we could talk.

Forty minutes later, I had told Sarah about Justine Russell—

she agreed Justine was a psycho—and about Emma Jenkins. All of it, even the nitty gritty. Even the "wanting to do unspeakable things" with her.

Guess what she did? Go on, have a guess.

She bloody laughed.

I was not impressed. How could she laugh when my heart was breaking? I think my expression said it all, because she stopped laughing, brushed her hands down her thighs and looked the picture of innocence.

"Oh, Laura, don't worry about things like that. You're only sixteen."

I glared at her.

"You will fall in and out of love many times before you meet the one."

I hadn't said that I loved Emma. I didn't know what she was talking about. She didn't seem surprised about me having a crush on, or having relations with, another girl. But why would she? She was with a woman herself.

She patted my arm and gave me a reassuring smile. "Whatever's meant to be, will be."

The next week went by without much happening. I saw Emma in the canteen on the first day back. When she waved from her table, I turned and left.

The following Monday came around too quickly. I had tried to get out of my mentoring duties, but I was still on probation for smacking the Psycho Bitch from Hell. Therefore, one o'clock saw me in the library, books out, hands twitching, and too many butterflies in my stomach to count. Yes. I was near shitting myself.

When you want everyone to turn up—nada; when you don't,

they all turn up at the same time.

Peter was completely oblivious to any undercurrents. He got out his books and pencil and waited to be spoon-fed. Justine was a total, and I mean total, bitch to me, and to Emma, too. I deserved it, I know, but Emma? What had she ever done to Justine? It was the longest half hour of my sad little life. I couldn't wait to get out of there.

As usual, Justine lingered whilst we were packing away. But so did Emma.

"Could I speak with you a minute?" As Emma spoke to me, she dismissed Justine with a look. And God, what a look. It could have frozen molten lava.

"Sure."

Justine snatched up her stuff, turned abruptly, and flounced away. Thank God.

"It's the English mocks next Thursday, and I really need some help, especially with the poetry." Emma looked almost bashful as she said, "Could you... Would you consider some one-on-one tutoring?"

Some one-on-one. I liked the idea. Tutoring her didn't seem too bad either. "Yeah, sure. Whenever." *Thank you, God.*

"How does Friday night round my house grab you?"

*Right in the crotch.* Sometimes I surprise even myself with my crudeness.

"We could study for a bit, then maybe watch a video."

I was ecstatic. Alone with Emma, around her house, invited by her. She wanted to be with me. Alone. Ditto. And no mention of what had happened on the field trip at Whitby. Added bonus. Yes, I know it was to study, and yes, I know there was nothing more to it, but I was euphoric anyway.

I nodded.

"Great. Give me the details, you know, address, phone number, et cetera, just in case something comes up."

I quickly scribbled my details on a scrap of paper, and she did the same.

"It's a date then." She smiled at me.

If only.

The rest of the week dragged along at a snail's pace. Nothing of note happened. I didn't get into any scrapes, kept my mouth shut, even though Geography had taken on a new aspect. Thinking about Ms Davies and Bulldyke performing the beast with two backs made me smirk inwardly. Then I remembered what I was doing at the time. Be still my beating heart.

Having an overactive imagination took its toll on me, and by Thursday I was a simmering pot of carnal desire. I couldn't go round to Emma's like that. As soon as she answered the door, I'd be on her like a sex-starved dog.

Now there was an image.

*Oh, shut up!*

Lying in bed, listening to the sound of the rain and thinking about the following evening, I began to twist reality into my own imaginings. Emma was the star of the show, of course, and I was her leading lady. I could feel the arousal seeping into my body—first, in my stomach, where it whirled around before venturing lower. My heart rate was beginning to pick up, my breathing became more laboured. God. What was I to do?

The only thing possible. Relieve the tension.

I slipped my left hand underneath my t-shirt and barely grazed the underside of my breast. The nipple, which at this stage was sleeping, bolted awake and stood to attention. Leisurely, my fingers circled the outside. I didn't want to hurry this—my hand was now Emma's. I trickled my fingers over the pert stump—

teasing, pulling, and pinching lightly.

Hating to be left out, my right hand sneaked past the elastic of my pyjama bottoms to fondle the soft, downy hair that covered my most intimate place. Left hand circling, right hand travelling—a perfect combination. Emma's face hovered in front of me—her eyes full of desire, her lips slightly parted and glistening.

My right hand ventured lower, eager to fulfil its quest. It slipped easily between my wet lips. A soft groan escaped my mouth as I unhurriedly pushed downwards, coating my fingers from the source of my wetness. I curled my finger slightly as I brought it back to the bundle of nerves at my core, and then back down again. Hips that had been lying dormant now moved steadily in a rhythm of their own making, trying to alleviate the fire that was pulsating through my body. Both hands were on the go—one pushing, and the other circling. Hips rocked more quickly now, attempting to keep pace with the building climax and the overzealous hands.

The pressure wasn't enough, so I abandoned my breast and sent the left hand to join the right. I separated my lips and rubbed the slick folds that protected my innocence, softly at first. I increased the pressure, using the flat of my hand. I needed release, and I needed it now.

I became more frantic. My eyes were beginning to glaze over. It was on its way. It started at my toes, the tingle that travelled up my legs to settle between my thighs. I could feel the walls deep inside me contracting, relaxing, then contracting again. My hand was rubbing uninhibitedly. I didn't give a fuck about anyone catching me. Shit. This was good. The heat coming from me could have toasted bread.

More frantic now, I was on the verge. Up down, up down,

up down—stroke, stroke, stroke—up down, up down, up down. I nipped my clit between my fingers and gently tugged. Every muscle in my body tensed, and over I went—crashing, thrashing, not a sound coming out of my mouth. My face was contorting into frenzied expressions, my teeth biting down on my lower lip to keep it all in. And it made it better. Much better.

I fell asleep, the smell of my orgasm clinging to my fingers.

Thank you, Emma.

# Chapter Nine

Friday night arrived, and I was beside myself with nerves. I stood outside Emma's house in Heaton Moor—yes, the posh end of town—and summoned the courage to knock on the stained glass door that separated me from her.

Tap, tap, tap.

So gentle, so unlike me. The images of last night were racing around in my brain, and I was feeling a little guilty about what I had done, who I had evoked to get me there.

"Hi, Laura."

She was resplendent, looking like a goddess brought to earth for my pleasure. Her hair was freshly washed, still a little damp at the ends. She wore faded blue jeans that hugged her hips and exposed part of her tan midriff. Her t-shirt was trying to connect with the waistband of the jeans, but to no avail.

My eyes devoured every detail of the image.

"Are you okay?" she asked.

Fuck. "Yeah. Sorry about that. Hi. I was just mentally (undressing her?) checking (her out?) that I had brought everything."

"Well, come in. You must be freezing standing out there."

She began to rub her arms, and I noticed that her nipples were reacting to the cold evening. Little devils. I mentally licked my lips. I was turning into a perv.

"My mum is out for the night, some work social or something, so I'll be your hostess this evening." Her smile was wide, and mine matched hers. "You look so pretty when you smile, Laura. You should do it more often."

My heart stopped in my chest, and time stood still.

"Come on, we'll never get finished studying at this rate." She turned and walked down the hallway.

"Being your slave, what should I do but tend / Upon the hours and times of your desire?" flitted through my head, and I waited a couple of seconds to get the blood flowing back to all limbs and away from that one special part where it seemed to go every time I was near Emma. I took a deep breath and tried to relax, then I followed eagerly.

In the kitchen we prepared sandwiches and drinks to take up to her room. It was fun. We chatted like we had known each other forever. Really, it felt like I had always known her.

Two and a half hours later we were slumped back on her bed, papers everywhere. Ben Jonson, Shakespeare's contemporary and rival, was exposing himself as usual. And me, for that matter.

*Drink to me only with thine eyes,*
*And I will pledge with mine;*
*Or leave a kiss but in the cup,*
*And I'll not look for wine*
*The thirst that from the soul doth rise*
*Doth ask a drink divine...*

Echoing his words, I heard my heart whisper inside me, "Just one sip. I promise that would be enough to quench my thirst for you. Parched. I feel like I've been in the desert, and you came along—fresh, clear, refreshing, the only thing that could save me." But like for the parched wanderer, too much water could be fatal; too much wanting something I just couldn't have would have the same effect.

"Ooo—I love that poem," she gushed. "Read it to me."

So, there I was, reading Jonson's *To Celia* to the one person I wanted to read it to. Under ideal circumstances, she would have had her head on my lap and her hand would be stroking my arm. I was getting goose bumps just thinking about it. Then, my over-active libido joined in, and all of my senses became heightened. I flushed furiously and jumped off the bed, nearly knocking her off it.

"Are you okay?" She looked concerned. "The poem hasn't upset you, has it?"

*If you only knew.* "No…cramp." I rubbed my leg for effect.

"Here, let me. I'm used to muscles tensing up after training."

Shit.

She had both her hands on my calf and was kneading and digging her long fingers into the flesh through my jeans. "It would be easier if you lifted these up," she said, tugging at my jeans.

I didn't answer, didn't move.

She continued up my leg and began torturing my thigh with her touch.

God, it was heaven. I did feel a little guilty, considering I didn't have cramp in the first place, and because I was enjoying it way too much.

She was on her knees in front of me, rubbing, pressing her strong fingers into pliant flesh. The top of her head was bobbing with the force she was using. The smell of her freshly washed hair wafted up towards my over-sensitised nostrils, and I furtively inhaled her essence.

"How's that?"

Heaven. I sighed, knowing I had to let her stop. "Loads better. Thanks."

"My pleasure."

*No. Definitely mine.*

We settled in the front room to watch a video. "Horror or Drama?" she asked.

I cocked an eyebrow at her that said "more info needed."

"Silence of the Lambs or Fried Green Tomatoes?"

Silence of the Lambs, it was. How can a girl resist Jodie Foster?

I was quite brave, honestly. I only jumped a couple of times. I didn't like the bit when they found the victim's nails stuck in the wall. To this day, that still makes me shudder. All the way through, I kept on stealing sly glances at Emma. She was totally absorbed in the film, her eyes wide.

Beautiful.

The climactic ending was very nearly climactic for me. Jodie was in the basement, and the killer was watching her through night vision goggles.

Emma grabbed my hand. Jodie's breathing became laboured as she swung her gun this way and that, trying to find something to aim at. Emma pulled my hand to her chest, where her very soft breasts were.

Bang. Off went Jodie's gun, and Emma ended up in my arms, head buried under my chin. God. She had a good grip, not that I was complaining.

Rejecting the moral high ground, I snaked my hands around her back.

A muffled voice came out from my jumper, her warm breath seeping through the corded wool to settle on my skin. "Did she get him?"

"It's okay." I tentatively stroked her back, to reassure her, of course. "He's dead."

Blue eyes blinked up at me, a look of embarrassment on her face, a crooked grin on her features.

"It's your film. Haven't you seen it before?"

Her head shook from side to side. "Too scared. Mum bought it last week, and I've been wanting to see it, but not on my own." A small smile quirked her mouth.

I looked down at her arms about me, mine about her, then looked at her face again.

For that moment, time stood still. Emma looked deeply into my eyes, so deeply, I felt she could read how much I wanted her. Guilt raced through me and I turned away, unsure of what I might do if I continued to look into those blue depths.

"Sorry." She scrambled back as if burned. "Bet you think I'm a right baby."

Babe, yes, but definitely no baby. Definitely all woman.

I shook my head. "I would have hid too, if I could have moved." I gave her a cheeky grin and raised one eyebrow.

She laughed and relaxed. "That's okay then."

We said our goodnights shortly before midnight. Elaine was outside in the car waiting for me. I shut the car door and waved vigorously at Emma as we pulled away.

"So, that is the wonderful Miss Emma Jenkins?" Elaine asked.

I nodded, content.

"You've got great taste…just like your aunt."

We both laughed.

"I think Sarah would agree with you there," I replied, feeling very happy with myself and with my lot.

I settled in for the short ride home. I was looking out the window, but my mind was solely fixed on a pair of twinkling blue eyes.

L.T. SMITH

# Chapter Ten

"Laura! Phone!"

What a way to wake up. I put my head underneath the duvet and ignored Sarah's voice.

"Phone!"

*Leave me alone. It's Saturday, for Christ's sake.*

The duvet was yanked back to reveal Harry grinning at me, his gap looking strangely bigger this morning. "Aunty Sarah said you gotta get up. Someone's ringing you."

"Tell them to ring back," I grumbled, patting around, searching for the duvet. I swiftly pulled it over my head and shut out the world again.

"Up, lady. Someone's on the phone for you, and you'd better take it." Sarah's voice brooked no argument.

I threw back the covers and plodded down to the lounge, feigning irritation. "Hello." I'm sure I sounded as pissed off as I felt.

"Laura?"

My heart beat triple-time.

"It's me. Emma. Look, if this is a bad time—"

"No, no, you're fine, it's fine. Go on." Was I rambling?

Elaine, Sarah, and Harry were making faces at me, putting their fingers in their mouths to imitate gagging. Harry began to play an imaginary violin. I glared at them and turned away.

"Do you fancy meeting up this afternoon? Grab a coffee, or do a little shopping?" She sounded nervous.

"Sure. I'd love to."

I could hear air kisses behind me. They were so immature. Honestly.

We made the arrangements, and I hung up.

The three of them were sitting on the sofa, looking like butter wouldn't melt in their mouths.

"Very funny." I about-turned and went to get ready. I only had three and a half hours!

It would be a rush, but I'd manage.

Manchester Piccadilly was heaving with people rushing from place to place. Mothers were dragging screaming kids behind them, threatening them with "Father Christmas won't bring anything to you at the rate you're going." Cars pumped out fumes that made the air thick, and noise assaulted us from every angle, penetrating deep within and vibrating through our bones.

I didn't care. I was with Emma again. Bliss.

The Arndale Centre was alive. Shops displayed promotions that lured the gullible shopper in with promises of a new look, how to keep your man happy in bed, tips on feeding your kids—because apparently you hadn't been feeding them before, and how to change your mundane world into something straight from the pages of *Hello* magazine.

I didn't buy it. No, not just *Hello* magazine; I didn't buy the whole shebang.

We wandered through shops, fingering the merchandise and commenting on how pricey things were. Miss Selfridges had a promotion on—what a surprise—20% off all t-shirts…in winter!

Emma picked up a short crop top and held it against her. It was black, silky black.

"What do you think?"

Nice. I nodded, as I had become utterly speechless just thinking about her wearing the top.

"I'd better try it on to make sure. Come in with me."

I nodded again. Shit. I was like one of those cheesy toy dogs in the back of an old, beat up Ford Escort.

The changing rooms were nearly empty, just a couple of other girls in the corner, giggling. It was a communal one—everybody had to strip in front of everybody else. I swallowed the gathering spit from my mouth. I was going to see Emma in a state of undress, and I was in panic mode. I was embarrassed by my own inadequacy to think pure thoughts. "Maybe I should wait for you outside."

Emma was already tugging at her top, arms over her head, completely oblivious to my condition and to what I had said.

Unexpectedly nervous, I stared at the floor. I looked around the expanse of the flooring, took in the entirety of the carpet's pattern, and then slowly raised my eyes to sweep around the walls, taking note of the posters of buff young men wearing jeans and a smile.

Unavoidably, my eyes eventually landed on Emma's exposed back. Firm, rippling, tan, it looked smooth and strong. I could see the line where she had worn a bikini top, because—I took a deep breath—she wasn't wearing a bra now. Her left breast was showing a little. I could see the curve of it, a hint of the roundness that lay hidden. I was spellbound. My tongue poked out to moisten my suddenly dry lips.

"What do you think?"

*I think you are the most beautiful woman in the world.*

"Laura? Earth to Laura."

I shook my head to clear it and looked into her concerned blue eyes. "What?"

"I said what do you think? I quite like it. Do you think it fits okay?"

More than okay—she was a vision. "It's all right, I suppose."

Well, I couldn't tell her the truth without drooling all over her, could I?

She was pulling it over her head, and I noticed the mirror in front of her. A full view of her chest greeted me like an offering—full, round breasts bobbing about as she pulled her arms from the sleeves. Dark pink nipples sat pride of place.

*Just one taste…or even a touch. Please.*

She was absolutely stunning, and my underwear felt soaked. "Ready?"

Becoming a mime artist once again, I could only nod.

We had spent a few hours in the town, and I didn't want it to end. I was in paradise and she was my angel. For today, anyway.

"It's been great, Laura. I really wish I didn't have to go, but I've got a date tonight."

I froze, rooted to the spot. *A date?* Jealousy surged through me. *Who the fuck with?*

"Rob Evans has been pestering me to go to the pictures with him for ages, and I agreed, just to get him off my back."

That bastard! He was known as Rob "The Octopus" Evans by half of the school. I fucking hated him, especially now. He prowled after girls, charmed them, shagged them, and then left. But what could I do? She was a free agent. "That's nice."

Well, come on—what did you expect me to do? Fall on my knees and beg her not to go? Or, better still, fall at her feet and tell her how I worshipped her, would die for her again and again, implore her to rethink this terrible mistake, tell her that we were meant to be together…we were always meant to be together?

Didn't think so.

"I wish I could get out of it."

So did I.

"But I promised. I'm having such a good time with you."

I smiled weakly.

Fifteen minutes later, I made my excuses and left.

Totally pissed off—that doesn't begin to describe how I felt. I felt cheated on. By Rob Evans, of all fucking people. Bastard. What were they doing? Was he mauling her, priming her to be his next conquest? Were they kissing? Was she offering him her mouth, lips glistening, tongue probing, sucking gently at his lip? Was he touching her perfect breasts, holding them, weighing them, softly squeezing before grazing the nipple with his fucking fat fingers? What if he ventured lower, you know, inside her pants?

Fucking bastard. I wanted to tear his head off.

I knew I was being irrational. I knew it was none of my goddamn business who Emma was with, and I knew deep down she would never be with me. But I was in pain. Hollowness had settled itself in my gut, and my heart was ripping apart. I wanted to curl up and die before I went out to rip that bastard's dick off.

*What if he forces her to do something she isn't ready for?*

Fear enveloped me.

*What if she can't fight him off, and I let her go without saying a word?*

I sunk my head into my hands, trying to block out the image of a frightened Emma fighting off the Devil himself.

Harry kept on coming into my room asking if I was okay.

When I snapped at him a third time, I felt like such a shit. He had been so pleased that his second front tooth had fallen out with only a little bit of wobbling and prompting, and was eager to find what the tooth fairy was going to leave him.

His face crumpled up, and he began to shudder with hurt, hurt that I had caused.

"I'm sorry, squirt. Come here."

He raced into my arms, flinging his smaller ones around my neck and hugging me as hard as he could. "I love you, Laurie. Don't worry about Emma."

How did he know?

"She'll soon see how special you are and love you nearly as much as I do."

What can you do, eh?

I agreed to watch telly with them in the front room, boring, shitty Saturday night telly, with everybody grinning like idiots. You know the ones—fake smiles, all teeth, not like Emma. Her smile was perfect, although a little crooked sometimes.

It was nearly nine o'clock when the phone rang.

"Get that, will you, Laura?" Sarah asked from her place snuggled up to Elaine on the sofa, Harry nestled between her legs on the floor.

"Hello." Totally pissed off.

"Laura?"

I swallowed. "Yes." I knew who it was, but I wanted her to say her name so I could roll it around in my head later.

"It's me… Emma."

There we go.

"Is everything okay?" Was that panic in my voice? "That bastard hasn't hurt you, has he?" My anger was up now and raring to kick the shit out of anyone who got in my way.

"No, no. Everything's fine. I just wanted to see if you were okay. You seemed a little out of it when you were leaving today."

"Just exam pressure catching me off guard," I lied. "I bet Rob isn't chuffed that you are ringing me on your big date, is he?"

"He isn't here. I'm at home. God, he was like a man with eight arms."

I did say octopus, right?

"He was forever trying to get hold of me, any part—he didn't seem to care where. So, I blew him out and told him I had to get home early. And here I am."

*Yes. There you are, my sweet, sweet angel.* My heart soared like a captive bird given its freedom once again.

We chatted for another half an hour about everything and nothing. Why was it so easy to talk to her?

"Are you free tomorrow? 'Cos we could get together and go to Lyme Park for the day…if you want to, of course."

Of course I wanted to, and we arranged to meet, with our study books, at ten o'clock the next morning.

Joy.

I skipped into the front room and was greeted by three sets of eyes—two knowing and one tired.

"Anyone fancy a cuppa?" I almost sang the words, I was so elated. I knew this was only the beginning of Emma's dating experiences, but this time she wasn't interested.

*What will I do when she does find someone who takes her fancy?*

I couldn't think about that today, I'd think about it tomorrow, in the words of Scarlet O'Hara "Cos tomorrow is another day."

As I was skipping to the kitchen, humming, I heard Elaine say "Well, she's brightened up."

Yes, I had. I bloody well had.

Lyme Park was beautiful. The weather was absolutely glorious and I was in my element; I was spending nearly the whole weekend with Emma. It was cold but sunny, good weather for nearly the end of November. Mock exams started tomorrow, but I didn't care—today I was free.

We walked around the woods for a while, watching the deer in their natural habitat, unaffected by our presence. The squirrels were getting prepared for the onslaught of winter, scurrying around in the leaves looking for stray nuts and berries to store away. It was perfect, and, strangely, it seemed as if we had walked together this way thousands of times before. I felt so at home with her, so comfortable, like we had known each other all our lives.

Lunch was sandwiches we'd bought from the local National Trust shop. They must think of a price and then double it. My facial expression told the woman behind the counter that she was a robbing fucker, but she just slapped the change into my hand.

Emma and I sprawled on the grass, lying on our jackets that we had been carrying around all day. We did a little bit of studying, but couldn't really concentrate on anything for very long.

The deer seemed fascinated with us and watched us from afar.

"So beautiful," Emma said.

I turned, and she was looking straight at me, a look on her face that I couldn't decipher.

She looked away quickly. "It was a nightmare last night."

*Yeah, tell me about it.*

"Rob acted like a total prick in the queue to the pictures. He was being rather personal to a couple of guys who were in line just ahead of us, calling them fags and the like." She shuddered. "I can't stand it when people are horrible about other people's life choices, can you?"

I shook my head and played with a piece of grass that had suddenly become extremely interesting.

She lay down flat, her hands on her stomach, and stared at the sky. I could see her eyes following a bird that had taken flight at the sound of a car backfiring in the car park. Such concentration. Her brow furrowed, and she tore her gaze away. A sigh issued from her.

"Wouldn't you like to be as free as that bird, Laura? You know—do what you want, when you want, and not worry about the consequences." Her dark blue eyes gazed at me.

"Well, yeah...I suppose." I chewed my lip. "But you must remember that even though we think the bird is free, it still follows the laws of nature. Every day is a fight, only the strongest survive. They can't cuddle up under the duvet and call in sick because they can't be bothered to get their backsides out of bed." I pushed my fingers through my hair. "So, in a way, no. I was only tempted at first because I imagined myself as that bird and nobody else knew me and I didn't have to worry about all the things I knew I had to do. So, I was free. Do you understand?" I turned over onto my back and stared into the powder blue sky.

Emma didn't answer straight away. "But at least I could fly away when I wanted to."

Was that another sigh?

We lay like that for a good thirty minutes, completely quiet, but it wasn't uncomfortable, it was...right.

"What's the story between you and Justine Russell then?"

I nearly died. What had brought that on? "What story?" *Yes. Be coy. Don't let anything slip.*

"It just seems that you two are always at each other's throats. Every time I've seen you together, you have been arguing or throwing punches. Even in the library on Monday, you could have cut the tension in the air with a knife." She laughed. "And I don't think she likes me very much, for that matter."

"That's because of me." Shit. What to say now? "Justine and I...er...have...er..."

Emma was listening intently.

"We…er…a history."

"Obviously." That crooked smile appeared on her face.

"Yeah…well…erm…it's a little bit more than that."

Even more engaged, Emma leaned in closer.

"We…" I couldn't believe I was going to come out to Emma Jenkins. "We…had a bit of a thing one time." I was blood red by the time I choked out the admission.

"It sounded like a little more than a bit of a thing, Laura. If my memory serves me right, she mentioned something about, and I quote, 'finger fucking.'"

I nearly died. Again. How dramatic. "But I didn't…we didn't…I couldn't…" What? Couldn't what? Finger fuck her because she had brown eyes? Or couldn't give her one because she wasn't Emma? "We only kissed and had a little fumble. That's it."

"Hey, I'm not judging you, just asking so I know what I'm dealing with." She smiled reassuringly. "So why is she so bitchy?"

I wanted to say "because she's a fucking psycho," but that did sound rather harsh. I explained how Justine seemed to think that there was something going on between the two of us, how she had told me that she had wanted me for a long time. Boy, did I feel embarrassed telling Emma that. I played it low key and tried to brush it off, wanting to change the subject but scared where it might lead. I was terrified that she would ask if I was a lesbian. To be honest, I wouldn't have known how to respond, as I wasn't entirely sure of the answer myself.

"One more thing, Laura."

I looked at her with expectation evident on my face, silently willing her not to ask.

"Does her quim really need a trim?"

A laugh burst forth and I joined her, seeing the funny side to this conversation at last. Although that was probably because of the relief I felt that she hadn't cornered me into coming out of, or staying in, the closet, rather than because I was thinking about Justine's nether region.

After packing away, we decided to investigate the house and gardens, our conversation staying light and friendly. Thank God.

We said our farewells just before six, because our first exam was after registration and we needed time to prepare.

A quick hug—yum, a peck on the cheek—double yum, and she was gone. I was left feeling relaxed, happy, and ready for anything.

L.T. SMITH

# Chapter Eleven

Monday. Library. Firstly, Peter didn't show up, and I knew it was going to be just the three girls together, alone. Not good.

The door to the library burst open, and in came a harried looking Justine. This did not bode well.

Emma arrived one minute after, looking decidedly worse for wear.

And then there was me. I sat there all prim, my blonde hair tied back away from my face in a loose ponytail, a pencil behind my ear and an aura of righteousness surrounding me. I had to keep my cool, act natural, drum up a big beaming smile from somewhere. "Hey, girls, glad you could make it."

This actually worked. They both stopped in their tracks and looked at me gone out for a second.

*Nice move, Stewart.*

"So, what do you want to look at today?" *Was that my voice, or the voice of Mr. Holmes, the English teacher?* I sounded really calm, in control. It's a pity that no one mentioned that to my stomach.

They plonked down either side of me like lambs. Ha! The

atmosphere, although strained, was okay. We all got stuck in discussing the novel we were studying.

"Poor George, he is tied to Lennie for obvious reasons. Can you think of his reasons for killing him at the end?" I asked.

"Well, Steinbeck uses the parallel storyline of Candy's dog."

"Good, Justine. Why do you think he does that?"

"I don't know."

Emma sniggered.

Not good.

"What are you laughing at, slag?"

"Excuse me. You…calling me…a slag? That's a case of the pot calling the kettle black, don't you think? I'm not the one stalking someone in hopes of a good fuck."

Shit! Ring any bells? *Bloody hell, Emma, where did that come from?*

Then it kicked off good and proper. I just sat there, frozen, pretending that I wasn't with them.

"Really? That's not what I saw in Whitby. You were stuck to each other like a couple of dogs in heat."

"And your problem is?"

"Everyone knew that Laura and me had a thing going, and you stole her away from me. How could you?"

Her voice broke, and I did feel sorry for her, but only a little bit.

Emma's eyes were cold, like slits in her face, and her lips pursed into a thin line.

*Uh oh. Here it comes.*

Emma leaned over Justine, her face mere inches away. "Stole her away?" she hissed. "Stole her away from *you*? I don't think *you* owned her in the first place, you fucking psycho."

Shit.

"If she did come to me, she would do so willingly. I don't have to steal anything, you got that?"

"So, you're not denying that you two are fucking each other's brains out, then?" Justine accused.

Was that a sob? I'm getting soft. Although you wouldn't even think I was with them, never mind the centre of their conversation—if you can call bad mouthing, bad language, and gross indecency a conversation. I didn't raise my head.

*Ooooh, look what Steinbeck has done here.*

"What if we are?"

That got my attention.

"What if we are fucking each other's brains out and loving every goddamn minute? What the hell has it got to do with you?"

Justine was gob smacked. So was I, for that matter, and slightly aroused at Emma saying the word "fucking" in conjunction with my name. Yes, I was a pervert, and proud of it!

"Come on, sweetheart." Emma grabbed my hand and pulled me up and into her. She possessively wrapped her arm around me and led me out of the library.

I didn't say a word. I was too stunned. So was Justine. And so was half of Year 11, who were studying in the library at the time.

Outside, Emma started laughing, hugged me close and then let me go. "Sorry about that. But I think that might have done the trick. She'll leave you alone for a while at least. Got to go, see you later."

I could still hear her laughing to herself as she hurried down the corridor, taking my heart with her.

L.T. SMITH

# Chapter Twelve

Exams took over our lives for the next two weeks. English was pretty easy, but Maths was a bugger, let me tell you.

Emma and I had lunch together every day. I even stopped going for a quick smoke behind the gym so I could spend more time with her. Justine would glare at us whenever we bumped into each other in the corridors, the dinner hall, even the exam room. If I hadn't known any better, I would have sworn that Emma was gloating.

Rob "Octopus" Evans would hover near Emma all the time, trying to get her attention in some fuck-witted kind of way. I wanted to knee him in the under-crackers and be done with it, but that would have meant explaining my actions to Emma. I couldn't reveal myself like that; I couldn't bear to see the look of disgust on her face.

"I could fix him up with Justine," my evil mind pondered— kill two birds with one stone, if I was lucky, though even maiming would have been good. But I doubted Justine would go for all the extra tackle. Pity. They would have made a perfect couple, and that would have gotten them off both our backs.

L.T. SMITH

I didn't know if Emma enjoyed the attention, or was just being considerate of Rob's need. She was such a sweet person, except to Justine, that I didn't know what to think.

With all the pressure of doing well in exams, Emma and I didn't get the opportunity to see each other in the evenings or at the weekend. She had to see her father in Chester from Friday night to Sunday night. I was gutted, but understood why she had to go.

I still hadn't met either of her parents. She seemed to shy off when I asked about them, not wanting to go into too much detail for some reason or another. Answers like "Oh, he lives quite far away now" and "She works late most nights" were the norm. I didn't press.

Christmas was on its way in all its gaudy glory. Every shop I went into had crappy songs playing from an album older than the Queen Mum. Bloody Band Aid. Yes! I know it's Christmas, and does the band bloody care, for that matter? I think they have more important issues going on than who is going to get the newest fad—things like famine, disease, AIDS, and drought, to name just a few.

I wasn't a "Christmas Hater" as such, but we have to prioritise, and my priorities came in a six-foot, dark haired, blue-eyed package labelled "Emma Jenkins." And I wanted to peel the wrapping off really slowly.

I just couldn't think of anything apart from her. She consumed me…all of me, her every thought, every action…everything.

The results from the mocks were quite pleasing. I got an A* for English; Emma got a B. She was over the moon with it, though, saying she had only been targeted a C. She wiped the floor with me in Maths—grade A to my C. I was quite pleased with the grade, as Maths and I had a history. We did not get along, and we both knew it.

All in all, life was good. Home was brilliant, with only the occasional drunken visit from the tart with no heart—our mother. Daddy dearest was serving three years in Strangeways for attempted rape and for being a twat. The last one was my description, not the court's.

Emma and I were inseparable. We spent all our free time with one another, and when we were apart, we talked for ages on the phone, about what, I couldn't tell you.

Lads were sniffing around her all of the time at school, and out of school, too. Well, she was one hot looking woman. She seemed kind of embarrassed when she told me who had asked her out; sometimes she seemed to be expecting a response. I had resigned myself to living in her shadow, my unrequited love sitting on my lap like an offering. I had no chance with her, but if you have hope, you have a reason to keep going.

Hope was all I had, but I had that in abundance.

# Chapter Thirteen

Christmas Eve arrived, resplendent in icy rain and sleet, but no snow. For God's sake—this was Manchester.

Emma and I were going to a youth disco at the Young People's Centre. It looked like it could be fun, and quite a few people from school were going.

At seven-thirty we trudged in, soaked to the skin, make-up turning into abstract art for the duration. We looked gorgeous, to say the least. Ten minutes in the girls' loos primping our look, and we were raring to go.

The room was heaving. I think every teenager over the age of sixteen had turned up, and the place was packed out. As the evening wore on, the temperature in the room rose considerably. Music blared out from speakers all around. It was deafening. Soft drinks were on sale at the bar, but alcohol was in the building, courtesy of the older kids. The innocent coke held aloft could have any concoction floating within it. Emma and I mingled in the crowd, never at a loss for people to chat to, but I had only one person on my mind.

"Hiya, stranger."

Cassie Phillips. God. Cassie and I went way back. She was one of my first inexperienced fumblings. She had shimmering black eyes and skin of ebony. Long, thick black hair completed the ensemble. She was nineteen, three years older than me, but at the tender age of fifteen, I pretended to be seventeen just to hang around with her gang.

"Long time, no see. What've you been up to?" she asked, stroking my arm suggestively.

"Oh. This and that." I was watching Emma on the other side of the dance floor, chatting to the Bitches of Eastwick. "Just had my mocks. Working hard. You know how it is."

God, she looked good—Emma, of course. She was wearing black, loose fitting trousers and *the* black crop top. Her flat, well defined midriff was on display to all, a sheen of sweat gracing it. I could just imagine my fin—

"Who are you looking at?" Cassie's eyes scanned the room until they landed on Emma. "Nice abs, I must say."

I just wanted to tell her to go away and leave me to my pervy little thoughts, let me just enjoy the vision undisturbed. Emma was drinking a bottle of water, holding it aloft, pouring the translucent liquid into her parted lips. It was all in slow motion, like snapshots in my mind.

Sweat shimmered on her stomach; hand raised above her head, her head tilted back; raven locks cascaded down her strong back; eyes closed; the lustre of perspiration coated her top lip; the excess water sparkled on her sensuous mouth.

I longed to lick the droplets, taking with them the dusky lipstick and then devouring the lips underneath.

She stopped drinking and turned to face me. Hooded eyes caught my gaze, and I willingly held it there. She hypnotized me. Her eyes looked almost violet in the dim light, and held a depth that I had not seen before. Her tongue poked out to capture the stray droplets of moisture that had mingled with the sweat, then swept deliberately around her mouth.

I stared. I wanted her. My heart hammered in my chest for just…one…kiss.

Emma began to walk toward me, a definite swagger in her gait. Her eyes didn't leave mine; mine didn't leave hers. Could this be it? Was this really happening? My legs were weak; my mouth was dry. I could vaguely hear Cassie vying for my attention, but I disregarded her. I was laser-focused on Emma.

As she was walking over to me, Rob Evans stepped right in her path. Damn fucking Rob Evans. Fucking octopus boy. Bastard. I was seething. He stopped her for a chat, a fucking chat! Emma, being Emma, chatted back, her eyes coming back to rest on mine. But less…and less. She was laughing now. He had his hand on her arm, rubbing up and down like he was wanking it off. She looked comfortable with him, at home, relaxed, while I stood there getting ever angrier.

Jealousy reared up from deep within me. How dare he… she…he… I couldn't even think straight. Who exactly was I angry at?

"Trouble in paradise, Laura? Your girlfriend sure looks happy to be chatting with Rob."

Justine. I should have known she'd turn up—Miss Fucking Bad Penny of 1991.

Cassie made her excuses and left. No surprise, really. There was me, for the most part ignoring her and then looking like thunder. To top it all, up strolls psycho-stalker to piss me off even more. I would have left too.

"What do you want, Justine?" My voice may have sounded bored, but my insides were on red alert. Evans was all over Emma like a second skin. Suddenly I erupted. "Why don't you just fuck off?" I turned and stalked to the ladies room.

Inside the loos it was quiet, just me, alone with my thoughts. I was shaking, especially my hands. I wanted to go outside and throttle the life out of Evans. How dare he! How…dare…he… come and take what…

*Take what, Laura?*

*Take what's mine, that's what.*

There was a lump in my throat the size of an orange. Inside this orange nestled a sob. Inside this sob nestled a broken heart. How could I liberate this ache, this orange, this broken dream? I didn't dare. Once it burst out, it could never be retrieved. Unfortunately, there wasn't anyone to stick her finger in the dyke until help arrived.

I gripped the edge of the sink, my hair tumbling over my shoulders and in front of my face. I was so wrapped up in my thoughts that I didn't hear the door open and close, didn't hear the footsteps approaching, only finally knew someone was in there with me when I felt the hand on my shoulder.

"Are you okay?" Softly spoken, so soft, but not Emma.

"Yeah. Never been better, Cassie," I sniffed.

She tilted my head back to look into my eyes. Her eyes shone with emotion. She touched the side of my cheek so tenderly, it was nearly my undoing. Her hands cupped my face. "It will happen if it's meant to happen."

Yeah. Heard that before.

Cassie stroked the hair away from my face. "Come on, precious. Don't upset yourself. Hey, you've still got me."

I looked her squarely in the eyes. She was serious. Who was I kidding? Emma Jenkins would never go for someone like me, not in a million years.

*Get over yourself, Stewart. Get it into your thick skull— Emma doesn't want you that way.*

Cassie leaned closer, expectant. I looked into the deep black depths and began to get sucked in. My breathing hitched, a solitary hiccup, and I was ready. My hand reached up and snaked around her neck, gripped her hair at the nape and fixed her in place. I leaned toward her, closing the distance between us. A gentle brush of lips, a meeting of tongues—

"What the…? Excuse me."

Emma. Shit. "Emma, wait! It's not what you think. Sorry, Cassie, I can't… I have to…"

"Just go." She smiled a truly genuine smile.

I ran out of the loos and back into the club. My frantic eyes sliced through the crowds, searching for Emma, praying that she hadn't left.

Then I wished she had.

She was in the corner, all over Rob Evans. She actually had him pinned against the wall, and he looked kind of startled.

If I hadn't been so revolted, so despairing, I would have laughed.

Her hands were all over him. She was grinding herself against him like two pieces of wood trying to light a fire.

I felt sick to the pit of my stomach. I had to leave or else I was going to make a bigger fool of myself than I already had.

Merry Christmas, everyone. I hope you all get what you deserve, just like I did. I was yearning for something that was out of my reach, and I knew it. But that didn't stop me from wanting it so badly that an ache throbbed throughout my whole being. I deserved to be reminded in the starkest way that I didn't have a hope in hell with Emma Jenkins.

As for you getting your just desserts—I hope you don't. No one deserves that. It hurts too much.

L.T. SMITH

# Chapter Fourteen

Christmas and New Year's were a mixture of pleasure and pain. The pleasure came on Christmas morning, watching Harry surrounded by a mountain of presents, eyes aglow and a smile almost slicing his face in two. He spent the whole day singing, "All I want for Christmas is my two front teeth" and flashing his comical grin.

I tried, really I did. I tried to join in the fun, but my swollen eyes were a dead giveaway. I said that I was coming down with a cold, but I doubt Sarah and Elaine believed me. Harry gave me loads of unexpected cuddles, throwing his arms around my waist whenever I was near. This only led to me going into my room for another session of sobbing, thumping the bed with my fist, anger and pain washing through me like a violent cleansing. I was wretched. I was in so much agony deep inside that I felt I wouldn't survive…couldn't survive…didn't want to…survive.

*Why had she kissed him? Why? She said she didn't like him in that way.*

The image of Emma grinding herself into him made my stomach churn, tied it into knots and left me aching, yearning, craving it to be me beneath her rather than him. Her mouth had claimed his. Her tongue had been thrusting into his mouth, possessing him. Her hands were pulling his hips against hers. You couldn't have gotten a hair between them.

*Why did you do that, Emma? If you wanted a quick fix, I could have been there for you...no strings, honestly. I would have done, been, anything that you wanted me to be. But no. You aren't like that, are you? You aren't a pervert like me.*

After holidays, we had been back at school for almost two weeks, and I had only glimpsed Emma occasionally, mainly in assembly. She looked ashen, withdrawn. Her blue eyes looked dead; her face was gaunt. She looked how I felt. Lost.

It was mid-January when the snow came. Fluffy whiteness coated the ground and hid the dangers beneath, like ice and holes in the ground. This being Manchester, the purity of the snow only lasted overnight, changing from an insulating bedspread of white to a sloppy mess of brown slush. Cars whizzed by, splattering unsuspecting pedestrians with the fragments of a city winter. The air was icy. Layer upon layer of clothing fought off the chill of the day and created staggering movements by people obese in their clothing. Heads were covered; eyes used peepholes to grope through the day whilst avoiding the dangers that surround blindness.

I was blind. I hadn't seen it coming. I must have worn my blinkers so close to my face, I didn't failed to see it. Emma and Rob, Rob and Emma. If you say it fast enough, without feeling, it sounds right, don't you think? Emma and Laura. Say that fast. No. It still doesn't make sense. Nothing did anymore.

# Chapter Fifteen

It was Saturday night and I was in my room, alone. Sarah and Elaine had taken Harry to Pizza Hut as a treat. As per usual, I had opted to stay at home. There was no reason to go out anymore. What was the point?

The shrill, insistent ringing of the phone broke my reverie and interrupted me drawing Rob Evans with eight arms, a small wrinkled dick, and a noose around his neck. The blackened teeth were a nice touch.

I answered flatly. "Hello."

"Laura."

My heart skipped.

"Laura, it's me. Look, I'm sorry to disturb you—"

"No, no, you're okay. I was just sketching."

Her sobs reverberated in my ears.

"What's up? Emma…love…" Panic invaded my voice, and it quavered. "What's the matter? Where are you?" I needed to get to her, to be with her…always.

"At home. Oh, Laura, I need to see you. Something's happened, and I don't know who to tell."

I bet it was something to do with that bastard. I'd fucking kill Rob Evans if he hurt her in any way. And I meant any way.

Twenty minutes later I was outside her house, dressed in a mash up of clothes selected from my bedroom floor.

When Emma answered the door, I sucked in my breath. She looked a mess—dishevelled clothes and hair, red-rimmed eyes, and shaking like a leaf. I took her in my arms like it was the most natural thing in the world.

"Shhh, baby. I've got you. Nothing can hurt you now."

She pressed herself against me, holding me so, so close that I could feel her body quivering.

I stroked her back, her hair, and placed delicate kisses on her cheeks, her ears, whilst tenderly crooning words of love and the promise of shelter.

Eventually we moved inside. I led her to the front room, sat her down on the sofa, and sat beside her. Holding her hand, I fixed my eyes on her angst-filled face and waited for her to speak. I didn't know what had happened, but she looked as if her whole world had crashed about her, smashing her life into smithereens.

"It's Dad," she eventually said, eyes closed, squeezing back the tears. I waited. "He's divorcing Mum."

Short and sweet, but it was a start.

"I honestly thought they'd get back together. How stupid. He's been shagging his secretary for years, and I've just found out they have a child together." She started crying again, her free hand angrily swiping away her tears. "I thought it was Mum who messed around."

I dug in my pocket and produced a tissue, handing it to her without saying a word.

She swiped at her face with it and then blew her nose.

I waited.

"Did you know I actually saw Mum fucking someone in her car?"

I couldn't keep the surprise from my face.

"It's true. She saw me as well, but just kept on going." She took a deep breath. "She had the audacity to deny it. Said I must have imagined the whole thing. But how can you imagine that? It's not something a person would make up, is it?"

She squeezed my hand more tightly, stopping the circulation to my fingers, but I didn't care. I looked at her with all the love I felt for her displayed right there on my face for the entire world to see, for her to see.

"Funny. You always hurt the ones you love." She looked deeply into my eyes as she said that. "Usually without knowing it." She looked away, looked down at our hands that were enjoying an illicit tryst.

My mind wandered. *Where's Evans? Shouldn't he be here comforting his girlfriend?* Bastard. "Where's Rob?" It was out before I could stop it.

She looked puzzled. "Why? What's he got to do with anything?"

"But…he's your boyfriend," I said, surprised that I had to remind her.

She emitted a sharp laugh. "Are you joking?"

I sat back and released her hand. My voice was cold, distant. "Well, if my memory serves me right, you were quite fond of him on Christmas Eve."

Was that embarrassment, confusion, or disgust on her face?

"Well," a dry humourless laugh, "that was then…in the past. Just put it down to spur of the moment. Better still, it was more like a reaction." She glanced at me.

"To what?"

"Life."

She turned away, and I couldn't see her eyes. God, how I ached to see her eyes.

L.T. SMITH

# Chapter Sixteen

I was floating. She didn't love Rob Evans; she thought he was a twat, like I did.

Belated Christmas gifts were exchanged. I gave her Sinead O'Connor's album highlighting *Nothing Compares 2 U*. It made me think of her and about the Geography field trip. But since our break-up—platonic, obviously, but not for the want of trying— the beginning of the song seemed more apt. "It's been seven hours and fifteen days since you took your love away" signalled the amount of time we had been apart and how I felt every minute of it, how I felt as if she had taken her love away from me. Even though she didn't feel the same about me as I did about her, the song still made me feel as if it connected us somehow.

Emma bought me a pen set with an engraving: *To my teacher and best friend. Love as always, Emma Jenkins.* I asked her why she had put her full name on there, and she said "In case you meet any other Emmas, then you won't mix us up."

How could I ever do that? There'll only ever be one Emma, one person my heart yearns for.

It was on a Thursday, the second Thursday in February to

be exact, and the reason I know that was because that was the day the school magazine came out. It was the Valentine edition. It was a lot of fun reading through the messages the rest of the lovesick school had put in there. At least it was funny until I saw the half page announcement—hearts and flowers border, the works.

*Laura Stewart*
*Loves*
*Emma Jenkins*

I nearly fucking died. I hadn't done this, had I? I couldn't remember posting it. Shit. What if Emma saw it? I'd be toast.

"Hey. What are you looking at?"

Fuck! Emma. "Nothing. There's nothing to see."

I sounded like the teachers when they were breaking up a scrap "Move along now, there's nothing to see. Come on, move along" whilst the two protagonists were deftly kicking the shit out of each other—blood everywhere, teeth flying, fists coming from all sides. And that was going to happen here if Emma spotted this posting.

"Let's have a look then." She leaned over and grabbed the edge of the magazine.

"No. It's really boring. Honestly."

"Let me be the judge of that." She smiled softly.

She nearly had me, and the magazine, but I pulled it away just in time.

She lunged and seized it. We tussled around, me squirming underneath her, both panting out phrases like "let go" or "it's nothing," "drop it," "it's boring."

With a triumphant pull, she had it in her grasp.

"Then why hang on to it like it's a lifeline?" Crooked cocky grin spread over her face, her eyebrow raised into her hairline, she smoothed the crumpled papers and assumed the mien of a newsreader. Her eyes skimmed over the pages, until they stopped, widened, and then squinted, then widened again.

"What is it?" I asked timidly.

Inch by inch, a smile formed on her face, her eyebrows raised, and then she laughed. Deep, guttural, sexy… Fuck was she sexy.

"Don't tell me you were worried about me seeing this."

I nodded.

"It's Russell. She's getting her own back."

That explained the heart and flowers border.

She laughed again. "Come on, you. Lunch." She got up and walked ahead, the magazine firmly in her grip.

I would have to get a copy for my treasure box.

I sat staring after her, sighing. I wished I had put the declaration in there…just to let her know. I did love her…and I always would.

# Chapter Seventeen

The real exams were done and dusted, and the school year had finished. All that was left was the school prom.

Emma was going with Richard Morris—Dick the Shit. He was a lad from her athletics club—tall and beefy, with the brains of a rabbit. I was going with myself. I couldn't hoist up the enthusiasm to ride with anyone but Emma, so she and I arranged to meet there, as I didn't think Dick the Shit would want to include me on his "date."

Everyone had scrubbed up nicely for the occasion. Even the school Pigpen, Tony Andrews, had sluiced himself. A blessing, believe me.

The hall was unrecognisable. Banners hung from the wall announcing "Good Luck, Class of 1992," and tables were set out filled with nibbles. The DJ was playing Lenny Kravitz's *It Ain't Over Till It's Over*, and the lighting was dim, with only a few laser lights intermittently dispersing the blackness.

I spotted Emma chatting with a group of teenagers, Richard hanging on every word that she said. She looked absolutely stunning. I noted every nuance, every curve and swell. Her lithe body was sheathed in a luscious black dress that hugged her figure before reaching the floor. A split from her ankle to nearly the top of her thigh displayed delicate slip-on shoes with a two-inch heel. The muscles of her calf and thigh stood out, and my eyes trickled slowly up her bare leg as I moistened my lips at the sight. Spaghetti straps finished the top of the dress, but the front plunged just enough to see the swell of her breasts. The back was cut away, revealing toned shoulders and back. Her hair was clipped back from her face, with stray locks dangling down to caress her cheek.

She was a vision. And I fell in love with her all over again.

I had actually made an effort with my appearance. It was the prom, after all. Sarah had helped me choose a full-length red dress, scarlet to be precise. Yes, the scarlet woman. She said that it would bring out the green of my eyes and reveal the strawberry essence of my hair. I wanted to look special for one special person. I did look good, if I say so myself. And the fact that the dress exposed quite a bit of my cleavage, and my breasts are my best feature, was an added bonus.

The DJ was now playing *I'm Too Sexy* by Right Said Fred.

Emma turned and looked directly at me. She smiled as if smiling at a stranger, and then she turned away. The smile fell from her lips. She scrunched up her face as if in thought, and then turned back. Her eyes bugged out, and she mouthed "Wow," and came over.

"You look fantastic, Laura. Good God, you scrub up good."

She hugged me hard, and I could smell her perfume, musky and sensuous with a hint of spice.

"What about you?" I held her at arm's length and looked her up and down. I pursed my lips and gave a low whistle. "You are one hot woman, Emma Jenkins, do you know that?"

She laughed and grabbed my hand. "Come and dance with me?"

Madonna's *Like a Prayer* was blaring out around us, and I allowed myself to get carried away with the mood. God she was a good dancer. She swayed her hips and clapped her hands, just like Madonna in the video. I was mesmerized, and a little turned on. Of course, I was always a little turned on as far as she was concerned.

We danced a few songs and finished on the Stone Roses' *Fool's Gold.* She led me over to where Dick the Shit and the others were standing. He was not at all impressed. Livid was more the word.

"Emma, sweetheart." He tried to put his arm around her, but she shrugged it off.

*Nice move, Jenkins.* I smiled smugly at him.

He glared.

I smiled all the more as I put my arm around Emma's waist. "How about a drink, honey?" I said.

Emma beamed at me as she threw her arm about my neck.

Leading her away with Dick's eyes boring through my back, I smirked. I knew it was Emma's way, that it meant nothing to her, but it meant the world to me. For five minutes, it seemed like she was mine.

As the night wore on, Emma and I got separated as we spent the evening mixing with people we would probably never see again for the rest of our lives. It was happy and depressing at the same time. School is the biggest thing in our lives for so long, and then it's over…gone…finished, and we are thrown out into the real world to survive on our own. The rules of the game change, and we haven't yet discovered what the new rules are.

The evening was drawing to a close. Emma was dancing with Dick (head) to Jimmy Somerville's *To Love Somebody,* and I was waiting in the wings, watching her every move. Jimmy was squealing about the object of his affection not knowing what it was like to love someone the way he loved them. Maybe Emma didn't, but I sure as hell did. It hurt like crazy.

Dick was trying to feel her up, and Emma was like a goalie, deflecting every move. I had to smile at that.

I sat down at a deserted table and fiddled with a flower from the table arrangement, stealing glances at the woman who held my heart so firmly and didn't even know it.

"Fancy a dance, Laura?"

"Fuck off, Justine."

"Suit yourself."

The song was coming to an end, and I vaguely heard the DJ announcing the last dance of the evening. I felt someone next to me, and I was on the verge of telling Justine to fuck off again when my eyes were caught in a blue gaze.

"Dance with me." It was not a question, or a suggestion, but a promise.

I held my hand up to Emma, and she took it firmly and drew me to my feet.

My heart was hammering in my chest; the rest of the room faded away. I was going to dance the last dance with Emma. And she had asked me.

She led me to the centre of the floor, and then turned to me, her eyes dark, hooded, her lips moist and ripe. I licked my suddenly dry lips. She pulled me to her, so close. I nestled the side of my face against the bare skin of her neck and breathed in deeply. My senses were overwhelmed. I couldn't think straight; my legs were feeling weak. The thought raced through my head that I might need CPR. My heart threatened to rip through my chest and dive right into Emma.

Her arms were around me, holding me tight. My hands snaked up her arms and draped around her neck as if it was the most natural thing in the world.

The music started, the first few bars drowned out by the dedication announcement. "And this one's for Laura. Thanks for being there, from Emma."

Sinead O'Connor's voice echoed out of the speakers—mournful, melodic, full of longing. I nearly passed out there and then. It was heaven.

Emma snuggled closer.

*Did she just kiss my hair?* No. Just wishful thinking. My heart thumped in my chest. My mouth was dry.

Emma pulled away and looked deeply into my eyes. Her own looked violet, smoky with… With what? I didn't know, I could only hope, but I knew it was probably just my overactive imagination.

She began to sing to me in a soft voice, beautiful, melodic. I hadn't even known she could sing. It seemed apt that she was singing about her putting her arms about every boy she could see, so fitting. But to have her say they would only remind her of me? Oh, my heart…my poor, poor heart.

The words coming from her beautiful mouth were the same words that I had heard whilst looking longingly at my heart's desire all that time ago. She clasped me to her as if I was somehow going to save her. Her hot breath fluttered against my ear as she sang the refrain "nothing compares to you" over and over again.

The funny thing was, I did not get aroused. What I was feeling was something far deeper than that. It was like a bonding, a connection, like I had found my path in life.

The song was ending. I didn't want it to end. Then I felt it—a soft kiss on my ear, so soft I could have mistaken it for a loose strand of hair brushing past, but it was definitely a kiss.

"Thank you, Laura," her husky voice breathed in my ear. Then she was gone.

I was left standing there, tingling in all the places that her body had come into contact with mine.

Justine Russell was glaring at me from the sideline, so I did the only thing I could think of—I blew her a kiss, winked, and skipped off the dance floor.

What a perfect end to a perfect night.

Emma and I never mentioned that night, not that we really had the opportunity to see each other. She was spending the summer with her father, his girlfriend, and her younger half-brother. We were going to start at the same college in the autumn to do our A levels.

Emma and Laura, Laura and Emma. It didn't sound so far-fetched now.

Anxious to see her again, I wished away my holiday.

# Chapter Eighteen

## TWO YEARS LATER

College was a blast from start to finish. The work was pretty standard for A level courses and not much higher than what we had studied at school. We got through it with no real problem. Exams were taken, and all we had to do was wait for the results. I was eighteen, would be nineteen in just over a month's time. Emma was nineteen in two weeks, and I had something special planned.

Throughout the past two years, Emma had dated on and off, leaving me in a state of purgatory. I wanted her so badly. She was my entire world, and she didn't know it. How could I tell her that when she went out with those boys, my heart was breaking? How could I tell her that I wanted her so badly, I cried myself to sleep at night? How could I tell her that I loved her more and more each and every day?

I couldn't.

I was frustrated beyond bearing, and consequently had liaisons with many willing, nameless people over the two years, but nothing that was remotely serious. I only did it out of desperation, needing to feel a connection with another human being. Every time, I imagined the woman to be Emma, even though her scent was enough to alert me it wasn't. I still hadn't given up my virginity; I was saving that for the right person. And we all know who I thought that was. Hope was still there, in abundance.

We applied for the same universities and both got accepted at Manchester Uni with conditional offers, meaning we had to get our grades at A level to get in. The two of us together for at least another three years, it was perfect. What more could a girl wish for?

Now that is an open question.

Deciding it would be for the best, Emma and I rented a place a while before classes were to commence. It would be easier than commuting, and I had the added benefit of seeing Emma all of the time. Heaven. We both had to get a job to pay expenses. I started shelf stacking at Waterstone's bookshop, whilst Emma got a job at HMV, the music store.

Sarah and Elaine were supportive of my decision. Harry was another matter.

"Why do you have to go and live somewhere else, Laurie?" His green eyes filled with tears. "I need you here. I'm starting big school soon. What am I going to do without you here?"

"Come on, squirt," I said tousling his hair. "You've got to be the man of the house and take care of Aunty Sarah and Aunty Elaine. They need you to be strong. Do you understand?"

He nodded, but I could tell he wasn't convinced.

"I have to move out. It'll be easier to go to the library and get to class if I'm closer to campus. I'll only be twenty minutes away. You can visit me anytime you like, okay?"

He hugged me hard, burying his face in my shirt. "Will Emma be there?" A sly grin grew on his face. He had a crush on Emma, big time. Like his sister.

"Yes. She'll be there. And no...she won't mind you coming to visit, and even staying over, okay?"

Big smile, with teeth now. "Okay."

# Chapter Nineteen

We moved into the studio flat, Sarah and Elaine helping me and Emma's mother helping her. It was the first time I had actually seen the woman in the flesh, honestly. I had spoken to her on the phone on many occasions, but every time I went to Emma's, her mum was either working or out. She was not what I expected.

She had black hair, like Emma's, and her eyes were a darker blue—but cold. She was stunning to look at, but there was something missing, something I couldn't put my finger on. It was only years later that I realised that what she was missing was a conscience. Her voice was refined to the point of being annoying, and she ordered Emma around as if she was a servant. Evidently she did not like the fact that her daughter was working in a music store when she could more than afford to pay for anything Emma could ever possibly want. Emma was embarrassed by her behaviour and kept making apologetic faces at every opportunity.

Clearly, I didn't really like the mother much.

It was heaven in our new "pad." Everything was ours—

crappy furniture, crappy dinner service, crappy everything—but ours, Emma's and mine. Life was sweet.

Results were in, and we had done better than we expected. I got three A's and a B, bloody History, but Emma got straight A's. That's my girl!

We were overjoyed with our results. Our place in university was in the bag, so we decided to celebrate in grand style. We invited all our friends to go into Manchester's Gay Village, then back to our flat for a shindig.

Canal Street was packed. Chairs and tables spilled out onto the pavement, music pumped through the windows, and the hot, sweet smell of summer was in the air. It was perfect.

Each club boasted the best beers, the best atmosphere, the best everything. One place even had "shag tags," where you were given a numbered badge and people could leave messages for you on a big notice board with their number written next to it. You would read the message and then hunt their number out, which they had pinned on their front. If you didn't like them, you didn't have to make contact. It was fun.

We ended up in Via Fossa, a trendy pub where all the action took place downstairs. It was dark and small, especially for our rowdy crowd, but we were drinking bottled beers by the caseload and nothing was going to dampen our mood.

Did I say nothing was going to dampen our mood?

That was before we bumped into Justine Russell and her girlfriend. I think her partner was either drunk or stoned. No, not because she was with Justine, although that was my initial thought. Her eyes were glazed, and her pupils were large enough to take over most of the colour.

Actually, Justine seemed to have changed quite a lot since school. She had lost that psycho edge that had been so endearing. I chatted with her for quite a while while Emma was having a heated discussion with her latest conquest, Mike Collins. I even invited Justine and her dopey girlfriend to the party at our place after the pubs chucked out. I knew Emma wouldn't mind.

I was totally engaged in conversation with a group of girls at the bar, hoping for a quickie in the loos. I know it sounds vulgar, but what should I do—sit at home waiting for the person I loved to notice that I was alive?

Didn't think so.

"Dance with me," a husky voice breathed in my ear.

Emma.

She looked deeply into my eyes. "Come on, dance with me."

Thoughts of prom night filled my head. Could I go through that again?

Without a doubt.

She led me onto the dance floor, and then turned as she neared the centre. She grabbed both of my hands and pulled me towards her, her eyes never breaking contact with mine. The dance floor was packed and we were snug in the core, hidden from prying eyes.

"Come closer...much closer," she murmured as she slipped her arms around my waist and pulled me tightly against her. "Oh, Laura. Hold me."

The rhythm of my heart increased its tempo, and I was nearly deafened by the thumping inside my chest. I could feel it flooding out of me from every pore...flooding.

My arms shakily circled her neck, and I looked into her face, which was leaning down towards me, her lips impossibly close.

I could feel her breath on my cheek. Tina Turner was singing in the background, and Emma was grinding her hips into mine, so fucking slowly, so sexy. She was staring at me, a question in her eyes.

Emma began to sing again in that low velvety voice that made my heart ache just from listening to it. The words to *Be Tender with Me Baby* seeped inside me, words about being confused, begging me not to give up, words that admitted fear. It was almost a plea.

Whilst she sang, Emma stroked the side of my face, fingers caressing my cheek or tracing the contours of my lips.

I placed a kiss on her fingertips, and she smiled and drew my head to her breast.

More words…more longing…more fear.

I was melting, morphing into her. Even when the words about it just being a phase trickled through my mind, I was too far gone to process what they meant. I was lost. Lost in her. Lost to her. Forever lost in Emma Jenkins.

She lifted my face up to hers. "Laura, please forgive me." And then she kissed me. Gently. So gently, her lips barely brushing over the surface of my lips.

My hand drew her head down so her face moved closer to mine to deepen the contact. The gentleness was replaced by something more carnal, more needy. My lips had picked up the tempo, and I was holding my breath. Her lips tasted like nectar. They were soft, wet, and inviting.

Her tongue came out and licked my mouth. I readily let it in, sucking it in, committing the feel of it to memory. Her hands began to move, sliding down my back. One grabbed my butt and pushed it into her groin. My own fingers were trailing along her collarbone. It was if we were daring each other to move lower. She moaned; I moaned.

Emma took the lead. Her left hand slipped between us and cupped my breast tenderly, as if it was breakable. "Oh God, Laura!" she panted when she came up for air, one of her hands still firmly on my butt whilst the other one was teasing my nipple through my top.

I lunged in for her lips, consuming her like a starving man would a dish he had coveted for years. My hand was wrapped in her hair, the other…the other was on its way to her breast.

Heaven. I was in heaven. Her breast was firm yet soft. She gasped at the contact and broke off the kiss, only to devour my throat in needy kisses. I was feeling lightheaded. After all this time of wanting her and believing she didn't feel the same about me, there I was in her arms, awakened to love and desire.

She pulled back from my neck and gazed into my eyes. "Your eyes are so green, Laura. Have I ever told you how beautiful you are?" I shook my head. "Then I've been a fool." She kissed me again, squeezing my breast tightly, like she was claiming it as hers.

My fingers sank into her raven locks and tugged at her hair. I was nearly frantic with longing.

She pulled away and looked at me, her crooked smile playing on her lips, her eyebrow raising in question.

I nuzzled my face against her neck, savouring her scent.

Long slender fingers raised my head to align with hers. Another kiss, gentle this time. "Until later."

By two a.m., we were all back at our place. The music was pumping though our tinny speakers, and the flat was smoky and hot. People were draped over every piece of furniture, lounging on the floor, and propping up the walls. Corners of every room contained couples getting intimate, oblivious to where they were.

I was in the kitchen getting ice out of the freezer when smooth, slender hands encircled my waist and firm thighs pushed into me. I stopped to enjoy the sensation.

"Come here, you."

I turned around and was caught in Emma's arms.

She nestled into my hair, drawing a deep breath like she was capturing it to memory. As I clung to her, her voice feathered its way through my hair, "Hey, it's only me."

God. Didn't I know it! That's what made me cling in the first place.

Lips met mine, not softly this time, but determined and experienced. I gladly followed her lead, crushing myself to her, heart banging in my chest, arousal subverting any rational thought.

She lifted me onto the cabinet and pushed my legs apart, not breaking the kiss for a single moment. Her hips came between my legs and thrust themselves into me, and I groaned. This was ecstasy. She started thrusting with more intensity, her hands roving my face, hair, breasts, and thighs like she was exploring new territory. One hand gripped my butt and pressed it into her. The rhythm pulsed, my need chafed by the seam in my jeans. I could feel my orgasm building.

Her hand slipped inside my shirt, resolute in its quest, pushing past the barrier of my bra to cup an exposed breast.

"Oh, God, Emma," I breathed.

That spurred her on. Her hips became frantic, gasping breaths entering my mouth and mingling with my own. "I want you, Laura, so…so…much." It was like a cry, a confession.

My heart reeled. "God yes!"

Her lips broke the contact and devoured my neck, biting the tender flesh, claiming my skin, not knowing that she had claimed it years ago.

My nails were digging into her back, spurring her on.

"Sorry to interrupt," a cold voice announced from the doorway. Mike was standing there with an empty glass in his hand, looking at us with hurt and hatred.

We sprang apart. Cold air separated us.

"Mike, I…"

"Forget it, Emma. I should have known." He turned and stalked from the room.

Emma turned to me. "Laura, I just need…" She chewed her

lip, the lip that had been trailing down my collarbone only a moment before.

"Go, see him. Go on." I gently pushed her away and smiled reassuringly.

She hurried after him, calling his name above the noise of the music.

I leaned back on the counter, the throbbing between my legs already beginning to subside. My heart was reliving our last kiss. I honestly wouldn't have thought that I could want her any more than I always had, but now… Sweet Jesus. She was everything I'd ever hoped for, and more.

"Hi, Laura." Justine was in the doorway, looking sheepish.

Now that was a word I never thought I would use about Justine Russell.

"Hey." I was in the mood to be pleasant. "Enjoying yourself?"

"I am now. I sent Trish home. She was well out of order. I don't think I'll be calling her in the near future." She laughed. "So, how are you keeping? Still studying hard?"

We began to chat about school days, and she looked embarrassed about how she had behaved with me then.

"Oh, I was truly fucked up. Especially all that with Bulldyke and the school magazine and all." She grimaced at the memory.

I squirmed a bit.

"She didn't even get a slap on the wrist for that bit in the school paper, you know. I got her out of it. Said there was no truth to it, that it was just someone stirring up trouble."

I had always wondered why Bulldyke hadn't got the sack for messing with a student.

"Then she went off with the Geography teacher."

Didn't I know it? I laughed to myself.

"So, you're living here with Emma now?"

I smiled.

"Her bloke seems nice enough. I was chatting to him earlier, and he said that he thinks she might be the one. Sweet, eh?"

I didn't answer. I knew better.

"Yeah, he said that they were getting on really well, if you know what I mean."

A flea of doubt jumped about in my head. But nah, she wouldn't, would she? "Excuse me, Justine. I've just remembered something. Help yourself to a drink."

I looked all over for Emma, without success. I eventually asked a couple leaning outside the bathroom if they'd seen her.

"Yeah." They pointed to Emma's bedroom. "She went in there with a blond-haired bloke."

I moved in slow motion. The door appeared gigantic in front of me. My hand reached out for the knob. *Quite steady. Good.* I turned the knob and pushed against the door. It was locked.

I didn't understand. Why would her door be locked? Fear crept up my spine. I knocked.

"Go away. We're busy!" Mike's voice.

Mike and Emma in her room...her *locked* room...busy. I rested my head against the wood and listened. I could hear Emma's voice, pleading. "Come on, Mike, we're both at college. These things happen."

He mumbled a response, and then Emma continued with something that sounded like, "I've wanted this for so long. I need this." And then the talking stopped.

I could hear the squeak of bedsprings as someone got on the bed. I couldn't stand it any longer.

The pain in my chest was exploding. She had led me on. I was a fucking experiment. The words to Tina Turner's song came back to haunt me...words about it being just a phase she was going through. She was trying to warn me, that's why she'd asked me to forgive her. I had been such a fool. I was a phase, a charity case that she had to help out before she moved on with that cunt in the bedroom.

Anger blinded me and I stumbled down the hallway, one hand pressing against my chest whilst the other clawed its way along the wall. I felt sick, my stomach heaving. I just made it into the bathroom in time before I lost everything I had consumed that day. Then I dry heaved, retching up the bile that I felt for Emma Jenkins…and for myself.

Gentle fingers combed through my hair, calming me, leaving me numb to everything around me except her touch. "Hey, baby. Ssshhh…don't worry, I've got you. I'm here. No one can hurt you now."

I looked up into Justine's compassionate eyes. Love was spilling over her lids and trickling down her face. She cupped my cheek and curled the fingers of her other hand around my own, bringing it to her mouth to lay gentle kisses on my finger-tips.

I watched transfixed, numb, an emptiness enveloping me from the inside out.

I don't know how we got there, but we ended up in my room. I don't know how I became naked, but I did. Justine was above me, her hands everywhere. I was flat on my back, my legs wrapped around her while she ground herself into me. My arm was over my eyes as I tried to stop the tears cascading down my face. I wanted to die. I wanted the pain to go away.

Justine straddled my thigh, and I could feel her slick need coating my leg. I could smell her desire; I could hear the loving words pouring from her mouth. Her hand gripped my breast, fingering the nipple crudely, pinching and pulling. I could not feel the elation I should have felt. I was numb to her, and to the world around.

Her excitement was growing, her strokes getting faster and faster—grunting and moaning, pinching and pulling. "Ohhh God, Laura. God…yes, yes. Oh baby…yes…this is so good. I love you so much. Oh, Laura!"

I pulled my arm away and looked at her face, contorted with her imminent orgasm. Her eyes were closed, her mouth open and panting, and she grunted as she came.

"Fuuuuuccccccckkkkk yeeessss!" She was pounding, unrestrained, her hips circling her mound against my leg, dragging out the little aftershocks.

She flopped on top of me, her breathing laboured.

I lay there staring at the ceiling.

"I've wanted this...wanted *you*...for so long."

Soft kisses moved down my neck. Her tongue circled my breast, teasing the nipple, which, like a traitor, stood erect at her touch. Her other hand began to play with the other breast before venturing lower, stroking my stomach, teasing the hairline of my crotch with experienced fingers.

Her head moved lower, lapped at the skin of my abdomen. She gently pushed my legs apart and nestled her head between them. Tender kisses touched the inside of my thighs, and then there was the sensation of a tongue trailing down, and then back up.

I closed my eyes when her mouth came to rest on my groin, her left hand parting the lips, and a featherlike touch sweeping across the opening bud. An involuntary moan escaped me, and this incited her. Her strokes became more insistent, more focused. I was drowning in my pain. I was allowing this to happen. Call it revenge, call it short-sightedness, call it what the fuck you want—I did not care. Emma had betrayed me.

She was in her room now, fucking someone else, fucking someone she had only known a month. I'd waited for her for so long, wanted her for so long. Now I wanted to die.

An unrelenting finger poked outside my opening.

What the hell? Let her have it. I didn't need it anymore.

"Yes. Go on, Justine." Her name burnt my lips. This should

not be happening.

Slowly one finger slipped inside until it reached a barrier.

"But, Laura—"

"Just do it." Was that my voice? Cold. Hard. Uncaring.

She pulled her finger out again and re-entered with two fingers. Half in, half out. Half in, half out. Justine kept this up for a few more strokes and then lowered her mouth to my centre again and took the hard nub in her mouth.

I moaned as she thrust the two fingers deep inside me and held them there until I could get used to the sensation of being filled. The pain of losing my innocence paled in comparison to the pain of what I had already lost.

I don't know how long Emma had been watching. All I know is that when I opened my eyes after Justine penetrated me, Emma was there, rooted to the spot, a look of bewilderment on her features. She still had one hand on the door handle, too shocked to move.

"How could you do this, Laura? To me…to us…and with *her* of all people?" Her voice broke, her face crumpling into a visage of misery. "Why!" she screamed at me. "Why did you lead me on?"

"Lead you on…lead *you* on?" The anger spilled out, vitriolic in its despair, taking no prisoners. "I'm not the one in there screwing Mike, am I?"

"But I—"

"Enough! Get out! And take that fucking cunt of a boyfriend with you!"

I roughly pulled Justine up by the hair, clamped my hands on either side of her head and kissed her hard, my tongue thrusting in her mouth so deep that I strained the underside. I heard the door slam, and I broke off the kiss.

"No more, Justine. I think you'd better leave."

She looked hurt. She knew I had used her. But hadn't she

taken advantage of me?

I know: excuses, excuses, excuses. "There's no blame here" should be tattooed on my forehead. It never even occurred to me then that Justine was just like me. She professed to have loved me for years, just like I had with Emma.

But that night, I was disgusted with Justine and I was disgusted with myself. The night had started out so wonderfully, and now I was left with a broken heart, a broken dream, and a broken future.

The next morning, Emma was gone. I don't know where—just gone.

I didn't see Emma again after the moment she slammed my bedroom door. She seemed to disappear off the face of the earth. I called her mother's just before the start of uni to ask if she was still attending. I can't repeat everything the woman said, but the facts were, Emma had moved in with her father. And no, she wouldn't give me his address. All I wanted to do was to look into Emma's blue eyes again, throw myself at her feet and beg her forgiveness…and forgive her anything. I didn't care if she screwed half of the football team, as long as she came home to me at night.

That's love for you. Whatever the one you love does to you, you still wait, still take it, still love them.

But, she was gone. Poof. Gone.

I was a total mess. Everything I'd ever known or cared about was gone. I was left with a gaping wound where my heart used to be—a void, an abyss, call it what you want, it's still there.

I couldn't take care of myself, didn't want to. Sarah and Elaine supported me through it all, as I had to move back with them for a while. Thoughts of ending it all were constantly racing through my head. I think the only person who stopped me from doing something foolish was Harry.

A whispered, "I need you, Laurie," as he snuggled against me, trying to stop me from crying, seemed to break through the walls I had erected. An eleven-year-old boy saved my life. I'll always be thankful to him. I honestly think I would have given up completely if it hadn't been for him.

But life went on, and so did I.

L.T. SMITH

Part Two

L.T. SMITH

2004

After attaining a 2.1 with honours, I did my teacher training. I loved it. Still do. What else did I have, except a string of one-night stands? Teaching was the only thing that could absorb me enough so that I did not feel the emptiness inside me.

I started at this school six years ago and have steadily made my way up to second in the English department, mainly because I threw myself into my work. I was "out" at school. Fortunately it wasn't a problem with the rest of the staff.

I think I'm going off point. Or am I clarifying it?

Teaching was all I had, and my students came first. Get in early, stay late, organise study sessions for the Year 11 students who were coming up to their GCSEs—nothing was too much trouble for good old Ms Stewart.

We always have a Parents' Evening for Year 11 about three months before the students take their exams. Reason being, we can give the kids a good old-fashioned bollocking in front of their mums and dads and frighten them into doing better. It helps focus the kids on the importance of getting a good grade, which is what it's all about, after all.

There was one student, Jack, a really good lad—tall, dark hair, blue eyes. He was one of my favourite pupils. He had an eager mind, and nothing was too much trouble for him. I think he had a little bit of a crush on me, too, probably because I was the only female teacher on the right side of thirty. I would do anything for him, within reason.

To get back to the point at hand, Parents' Evening was a big deal.

"Miss?"

Why do students always say "Miss" as a question?

"Yes, Jack."

Why do teachers always answer as if they are bored shitless?

"My parents can't make it on Wednesday. They're away on a business trip."

"Really?"

Why do we always say it like we think they are lying? Probably because they usually are.

A crooked grin lighted his face. "Yes, *really*, Miss."

I laughed and put down my pen. "And?"

"Can my sister come and see you instead?"

I looked at him in puzzlement. "And why would she want to do that?" An image of a twelve-year-old with her hair in bunches popped into my mind.

"Well, she's looking after me while they're away. I'm staying with her for a while."

"Okay, then. Don't forget to fill in the slip."

"She can't make it on the night, but she said she could squeeze you in on Wednesday morning."

Cheeky cow. Squeeze me in! I'd squeeze her—

"Is that okay then, Miss?"

He looked at me with those big blue eyes, and I was lost. "Go on then, Jack. I'm free period four. Tell her to sign in at reception, and they'll send her to my room."

He flashed me a big smile and raced off to his next lesson.

How could I know that was going to change my life as I knew it?

As I said—it's all retrospective. We live and learn.

L.T. SMITH

# Chapter Twenty-One

It was Wednesday morning, and I had forgotten about the visit from the cheeky cow of a sister. It was one of those mornings—you know, the ones where you get up late, get stuck in traffic, have a blazing row with some dickhead who cuts you up, get caught in staff briefing applying lipstick at the back of the room. It was one of those mornings, although nothing truly out of the ordinary.

The first two lessons went okay. The kids were nuts on account of there being a drop, and I mean a single drop, of rain splattering on the window. They were fascinated with it. I was just glad it wasn't windy. They were even worse then.

Period three, I was teaching *Of Mice and Men* to Year 11. God, that brought back memories. A heated discussion about the importance of Curley's wife and why all the characters—apart from George and Lennie—used fake names, took up half the lesson.

Stevie Daniels put up her hand. "Miss?" The question in the voice again. "Why does Steinbeck have George kill Lennie at the end?"

I flashed back to nearly thirteen years earlier and being in the library with Justine and Emma Jenkins—the snigger, the argument. A small smile curved my lips. "Good question, Stevie. Anyone?"

That kicked them off good and proper. I had to call it a day when two of the students were approaching a fistfight. God, I loved my job. Never a dull moment. "Right, everyone. Don't forget your anthologies tomorrow. We are studying Pre-1914 poetry."

There were groans all around.

"Get over yourselves. You should feel privileged to read such works of wonder."

They all started to pack away, mumbling about me being a slave driver and other things that I can't mention.

I started to quote Blake at them, just to piss them off even more.

"But to go to school in a summer morn, Oh it drives all joy away; Under a cruel eye outworn, The little ones spend the day In sighing and dismay."

I walked around the classroom quoting directly to individual students and checking the floor for the limitless crap they could leave behind. When I reached the front, I ended with,

"How can a bird that is born for joy Sit in cage and sing?"

"Dead right," someone muttered.

"Well done, Anthony."

He looked at me gone out, like he didn't quite get what I meant.

"At least you understood it."

The bell rang, ending the lesson, and they all rushed out.

I guessed it must be me.

"You haven't forgotten have you, Miss, about my sister coming?"

Jack was behind me. I didn't even know he was there.

"Of course not," I lied.

And out he went, whistling.

I thumped down in my seat at my desk. That was all I needed—some stuck up piece of ass coming in here, thinking she knew everything. Squeeze me in, indeed. The cheek of it.

Tap tap tap.

"Come in." The authoritative directive came out of my mouth in my teacher tone. Here came Miss Bossy Boots now.

That was the last lucid thought I had for a while.

## Chapter Twenty-Two

Emma looked good. I'll give her that. She was dressed in a classic black suit, the jacket slung over one shoulder, an open collared, short-sleeved white shirt finishing the look. Her raven locks were shorter, dancing just below her shoulders. The blue eyes were the same. Older and wiser, but the same.

After I came around from my dead faint, I blamed a lack of breakfast and too much caffeine for my behaviour, made my excuses, and scampered off to the staff room.

Inside the room, I let out the breath I had been holding. Ten years. It had been ten years since I had looked into those eyes, those blue, blue eyes. The feelings that washed through me were feelings I had thought were dead and buried a long time ago. When I lifted my hand to push strands of my hair away from my face, my hand was shaking. I was shaking.

"Pull your socks up, Stewart. You can get through this."

Why hadn't I made the connection? Jack Jenkins…Emma Jenkins. Probably because I knew she didn't have a brother.

But she did have a half-brother.

I took a deep breath and went back to my room. "Sorry about that, Ms Jenkins."

"Sanders, *Mrs* Sanders, actually, Ms Stewart."

She was married. My heart sank, and I wondered why my heart would sink at hearing that she was married. Probably that hope coming back to bite me in the ass one last time.

"Sorry about that, Mrs Sanders." I forced a lovely fake smile. "So, you have concerns about Jack's exams?"

Off I went into teacher mode, totally professional, showing his target grades and previous marks. I passed the mark sheet over to her, and she studied it intently. I took the opportunity to take in everything about her: her concentrated gaze, her pursed lips, lips that I had kissed, that had kissed me, the stray lock of hair that was hanging across her chiselled features. She was stunning. Her husband was a fortunate man.

I tore my eyes away.

"Looks good, Ms Stewart." She met my gaze, and then sat back on her chair and looked me over. "The years have served you well, if you don't mind me saying."

I flashed her a smile.

She looked down at her lap, then back at me. "I wondered if Jack's Ms Stewart was my Ms Stewart, my Laura. I just had to come in and have a look."

I gazed steadily at her as I swallowed the lump in my throat. *My* Laura. My heart began to beat again.

"Yes, it's me—in the flesh." I was sure she blushed, but then decided that it was just hot in the room. "So, how have you been? It's been a long time." An eternity.

"Jack raves on about you all the time, says how you inspire the kids and you seem to be the only one that doesn't have a stick up their arse."

I laughed out loud. That was the Emma I knew, and loved.

"I'm okay. Busy most of the time with school, but okay. How are you? What are you up to now?"

She began to tell me about her job as a systems analyst. I didn't have a clue what she was talking about, but I enjoyed listening to her voice. "And that's where I met David, my other half."

I understood that all right. I had almost forgotten that she was married.

"Well, I say 'other half,' but we're not together anymore."

Sweet love, renew thy force.

A sad smile traced around her mouth, and I felt guilty for being happy.

"We were only married for just over a year when I told him it wasn't working," she said.

"I'm sorry." What else was there to say? "Yippee" came to mind.

She looked at me in confusion. "But why should you be sorry? I was the one who made the mistake of marrying a man I didn't love."

From my perspective, this was getting more and more interesting.

"Anyway, Laura— Do you mind me calling you Laura?'

My expression said it all.

"Thanks for your time. I know how busy a teacher can be." She stood up and extended her hand. "Lovely to see you again. We should meet for a drink one night."

"That'd be great." Did I gush? Probably.

I took the offered hand for an innocent handshake. And there it was...the connection on contact. She must have felt it too, because she looked startled and pulled her hand away as if she had been burned.

Then she was gone, and I was left wondering if I had dreamt it all.

# Chapter Twenty-Three

Two weeks rushed by, as I was working harder than ever. I got in to work early and left as late as possible. I had rewritten three schemes of work in my spare time. It seemed as if I was running away from something, but from what, I didn't know, or if I did, I was ignoring it.

When I entered the staff room at lunch, I was accosted, yes accosted, by the school secretary. That woman was like an octopus; she must've been a relative of Rob Evans'. She was forever stroking my arm, patting my hip, or just generally getting on my tits.

"I've a message for you, Laura."

It beats me how anyone can say a name and make it sound so vulgar.

"A Mrs Sanders has called in, something about Jack Jenkins."

Had the staff room always been so small? My hands looked

huge holding the pink slip between my fingers. I scanned down to the boxes at the bottom, and my breath caught as I saw which one had been ticked: Please call. And there was her mobile number.

I didn't count how many times I picked up the phone to call, and then put it down. I didn't count the times I began to dial the number. I was such a coward.

"Hello. Mrs Sanders? This is Laura Stewart calling in regards to Jack."

"Hi, Laura. I was hoping you'd get back to me. Sorry to deceive you, but I didn't really want to talk about Jack."

The silence was deafening, as she was apparently waiting for a response. When I didn't reply, she continued.

"What are you doing on Friday night? Do you fancy coming out for a drink, or maybe catching dinner?"

Did I want to go there again? "Love to."

Hey! I hadn't gone through the whole patter yet. Crabbe sprang to mind: "No more debating, take the ready hand."

God. More quotes. *Get a life, Stewart.*

"Great. I'll pick you up about seven-thirty?"

I agreed and gave her my address.

My hand was shaking as I replaced the receiver. I was meeting Emma Jenkins, uh, Sanders—"a rose by any other name… "—in two days.

Shit. Two days! It would be a rush to get ready, but I'd manage.

# Chapter Twenty-Four

Friday night I was in a state of panic. I didn't know what to wear. No, that wasn't the problem. I didn't know what I was do-ing, setting myself up to get hurt all over again. I thought I might be putting the cart before the horse again.

My stomach was dancing around, performing cartwheels and back flips, and I was definitely nauseous. Every time I thought of Emma—her eyes, her smile—the butterflies would climb up my throat, nearly choking me. I couldn't imagine how I could spend five minutes in her company, never mind a whole eve-ning. But I wanted to. So much. I could feel it inside me, behind my breastbone, in the place where my heart used to be.

I didn't want to go all out, so I vetoed my evening dress and tiara. I went for the casual look—jeans, white shirt left open with a skimpy top underneath, and a little mascara and lipstick.

The shrill ringing of the doorbell broke through my thoughts and made me jump like I'd had too much caffeine.

She was here, and on time.

I stood at the door trying to control my breathing. I couldn't let her in with me panting like a knackered dog. She would definitely make her excuses and leave.

I actually considered that briefly before resolutely opening the door.

"Hi, Emma." My voice sounded steady. Tick. My hands didn't shake. Another tick. I digested her outfit, her body, her smile, those eyes…all in one quick glance.

Big cross.

She looked radiant. I could smell her scent. Mmm, *Gucci Envy, sexy*. I subconsciously licked my lips and wondered what her perfume tasted like.

Another big cross.

"Come in," I gushed. "I won't be a minute. Take a seat."

In she strolled, confident, the sexy swagger still there and even more entrancing.

I pointed her into the lounge and then bolted to the bathroom. "I can do this. I can do this. I can do this." I stared at my reflection in the silvered glass. Not bad, quite sexy. I pouted my lips and tilted my head back, which made me look as if I had special needs. A laugh broke out, relieving the tension. "Come on, Stewart. It's only one night."

"But I want more," said a small voice inside me.

I think it came from my heart, but I couldn't be sure. It had been quiet for so long, I didn't recognise its voice, didn't really know if I wanted to listen to it, either.

When I returned to the lounge, Emma was seated on the sofa, totally at peace with the situation. I drank her in. Ten years had only made her more beautiful. She wasn't the girl I knew back when, but she was, too. Does that make any sense?

Emma Jenkins was in my home, sitting on my sofa, waiting

for me to get my act together so we could go and eat.

Shit. I realized that I'd better put a spark to it.

"Nice place," she said, nodding her head in recognition of her surroundings. "Do you live alone?"

"Yeah. I bought this place three years ago when I was more financially stable after uni." I puffed the cushion, more out of nerves than anything else. I was a little manic, to say the least. "I always wanted a dog to greet me at night, but being a teacher… well, it would be cruel to leave it alone all day. Maybe one day, eh?"

Why I said that, God only knows.

She smiled, though I thought she looked a bit wistful. "Ready?"

"As I'll ever be. Lay on, Macduff."

Italian. Mmm mmm mmmm. Have I mentioned how much I love Italian food? Well, I do. It's more filling, for a start, and the desserts… Oh God, I could get aroused just thinking about them. I was surprised that Emma had remembered this little detail, happy, but surprised all the same.

The restaurant was totally couple-oriented, with dimly lit tables for more intimate liaisons. Single roses posed in crystal vases, and soft music promising undying love filtered through hidden speakers. I captured it all and filed it to memory.

I looked at Emma, who smiled at me and winked.

"You like?" she said.

I nodded like a prepubescent teenager.

"Good. I know you like Italian—bigger portions."

A soft laugh escaped that wonderful mouth. I wanted to capture it in my own. *Get a grip, Stewart.*

The meal was wonderful, appearing in the aforementioned

bigger portions, but the company was even better. We chatted about our lives, our jobs, everything. I couldn't believe how quickly we seemed to drop back into our roles.

"I attended Cambridge University, Queens College, and got a first class with honours. That set me up, really."

Bloody Cambridge. No wonder I hadn't seen her.

"I now work mainly from home, which is good, because I can look after Jack when his parents are away." She sipped at her water.

I was the only one drinking a lovely Shiraz.

"But I do go on business trips occasionally. Actually, I'm off to Rome on Monday for four days." She took another sip as she looked about for the waiter.

The candlelight was doing something to her face. She seemed vulnerable, beautiful, distant. I wanted to put my arms around her and tell her she was safe, that I would take care of her. I felt a surge of emotion clambering up my throat. I wanted to cry, and I didn't know why.

"Excuse me," I stumbled from the table and headed to the restroom. I could feel her eyes on me, but I couldn't turn around.

After splashing copious amounts of cold water on my cheeks and neck, I was a little calmer. "What are you doing, Stewart? She doesn't feel that way about you, or have you forgotten?" A sneer twisted my face.

No. I could never forget that.

Before I knew it, the night was drawing to a close and she offered me a lift home, which I graciously accepted. Anything to have a little more time with her. All the while knowing that however long I was with her, it would never be enough. Sitting in her car, watching the streets of Manchester rush by, I had a feeling of true contentment.

"Put some music on if you want. There's case of CDs in the glove box."

I sorted through them and picked one that was labelled *"Faves."* As the first track began to play, I felt as if I was being transported back in time. Sinead O'Connor's voice filled the car, and my stomach clenched.

A strong, slender hand shot out to the player and ejected the disc. "Not that one. It jumps like crazy."

Was that a blush? Was it the song or the situation that embarrassed her?

I leaned back in my seat and looked out of the window, afraid that I would expose my feelings if I looked at her right then.

The car was silent; she was silent. I was kicking myself. I should say something, something to break the tension.

"Lovely meal. Thanks." What a golden-tongued charmer I was. No wonder I was on my own. "The lasagne was lovely, just lovely."

*Think of another word apart from lovely, you moron.*

"The wine was nice, too."

*Nice? Nice? Could you not think of a weaker word? What about okay? The dessert was okay.*

My inner voice was getting on my tits.

We pulled up outside my house. "Fancy a nightcap? Coffee?" For a moment I thought she was going to refuse.

"Sure, that'd be great."

My heart began thumping again, and I realised I had been holding my breath.

We sat either end of my sofa, shoes off, coffee in hand. Perfect. I had put *Dido* on the CD player, just to fill the air.

"I can't believe you're still single. I thought they'd be queuing up outside your door."

I blushed at the compliment. "Well, I have just come out of a relationship."

Her blue eyes held my gaze for a while and then dropped. "Oh, really?" Her voice seemed strained. "What happened?"

L.T. SMITH

*You. You walked back in my life, and I was lost.* "It wasn't working. Jenny was nice enough, but not for me." I tried to sound wistful, but it came out as lame instead.

"Were you together long?" Her voice sounded faint, controlled. She looked up at me again. "You don't have to answer if it still hurts." Her smile was gentle, reassuring.

"Nearly a whole week."

She laughed out loud at my confession. "A week! God, she did well."

"Yes. She's been the longest so far." I produced a full out grin.

Her face became reflective as she pondered what I had said. She tapped my leg and giggled almost girlishly.

*God. I love you, Emma Jenkins.*

I felt a sharp pain in my chest. I knew I was leading myself down a very dangerous path by allowing this woman back into my life. I shook my head, trying to dispel the images dancing there, taunting me, reminding me of the heartbreak that had nearly killed me ten years earlier.

But that was the past. We'd both grown up since then. We were different people, different women, with different lives and different goals. I took a sip of my coffee, drowning my emotions in the dark, hot liquid swirling in the mug.

Our conversation led to her asking about Sarah and Elaine, and not forgetting Harry. I became animated when I spoke about them. Understandable really, as they were the people I was closest to in my life.

"And how are your parents?" I asked, realising too late it was a question that Emma would probably be uncomfortable in answering.

Her voice became bitter when she spoke about her mother. I hadn't known how much she hated her, couldn't believe that I had missed the revulsion she felt for her own mother.

"So, you haven't seen her in three years? That's a long time, Emma." I sipped my coffee. "Of course, I haven't spoken to her since—" I stopped abruptly when I realised where that statement would lead.

Her eyes flamed. "Since when?"

I had to go on. "Since just before I started uni. I called to see if you were…um…coming back and…erm…where I could reach you…" That was as far as I could stretch my strangled breath.

She sat forward and stared right into my eyes, as if she was willing me to say something. "What did she say?" The blue eyes looked dark, and almost a little wild.

"Said you had gone to your father's and wouldn't give me your address."

"Fucking bitch!"

I jumped.

"The lying fucking bitch!" She slammed her fist on the arm of the chair. "I fucking well told her— Of all the— Fuck!" She leapt out of her seat and began to pace. "I can't believe she'd do this. What a…"

I stared, dumbfounded. "Emma, what do you mean?" I almost didn't want to hear the answer.

"I told her…fucking told her…if you called, she must, and I repeat *must* give you my number. No wonder you never contacted me." She flopped down next to me and buried her face in her hands. "No wonder I never heard from you again," she said in barely a whisper.

I stared at the wall, willing my insides to stop boiling.

I told you it wasn't until years later that I realised that her mother was missing a conscience. I would now like to add—she was missing a heart, too.

Emma left shortly after that. She snatched up her car keys, saying she had to pay someone a visit. I knew who she meant, but I didn't say anything to her. What could I say?

She hugged me at the front door, and I inhaled her scent—not just her perfume…her, all of her.

I heard from Emma a couple of times when she called to chat, and we even grabbed a coffee one Saturday, but there was still a distance between us.

On one occasion, I asked Jack how she was, and he said that she was really good, that she seemed happy. He put this down to her having "found someone," someone he thought might be "someone special." Obviously, I didn't ask him again. I knew it had been a mistake to let myself get involved again. I should have remembered that loving Emma Jenkins could only lead to heartbreak.

After that, I ignored her calls. I knew it was the coward's way out, but I couldn't go through needing her again. I hadn't actually ever gotten over her the first time.

Chapter Twenty-Five

The next two weeks flew by in the scurry of work. The end of school production was underway. It was called *A Wilde Evening*, a presentation of plays and poems by Oscar Wilde. Jack was in the lead role as the great man himself. He was perfect for it, too, although I doubted he was gay, as my radar didn't register even a slight ping when he was about.

I had to collaborate with the Art department concerning the backdrops for the play. It was usually the Head of Drama's job, but he said Claire Hepworth had specifically asked for me. In other words—he couldn't be arsed.

Claire was nice enough, and quite attractive, really. She was a little taller than me, with brown shoulder length hair and fiery brown eyes. Nice tits, too. And she was straight, although even if she'd been a raving lezza, I still wouldn't have been interested.

School was ultra-demanding, even more so than usual, so

Claire and I arranged to get together at the Elizabethan pub on a Friday night to iron out the details.

We met there, both of us weighted down with notebooks and sketches—hers better than mine, obviously. It was nice, in a boring kind of way. Usually when I'm with a woman, I've only got one thing on my mind—how quickly I can get her into bed, which leads to how long do I have to wait before I make my excuses and leave. Don't get me wrong, they always knew it was a casual thing. I would never lead someone on. I knew from past experience how much that could hurt.

For half an hour, we were totally immersed in our work and conversation. Then I felt it. It suddenly seemed as if all the hairs on the back of my neck were standing to attention, like a charge of electricity had raced through them, scaring them into action.

I turned. Emma was just coming through the entrance with a tall, distinguished looking man. I had to give her credit—he was handsome in a hetero kind of way. My heart sank. I felt as if I had been punched and punched and punched.

"Are you okay, Laura?"

I nodded at Claire and desperately began to sort through the sketches again, pretending that I gave a fuck. My eyes were drawn to Emma. She was laughing as she slapped him on the arm. I would have liked to slap him too. He was loving it, kept looking around to see who was watching him with the hot date. Bastard.

She was beautiful. She was sexy. She was…with him.

I looked away, looked down, then looked up again and was caught in blue eyes. The room faded out, and only Emma was there.

The soft smile that graced her lips steadily grew into a wide, crooked grin. She waved, then she shifted her gaze to Claire, and her facial expression shifted into neutral. She looked back at me with a sad smile, and then turned back to her date.

Ten minutes later, I was in the toilets banging my head against the wall. Why was I such a coward?

"New treatment for an annoying headache? I'll have to try it on David out there."

Frozen by the sound of Emma's voice, I stopped thumping my head. That man was her husband. *Ex–husband* a little voice inside whispered. I laughed, a patently fake laugh. "No. Just having one of those days again."

"Tell me about it." She sighed and entered a cubicle.

I was just about to leave when she spoke. "So, a new conquest, eh, Laura?"

I could tell she was trying to sound light-hearted, but there was an underlying tone that I couldn't quite put my finger on. "Just a work thing, actually. Thought we might as well take it to the pub instead of sitting in my classroom."

The toilet flushed, and Emma was grinning when she came out.

"Speaking of love life—how's yours?" My head nodded toward the door. "Jack said he thought there was someone special in your life." I was embarrassed that I had pumped information from a sixteen-year-old boy.

She laughed again. "No. No one special." She began to wash her hands, her back to me. "And as for David…he's in town for a couple of days. Probably thought he could get in a quickie while he is here."

"And?" It was out before I could stop it, but I held my breath waiting for the answer.

Emma studied me through the reflection in the mirror. "Been there. Done that. Think I have the t-shirt somewhere. Anyway…"

I released the breath that I had been holding.

"What are you doing tomorrow? Fancy going to the flicks?" Her smile was teasing.

How could I resist?

Saturday morning I was at Sarah and Elaine's, early. After the usual jokes of "Have you wet the bed?" they settled down enough to let me unburden myself. I told them about Emma re-entering my life. They looked at each other with raised eyebrows and knowing smiles. I ignored their childish behaviour, as I was caught up in wallowing in my own misery. At one stage, I contemplated sucking my thumb, but thought better of it. That's not good for the reputation.

"You don't understand. Emma broke my heart. I can't go through that again," I wailed as I stamped my foot.

"Has she led you to believe that there is a chance of taking up where you left off?"

Trust Elaine to be analytical. Why couldn't she just agree with everything that I said and be done with it?

"Or are you jumping the gun here?"

I hadn't thought about that. All I had thought about was how I was feeling about seeing Emma again; I wasn't even thinking about what was being offered. "Bloody women," I sighed. "I don't know. What do you expect me to do, ask her?"

They both nodded.

"Have you completely lost your marbles?"

More nodding.

"Are you pulling my leg?"

Vigorous nodding accompanied by huge grins.

"Look, Laura, we both know that losing your relationship with Emma nearly destroyed you. We also know that being without her nearly destroyed you, too." Sarah stepped forward and rested her hand on my arm. "You have to grab what you want in this life, nobody will give it to you on a silver platter.

Tell her how you feel, tell her how you felt back then. Be honest with yourself, and with her, for that matter."

I digested Sarah's words. How on earth could I tell Emma how I felt? She'd run a mile. But then she'd know. But she'd still run a mile.

I sighed.

"Laura, always remember—whatever will be, will be."

Sarah's wise words. I remembered them from the first time around with Emma, and look what good that had done me.

L.T. SMITH

# Chapter Twenty-Six

Standing outside the pictures on a Saturday night in Manchester Piccadilly was no picnic. I had been propositioned twice and accosted by an old lady who swore I was her twin sister. I was just in the middle of directing some pervert to "Turn left at the end of my finger and continue going" until he fucked off out of my sight when I heard Emma's dulcet tones behind me.

"Well, that's a sight for sore eyes."

I was leaning over, shoving my middle finger repeatedly in the air at the unfortunate bloke who had asked, "How much?" in a gravelly, Secret Squirrel kind of way. The pervert was forgotten, although I was sure I taught his son in one of my classes.

"Come here, you." Emma grabbed hold of me in a bear hug. Flashback? Most definitely.

"Are you ready to have the bejeezus scared out of you?"

I feigned fright in an overly dramatic kind of way, you know, like in the 1920s silent movies. That made her laugh.

"Okay then, big guy, you can buy me the biggest popcorn in the house." She grabbed my hand and led me to the entrance. "And if you're a good girl, I'll let you hang on to me during the scary bits."

"In your dreams, Jenkins." There was no reaction to me using her maiden name. "If I remember rightly, you're the one who nearly wet herself while watching *Silence of the Lambs.*"

"From laughing. Yes, I remember it well." She playfully shoved me and ran inside.

I was mesmerised. The only thought I could think was "Girl, you blow me away." And she did…still.

*Gothika* was okay, I suppose. I was expecting something a little more frightening, but seeing Halle Berry certainly made up for what the film lacked. I'm not saying that I didn't jump three feet into the air on numerous occasions. Especially when Halle was in that bloody cell, on her own, then she wasn't alone. Christ. That was one fucked up vision. Me being me, I leapt into the air at that point and grabbed hold of Emma's arm. She wasn't expecting it and screamed at the top of her lungs. I thought she had seen something I hadn't, and I joined in with her scream.

Believe me, it was funny, but I guess you kind of had to be there. Actually, thinking back on it, the people who were there didn't find it very funny. Whatever. They needed to get a sense of humour transplant.

As the film was reaching its climax, Emma began inching closer and closer to me.

That brings back memories.

Another reflexive jump, and she was gripping my arm. Another, my hand. I prayed for there to be one more.

By the end of the film, she was almost in my lap. I was in heaven, but I assumed a smug smile. I couldn't resist teasing her. "Nice to see you've toughened up, Jenkins."

"I thought I did great," she said as we left the cosy interior of the movie theatre and made our way outside. "I usually get scared at things like that, but I had 'Stalwart Stewart' to protect me," she crooned.

I laughed and hit her arm.

The fresh air outside was like...um...a breath of fresh air. It was too early to go home, so we decided to go for a stroll, see if I could tout for some business. As my earlier encounters had highlighted, I had the presence of a hooker.

Manchester was alive with activity. Cars lined the streets, pumping out music that could make your ears bleed. The night smelled of smoke, car fumes, and beer—nectar to a true city girl. The streets were packed with clubbers, mostly teenagers, students, and twenty-somethings.

We strolled along, side-by-side, chatting inanely about what was on display in the shop windows. Before we knew it, we were on Canal Street, standing outside Via Fossa. I walked on, then noticed that Emma had stopped and was staring at the outside of the club. A burly bouncer gruffly asked if she was "Coming in or not?"

Emma looked startled, like she had just awakened from a trance, and her eyes searched out my own concerned gaze. After one last glance at the bouncer, she hurried to catch up to me.

We walked in silence, until Emma said, "Do you still see Justine?" Her voice was decidedly cold.

"No. Well, yes, but only at a distance."

"So, not up close and personal then?"

There was bitterness her voice, and anxiety flared in my gut. It had been ten years, but I still felt as if a part of me had been lost that night, and not just the obvious part, either. I tried to keep my tone light, but it came out strained and forced. "Been there; done that; never to be repeated."

She was silent, lost in thought. "We'd better get going, it's getting late."

The drive home was uncomfortable. The silence screaming around us made my ears hurt.

"Fancy a coffee?" When there was no response, I shrugged. "Okay. Thanks for a lovely night." I grasped the door handle.

A hand gripped my arm, holding me fast. "Are you free tomorrow?"

I nodded.

"How do you fancy me, you, and a picnic, provided by me, of course," she gestured toward herself, "…a book of poetry, provided by you, and a day at Lyme Park?" The smile on her face made the last twenty minutes fade away. "Maybe that'll bring back happy memories, eh?"

"Love to."

She grinned. "It's a date, then."

If only.

Chapter Twenty-Seven

It was beautiful. I hadn't visited Lyme Park since…well, since…you know.

We were surrounded by trees robed in all their late spring glory. Budding leaves waved in the light breeze, and the woods were becoming shaded once again. The deer were there with their young trailing after them. It was like watching a nature channel with the volume turned down low. So peaceful.

We walked through the woods to the far side of the park and set up our picnic. After throwing a chequered blanket down on the grass, boxes of goodies were brought out by my Emma's beautiful hands, and I "ooohed" and "ahhhed" in all the right places. It made her laugh.

"You're always thinking of your stomach, Stewart."

"Not always." I gave her a saucy smile.

"Well, your appetites, then." She smiled crooked grin, just

for me.

Faultless. That's what it was. A beautiful day with a beautiful woman. What more could a girl ask for?

Our patch of the park was secluded, the only company being the flora and fauna. It was perfect, and an opportunity to make the most of our time together alone.

I read some poetry—some funny, some sad, and some crude, just to keep the balance.

She listened intently, her eyes devouring every word, especially the ones about love and loss. She gently took the book from my hands and scanned the index. Frantic fingers sifted and separated the pages.

"This one."

I looked down at the open page. *To Celia.* I stared at it, trying to control my breathing. "Sure."

Was that my voice? It sounded like a teenager, a teenager who had sat in Emma Jenkins' bedroom thirteen years ago.

I began to read, stumbling over the first few words, apologising, and then starting again. My eyes flicked intermittently to Emma.

She was sprawled out on the grass, her eyes fixed straight ahead, her face blank. "You read aloud so well, Laura."

"It's my job." I smiled at her as her eyes met mine. A sad smile came back to me. Why did she look so sad? She must have her reasons, reasons that, in a way, I was too scared to know.

I lay back on the blanket and absorbed the springtime sun, listening to scampering and the rustle of leaves around me. I could also hear Emma's laboured breathing.

And then it just popped out of my mouth, completely unbidden. "About that night…" I heard her sit up, so I cracked open an eye to look at her. "With Justine…" I sat up and looked squarely at her.

"I don't want to know. It's in the past."

Her voice was cold, hard, so unlike her. I tried again to explain, but she cut me off.

"I said I don't want to know. Leave it."

"But I need to explain—"

"What?" Her voice was forceful. "That you fucked that slag in our flat while I was in the other room breaking up with Mike?" The colour had completely drained from her face. "You fucked her right in front of me, Laura! For Christ's sake—you even kissed her when you knew I was watching." Her voice dripped venom, rising in volume and scaring the birds from their perches.

"Breaking up with Mike! Right. Didn't sound that way to me," I threw back. "Funny how loud bedsprings can sound through a locked fucking door!" I shot to my feet. "I heard you, Emma, pleading with him to forgive you, to screw you, and I quote: 'Ooooh, Mike...I've wanted this for so long...I need this...please...'" My own voice was childish, ugly.

She looked shocked.

*Yeah, caught you out good and proper, Jenkins.* "I know you played me for a fool. And like a fucking fool, I fell for it again."

"But I didn't...I wasn't..."

"Fuck you, Emma Jenkins." I grabbed my jacket. "I'm going. See you around."

I stormed off, my legs moving so quickly, I thought I would topple over. "Play me for a fool. Not again," I muttered under my breath.

Shakespeare's sonnet sprang to mind *"Being your slave..."*

I wasn't in the mood. "Fuck you, too, Shakey."

I was livid. How dare she? How dare she tell me she hadn't slept with Mike Collins? Did she think I was that fucking naive? Well, she could kiss my arse.

I could hear her behind me, calling my name. I ploughed on. People were beginning to stare. One poor unsuspecting bloke happened to be in my line of vision. He became the target of my wrath. "What the fuck are you looking at, twat?"

He shook his head, bewildered, not wanting to get on the wrong side of a five foot-four bundle of anger.

"Laura, wait!"

*I did wait, Emma. For three years I sat on the sidelines and watched you with all your boyfriends, patiently waiting for my turn. Yeah, and look where it got me.*

Strong fingers grabbed my arm and forced me to stop, spun round to face her. "Don't leave me, Laura. Not again!"

I stared at her hand. "I didn't leave you in the first place. You left me, remember?' The words almost spat from my mouth. I tried to move.

"Please?" It was barely a whisper. She pulled me into a hug, crushing the breath out of my body. "Don't leave me, please?"

The pleading note in her voice stopped me.

"Do you know how many times I wanted to come back… speak with you…hold you? Do you know how hard it was not to get down on my knees and beg your forgiveness?"

A sob broke from her, but she caught it and swallowed it back in. "I've watched you for the last ten years, Laura."

I grunted my disbelief.

"Yes. I have. I used to drive past your house, sometimes park up and watch you. You seemed so happy, how could I…" She drifted off. "We were both so young, Laura. We wanted different things."

I broke away and fixed a stony gaze on her tear-filled blue eyes. "Still do." I turned and left her there, still holding my beating heart.

"I didn't sleep with him," she called after me.

*Liar. Fucking liar!* I kept on walking.

She didn't follow me this time. It was for the best. Wasn't it?

I could still picture her standing there, looking lost, rejected. I pulled my jacket around my shoulders to ward off the chill caused by the gaping hole in my chest.

I was fuming, sitting on the bus, on my own, fuming. I was mumbling to myself, arguing with myself, and people were beginning to move away from me. I didn't care.

How dare she? How dare she try and get out of sleeping with Mike Collins. I knew what I had heard that night. If she was so adamant that she hadn't slept with him, why did she say she wanted to beg my forgiveness? What was there to forgive?

Yes. What was there to forgive? Maybe that she had lied to me, had led me on. Had made me believe that I had a chance, a chance with her!

"Fuck her!" It shot out of my mouth before I had time to stop it, and I could hear people muttering behind me about the youth of today. "And fuck you, too!"

It was two old blokes sitting there, expressions grim, probably thinking about how they had fought in two world wars for the likes of me. "There's no need for that, young lady. Think about the children."

I looked about me. There wasn't a child in sight. I was just about to go off on one of them again, when I felt all my energy seep out of me. I could still see the rejection on Emma's face, hear the whispered, "But I didn't sleep with him."

I rubbed my eyes to try and stem the flow of tears that would expose my pain.

I had lost everything.

Again.

# Chapter Twenty-Eight

I didn't hear from Emma. It was a strained week at work, during which I chewed the heads off students and colleagues alike for no reason other than that someone besides me had to suffer.

Saturday morning I was lying in bed, staring at the pale constellations I had put on the ceiling as soon as I moved in, tracing the star patterns with my finger. The whispered "But I didn't sleep with him" danced about in my head like a macabre mantra. I didn't feel the all-consuming anger now, only grief.

An insistent knocking at the front door broke my reverie, and I thudded to the front door.

"Flowers for Stewart." The deliveryman smiled at me, all the while overtly taking in my rumpled hair, puffy eyes, and skimpy pyjamas. "Someone loves you."

I smiled at him, but I really wanted to tell him to shove his comments up his…

"Have a good day." And he was gone.

I shut the door, still a little too shocked to think straight. It wasn't my birthday; who on earth would send me flowers? The bouquet was huge. A myriad of smells wafted forth, jousting for attention with the vibrant colours of the arrangement.

A small card stuck out from the greenery, and I took it out cautiously, as if it was going to explode in my hand.

*Sorry about Sunday. Please forgive me.*
*Can I see you again? Maybe tonight?*
*We need to talk.*
*Love, as always, Em xxx*

I reread the words "We need to talk." I didn't think I could stand another confrontation. An image of Emma's face floated in front of me—blue eyes filled with pain, pain I had put there with my cruel words. Whatever had happened in the past, happened in the past. What was the point in dragging it all up to analyse and confront. It wouldn't, couldn't change a thing.

I sighed, one of those sighs that move your entire body. It was like a coming to terms, a release, a pressure valve hissing out the pain and fear held inside for far too long.

Emma was right. We needed to talk, to get things out in the open and resolve the events that had haunted my life for ten years.

I looked at the card again, and a smile crept onto my lips. Em, eh? It was only then that I noticed the hearts and flowers border. A laugh welled from deep within me, a real laugh that released even more from the pressure valve. It felt good. I felt lighter and freer than I had in years.

Life's too short to be so damn angsty.

Being a woman, I let her stew for an hour before I called her. The phone rang and rang. Maybe I had left it too late. Maybe she'd dec—

"Hello?" She was panting, like she had been running.

"Hello there, Em."

"So you got them, then? Well?"

"They're beautiful."

"Not the flowers. Tonight?"

Her voice sounded urgent, like her whole life depended on my answer.

"I don't fancy going out with you tonight," I said.

"Oh. Okay."

I could hear the hurt in her voice.

"But I'd love to cook for you here. Seven-thirty?"

A smile appeared on my lips as I heard her muffled "Yes" on the other end of the line. I could picture her pumping her fist in the air.

"That'd be lovely, Laura. Do you want me to bring anything?"

*My heart, please.*

God. I felt like a caricature for the romantically addicted, but it felt good. I felt good. And for the first time in years, I felt a little in control. A little. A bit like being a grown up and taking responsibility.

"I said, do you—"

Shit. I had been caught daydreaming. So, I coughed, and began to reassure her I was more than capable of shopping for food and purchasing a bottle of wine on my own. "I'm a big girl, after all."

"Don't I know it?"

Her voice trickled sex, and I don't even think it was intentional. Fuck. It felt like I had just cum in my pants. *Oh, Stewart, get your mind out of the gutter and get down to business.*

I clasped the phone between my fingers like a weapon. It was now or never. "So, you think we need to talk?" There was a lengthening silence on the other end, until I finally let Emma off the hook. "So do I."

She was still quiet, so I continued. "We need to get this out in the open so we can move on with our lives."

"Okay." She sounded distant, like she was going back into her shell.

"Seven-thirty."

"Okay." Her voice was a little stronger; I could hear the resolution kicking in.

We said our goodbyes, and I began to plan. I had only eight hours to prepare. It would be a rush… You know the rest.

Dinner was a success. Chicken breasts cooked with leeks and mushrooms, followed by warm chocolate fudge cake and cream. Emma made orgasmic noises throughout, tantalisingly licking her spoon with the flat of her tongue, alternating that with using just the tip. My dessert was cold by the time she had finished. I was close to my own mini orgasms just watching her eat.

My God! If she could eat a cake like that, what would she be like…

We took our coffees into the lounge and sprawled onto the sofa.

"Do you mind if I unbutton my jeans? I'm stuffed."

I managed a weak nod. She could take her pants off if she wanted, I wouldn't have minded. No sirree, not at all.

At first the conversation was light, as if neither of us wanted to spoil the evening, but we both knew what was coming.

Finally, I took a deep breath. "So, you said we needed to talk."

She sat a little straighter in the chair.

"I'll start, shall I?"

Emma looked down at her hands that were fidgeting with her

pinkie ring. Her face was a mask.

"I slept with Justine Russell."

Her head shot up, her body stiffened.

"I can't deny it. You saw me…us, not that I would deny it anyway." I took a deep breath. "That night, I came looking for you, and—"

"Laura—"

"No, Emma, please, let me finish." I took a deep breath, exhaled. "I got to your bedroom door, and it was locked."

Her mouth opened, and I just looked at her, my eyes pleading with her to keep quiet. "As I said, the door was locked, so I knocked."

"That was you?" She seemed incredulous.

"Emma, please?" I sifted my hands through my hair. God. This wasn't easy. "Yes, it was me. Mike told me to go away, said you were busy. I couldn't believe it—one minute with me, the next with him." A lump formed in my throat, but I had to continue. "I could hear your voice inside the room saying that you were both at college, these things happen, and about how much you needed this." I stopped and picked up my wine to guzzle a large mouthful, hoping it would take the lump in my throat with it.

"Laura, it wasn't like that. It was you I was talking about, not Mike." Her voice was a mere whisper.

My eyes widened at the revelation, and then retreated into slits again. "I need to tell you the rest, Emma. I need you to know."

She nodded, her eyes full of something I couldn't identify.

"You may say that you didn't sleep with him—" I put up a hand to stop her protestation. "Let me finish! But I went on the evidence I heard with my own ears. I left your door and headed for the bathroom, where I lost what little I had eaten that day. Justine found me there, comforted me."

Emma's face showed her disgust at what was obviously the memory of what she had witnessed that night. Blue eyes sparked with bridled anger, and I was sure I could see her lips quivering as if she was struggling to keep from interrupting me.

"You must understand, I was devastated, Emma. I couldn't think straight. Justine offered me a release. She said all the right things, told me that she loved me, pressed all the right buttons. Next thing I knew, we were in my bed. I couldn't even remember getting there."

I couldn't look at Emma. I knew she would be looking at me with the same revulsion I was feeling for myself. What if she had slept with Mike? At least she had done so for the right reasons. She broke my heart in the process, but for the right reasons nevertheless.

"It was the first time I had ever slept with anyone. I lost that, too." I didn't say what else I'd lost; I thought it was obvious. "The next thing I knew, you were standing there. I felt so ashamed, Emma, so dirty. I wanted to hurt you as much as you had hurt me, as much as I'd hurt myself. When you left, I told Justine to go. I used her to get back at you. I couldn't help but feel sorry for her."

She huffed at that, but I ignored her.

"I was to her what you were to me—a pipedream. Neither of us seemed worthy of the one we really wanted." I picked up my drink and leaned back into the sofa, eyes staring straight ahead.

"It was never a pipedream, Laura. I wanted it then as much as you did."

Then. She said "then."

"I just...well I couldn't just cheat on Mike. I had to sort things out first. I didn't know he had locked the door to the room until I was coming to find you."

My chest was rising and falling erratically, and I couldn't breathe properly.

"He tried to make me stay, said all I needed was 'a good see-ing to.' He got quite aggressive at one stage, and I had to force him…force him away. I was still a virgin, Laura. I didn't lose my virginity until I married David."

My eyes shot around and stared at her. A virgin! Emma? But she… My brain couldn't finish the sentence.

Her eyes were tearing. "Straight away I came looking for you to tell you what had happened. I couldn't believe it when I saw…when you and… Why can't I even say her name?" she wailed. "Why has she still got a hold on our lives?"

I moved closer to her and put my hand on her leg, patting it reassuringly. I could feel her trembling beneath my fingertips.

Emma took a deep breath. "I hate her so much, Laura. It had to be her, didn't it? All the way through school, she used to taunt me about you and her. How you two had a past and I was no part of it and never would be."

Tears slipped silently down her cheeks. I wanted to catch them, brush them away, but I still had a niggling doubt.

"Sunday, at Lyme Park, you said you wanted to beg for my forgiveness. Why?"

"It doesn't matter."

"Yes it does, Emma. We need to get this all cleared up. We've lived with it hanging over our heads for too many years."

The air was thick with silence. It seemed to drag on, suf-focating everything under a thick cloud of deceit, shame, and misunderstanding.

It wasn't until her voice splintered through, breaking the tense molecules into smithereens, that the clouds of the past were dispersed.

"Okay." Emma cleared her throat. "Cards on the table." She leaned forward and filled her glass with wine, delaying the mo-ment. She gulped half of the contents and then wiped away the droplets on her lips with her thumb. "You really want to know why I asked for your forgiveness?"

I nodded, transfixed.

"I wanted you to forgive me for not fighting for what I wanted, for running away that night instead of dragging that bitch off you. I wanted you to forgive me for being a coward, for taking the easy way out. I wanted you to forgive me for leaving you. I knew that you would regret what you had done and you would hurt, but I just couldn't stay."

I dipped my head in understanding, tears trailing down my cheeks too.

"It didn't stop me, though."

I looked at her questioningly.

"Two days later, I waited for Justine Russell to come back from the pub and I confronted her."

My eyebrow shot up.

"I threatened her, told her to stay away from you or she'd be sorry."

Both my eyebrows were nearing my hairline now.

A sardonic grin crept over her face. "You know what she did?"

I shook my head.

"She laughed. Said that you'd been the best fuck of her life, and you loved it." Her eyes flicked to meet mine before skipping away again. "I don't know what got into me, Laura, but I pasted the shit out of her. I couldn't stop hitting her and screaming at her to stay the fuck away from you." She turned and faced me full on, her expression begging for understanding.

My face must have said it all.

She swallowed nervously. "That's not the worst of it." Her eyes misted over, and she looked away again. "She pressed charges. That's why I had to move away to my father's—I was bound over to keep the peace."

Her hands agitatedly plucked at an invisible thread on her

top. Blue eyes hesitantly glanced up into my own, expecting some form of rebuke.

I sat silent, waiting for her to continue.

She swallowed again. "If I was seen anywhere near her, I would have been up in court. That would have been the end of my career." She looked down to her lap again. "That's why I didn't come back—I couldn't."

"So—you didn't sleep with Mike, and you beat the shit out of Justine Russell?"

I felt like such a shit. I hadn't trusted her enough then to not let me down, and I hadn't trusted myself enough to think I deserved her. What more was there to say?

She looked miserable. She had exposed her innermost thoughts, revived memories that should have stayed buried. And for what? For someone who wasn't fit to clean her shoes.

Her eyes—so blue, so vulnerable—looked directly into mine, and she whispered, "Can I have a hug?"

Who was I to resist?

We had drunk wine with our meal and quite a few glasses whilst we had been talking, and I was coaxing her into having a Scotch to round off the night.

"I've got plenty of room. Stay over. You can stay in the guest-room, or on the sofa, wherever."

My heart was pleading, *My bed. Please choose my bed. I won't hurt you. I just need to feel you next to me again. Smell you. Watch you when you sleep. Push stray locks away from your face. Know you are there…with me. No strings.*

"Thanks. That'd be great." She took the offered glass and raised it in the air. "To friendship, and all who sail in her."

We both laughed, totally at peace on the outside, but my insides were in turmoil.

It was past midnight when we decided to call it a night. I offered her some large sweats and a t-shirt to sleep in.

She accepted with a smile. "I usually sleep in the buff, but tonight I'd better make an exception. Don't want to frighten you in the middle of the night when I nip to the loo, now do I?"

Yes, please. But I thought I'd frighten her with my reaction, so I just shook my head. A close hug allowed me to breathe her in.

"Night, Laura. See you in the morning."

I left her outside the guestroom and went to the bathroom to get ready for bed. Shit. I hadn't told her about the spare toothbrush.

I trooped down the hall, my feet not making a sound. Her door was ajar, and I could see her stripping off. I felt like a voyeur, but I couldn't take my eyes away. Her skin was smooth, legs strong and firm, thighs toned. She bent over to put her folded clothes on the chair, and I saw her butt—two rounded spheres of muscle. God, how I wanted to run my hands over them.

She turned to face the door, and I was captivated by her breasts—full, curved into a swell, and with dark nipples that were half erect. I held my breath as my gaze slid lower. Dark, coarse hairs guarded her beauty—neatly trimmed and begging to be ruffled. I was riveted. My heart was drumming inside my chest.

"Laura?" A question, softly spoken.

I looked up into dark blue eyes that were fixed on my face, the expression in them unreadable.

"Are you okay?" she asked.

Why did she just stand there naked? Why didn't she cover herself up, put on the t-shirt, cover the objects of my desire? Why did she have to be so beautiful? So unobtainable?

"Toothbrush," I squeaked out. I cleared my throat and tore

my eyes away. "Toothbrush. For you. To use. Night." And off I went at the speed of light, embarrassed at my Tarzan impression and my inability to stop staring. I thought I heard a giggle as I shut my bedroom door.

The next morning I woke to the sounds of music floating up the stairs accompanied by the delicious scent of bacon. My stomach ordered me to get out of bed and investigate. I stumbled downstairs, rubbing the sleep from my eyes. I hadn't slept much, there were too many emotions running around in my head, and my body, for that matter. I had lain awake for hours thinking of everything that had been said, of everything that had been confessed.

Basically, guilt had kept me awake.

Guilt at the thought of Emma beating the shit out of Justine Russell, and then being charged with GBH.

Guilt at Emma having to move away from all her friends because of my weakness. It made my heart ache.

Guilt because of the knowledge that Emma hadn't slept with Mike…had still been a virgin, and I had slept with Justine. If I hadn't been so quick to think the worst, our first time could have been together. In a way, that hurt the most.

Still dressed in the sweats and t-shirt, Emma was in the kitchen cooking breakfast and singing along with the radio. It was a memory, ten years hidden—Emma, in our flat, cooking breakfast.

I stood in the doorway and watched her, the wiggle of her hips, the bobbing of her head as she stirred scrambled eggs around the pan. She held the spoon up to her mouth and belted out the slow song that was blasting from the radio. Texas was accompanying her…words that spoke of being in love…so in love. Words that spewed out promises of being all she ever needed.

And the begging...the needing to know...the longing to know if the object of this woman's love felt the same way.

It would have been so easy to just say, "Yes. I'm so in love with you, too, Emma Jenkins." But I couldn't tell her. Couldn't. Instead I said, "Nice eggs," and nodded at the pan while flashing her a smile. A little different from what I wanted to say, but, once again, I couldn't.

"Oh, you're finally out of the pit then, lazy bones. I've never known anyone who could sleep like you."

Was that an embarrassed smile on Emma's face? I hoped so.

"Nice hair," she added.

I tried to flatten the haystack mass of blonde, but it wasn't haven't any of it. I think it was aroused.

Breakfast was relaxed. It seemed as if last night had been a cleansing of souls, something we had needed to do for so long but hadn't, because we were too scared of the outcome.

We shared the *Telegraph*—her having all the boring financial bits while I looked at the newly released books and the comic strips. Good division. It was, in a word, bliss. I had never felt such contentment. Well, I had, but not for ten years.

"So, what are your plans for today? I'm away again tomorrow, and I hoped you might want to do something before I go."

Did I say bliss? Perhaps I should change that to euphoria. Nah—bliss will do.

I nodded, a piece of toast seeming awfully dry in my mouth.

"Then I'll have to go and get changed. We could do that on the way, if you wouldn't mind stopping at my place?"

I shook my head. I'd follow her anywhere, anytime, and for any reason. I was in big trouble. I was captivated by her again. That couldn't be good, but I couldn't help myself. I was caught like a little fish—hook, line, and sinker.

Chapter
Twenty-Nine

Her house was classic modern, and it suited her perfectly. Although it had the ambience of the present, it exuded a feeling of timelessness, a familiarity.

Before she went upstairs to shower and change, she told me to have a poke about. So I did.

Books lined the shelves, from modern mathematics—yawn— to computer manuals. I wasn't even tempted enough to take one down and have a peek. Then I saw it, tattered, dirty and stuffed in the top corner of the bookcase. It was her poetry anthology from school.

I slipped it from its slot and looked it over. Youthful handwriting adorned the cover in both Emma's hand and mine. Things like "Justine Russell is a twat." My handwriting. "A big twat at that." Emma's. Pop groups' names were scrawled on there, exposing our bad taste. I laughed and began flicking through it.

It fell open on its own to reveal a crumpled piece of paper. The hearts and flowers caught my eye:

*Laura Stewart*
*Loves*
*Emma Jenkins*

With a shaking hand, I moved it aside to reveal Jonson's To Celia. I almost expected it. The annotations were smudged, the writing nearly invisible, and there seemed to be something spilled on it—drops of something. She had underlined:

*I sent thee late a rosy wreath,*
*Not so much honoring thee*
*As giving it a hope that there*
*It could not wither'd be;*
*But thou thereon didst only*
*breathe*
*And sent'st it back to me*

Why had she underlined that particular part? I shook my head and carefully put it back. I couldn't deal with the memories; they were too painful. I would have to think about it later.

I went into the front room. It was bright, cream walls with two large brown leather sofas in the centre. The stripped pine floors were varnished. A large white rug sat pride of place in front of the open fire. It was exquisite, very tasteful—like her.

My eyes drifted to a framed photograph on the mantelpiece. No. It couldn't... I stepped closer. It was. A framed photograph of Emma and me at college, arms wrapped around each other and laughing at the camera.

My hand shook as I picked it up. We had been so happy, content just to be together. If the world had stopped spinning at that exact moment, the events that had come after it would never have happened, and my life would have been so different.

I remembered that day so well. It was taken just after we had received our A levels results.

But that meant…that meant it had been developed after the Justine Russell incident. I didn't understand. Why would she want to be reminded of that?

"Those were the days, eh?"

Her voice startled me, and I mumbled an apology as I thrust the photograph back onto the shelf.

She came and stood next to me, I could smell her freshly washed body, but it didn't cover the smell of her…*her* smell.

Her hair was towel dried and strands of it still clung to her face. She gently lifted the photograph, her eyes sparkling. "Who would have thought that in a matter of hours, everything we knew would be turned upside down. Life, eh?"

What could I say? There was nothing that could excuse what had happened, especially now that I knew she was an innocent in the events. I had followed my own vulnerability, believing that no one could possibly love me, especially Emma. She was too good for me. Still was.

"Has Jack seen this?"

A small smile crept over her face, and she gave a slight nod.

"So he knew who I was?"

Another nod.

"So you knew it was me before you came to school?"

Her wide smile was almost sheepish.

"You little bugger."

The smile was replaced by an all out laugh.

"You two set me up!" I feigned shock. "Why you…" I tickled her right in the ribs, the place where I knew I could get her.

She wriggled like crazy, spluttering, laughing, and trying to catch my hands. We staggered backwards until I felt her legs meet the sofa.

I shoved. Down she went, me on top of her. "Give up!" I

tickled more frantically. She was laughing unreservedly now. "Come on, say it! Say 'Laura Stewart is the Champ.' Go on, say it!" Demon fingers dug into her.

"Okay! Okay! Laura Stewart is the Chump!"

"Why you little…" My fingers dug in again.

"Okay! I give in. Laura Stewart is the Champ!"

My hands stilled but stayed on her sides. We were both panting. Blue eyes locked on my green. The air was thick with expectation. Our breathing was beginning to slow from our exertions, but still had an occasional hitch. Her face wore an unreadable expression. She was so beautiful, and it felt so natural to have her underneath me.

"'Bout time. And don't forget it." I grinned as I spoke, and she returned it with one of her own crooked ones.

"Are you going to let me get up, or are we staying like this for the rest of the day?"

Now there was a thought.

Style Woods was any naturist's dream. No, naturist, not naturalist. Perv. We stopped at the Ship Inn for Sunday lunch and a shandy before we headed into the woods. God, the food was good—Yorkshire puddings the size of tennis balls, and so light and fluffy. Once again I was thinking about food. At least it gave me a brief respite from thinking about Emma, the announcement she'd tucked away, and the underlined passage. I would make a meal of those snippets later.

The woods themselves were coming to life, just like I was. Musty smells seeped up from the undergrowth after the initial rain of spring, and birds warbled their songs from up above us. The river was calm, almost achieving the stillness of a lake in its tranquillity. Ducks charged over in the hope we had some offering for them, like they were pagan gods.

We stood in silence, the need for words redundant. How could anything top this perfection?

Easily.

Emma took my hand into hers. Honestly, I wasn't expecting it. Her fingers curled around mine in possession, holding me fast. I swallowed my heart back down.

"Come on. Let's go."

She led me back along the path to the car, still holding my hand...and my heart.

She took me home and escorted me to my door. Her face was so beautiful, the dying sun casting shadows over her features. "I'll see you soon, okay?"

"When?"

"Not sure. I'll try and make it back for the play?" She put her arms about me and slowly drew me to her.

I melted at the contact. "You take care, okay?" I had choked back the "Please take care, for me," not wanting to ruin the moment with words of possession.

I could smell her spicy scent. Not perfume, her scent, her smell. Her hand came up to my hair and brushed back the stray locks. I looked up into her eyes and drowned. She looked so serious, like this was the most important minute of her life. She kissed my forehead, featherlike. A sigh escaped me.

She placed another gentle kiss on my cheek.

I gripped her waist in ownership.

On the lips. So light, so tender, a gentle brushing of lips, but with that kiss I was truly lost.

A connection in my breast struck me so hard, it took my breath away. It felt like my soul had reached out of my body and pulled hers in. I was whole again.

Then she was gone, and I was once again left wondering whether I had dreamt it all.

L.T. SMITH

# Chapter Thirty

I didn't hear from Emma for two weeks—not a postcard, phone call, text message, nothing. I felt empty without her. I couldn't concentrate, couldn't sleep, even my appetite had died off. Honestly.

It was the opening night of our *Wilde* production, and everyone was in a state of anxiety. Rehearsals had been a nightmare. The kids had buggered up nearly every line in the whole thing. Oscar Wilde was undoubtedly spinning in his grave. I was the only one who seemed unruffled, probably because I had other things on my mind, more important things.

I had to keep busy some way or another, so I sorted out make-up, lights, props. You name it, and I was there. What else did I have?

Jack looked fantastic in his costume—a smoking jacket and cravat, with just a touch of make-up for the people at the back. I never asked him about Emma. It wasn't fair to put him in the middle, and I didn't really want to know if she was with someone else.

She didn't turn up for the opening, or the second night. Jack didn't seem bothered about her absence. It was on the final night that I saw her again.

I was bollocking some Year 9s who had been pissing about with the props the night before. I was in mid rant—real "teacher angry," you know—give the impression that you are boiling mad, but in reality it is all an act. It was also a good way of relieving the tension that was building inside me because I hadn't seen Emma, although the up and coming performance didn't help my nerves either.

"It's not you that I'm disappointed with, just your behaviour." Yeah, right. "Now go away and think about what I have said."

Off they scampered, probably going for a ciggie before the play started, the wise words I had bestowed on them completely forgotten, if they had even heard them in the first place.

"Hello, stranger."

At hearing that voice, my heart cheered, flooded with warmth, then cheered again.

"Oh, hi." I tried to sound aloof. After all, I hadn't heard a word from her for two weeks!

"Come here, you." She grabbed me and wrapped me in a full body hug.

I began to dissolve, then thought better of it and drew back.

She smiled at me, a full crooked one—the ones I loved best— and grabbed me again, crushing me to her breast.

That did it. The feel of those weapons bobbing underneath her shirt was my downfall.

She placed a gentle kiss on my hair. "I really missed you." A soft kiss grazed my ear. "Sorry I couldn't get in contact. You know how things can get."

Before I could answer that actually, no, I didn't, Jack came up to greet his sister. "Hi, Emma. Glad you could make it tonight. Just get in?"

"About thirty minutes ago. I haven't even been home yet.

Had to get here to see my best people." She turned and smiled at me.

I blushed.

"Is Dad here?"

Jack nodded and pointed into the audience to a handsome man in the third row, sitting with a pretty blonde.

"Better get this over with. Are you free later, Laura?"

"Well, I'll have to clear up a bit, keep the caretakers happy, and then I'm all yours."

Her face lit up. "Until later."

"Later it is."

Emma stuck in to help with the cleaning too, making the kids laugh with her antics. After we had cleared up, she and I went to a local wine bar not far from school. I had been there before, as it was gay friendly. The atmosphere was light-hearted yet sultry, although that could have been just my take on it. Maybe I just wanted it to be sultry. A piano sat centre stage, and a middle aged crooner was singing songs from all eras. It was soothing. He took requests if you gave him a decent tip.

Emma ordered a bottle of wine and settled in her chair. Blue eyes flicked over the candle that was standing right in my line of vision. I didn't want anything to spoil my view of her, so I unceremoniously shoved it to the side.

She laughed, and then became serious. "I'm sorry I didn't get in touch with you, Laura. I...I had a few things I had to sort out in my head, you know? I...well, I'm sorry anyway."

"Did you practice that?" I paused for effect, then I grinned. "Cos you should have." I didn't care that she hadn't called, or e-mailed. She was here now, and that's what mattered.

She beamed that smile again, and it was definite—the room

lit up.

We chatted for about half an hour until she excused herself to use the bathroom.

I sat there twiddling the drinks mat, then reading the bottle of wine. *Mmm...good year.* As if I had a clue.

"Excuse me, madam."

Startled, I looked up from my scattered thoughts and met brown eyes.

The waiter stood next to me, holding out a single red rose. "This is for you."

I looked at him dumbfounded.

"And there is a message I am to deliver to you." He cleared his throat. "I sent thee late a rosy wreath, / Not so much honour-ing thee /As giving it a hope that there / It could not wither'd be." He bowed and moved toward the kitchen.

My eyes filled with tears.

"This one's for Laura."

My head snapped around to locate the woman who belonged with that voice. Emma was on the stage, microphone in hand. The music began, the pianist accompanied by a faceless man with a guitar. Emma's voice was deep, soulful, full of emotion, and I was transfixed.

The lights over the stage silhouetted her frame, but I could still see her face, her eyes. I was almost sure the song was by Melissa Etheridge. It was full of love and acceptance, full of completeness. Finding the one...finding the one...she was sing-ing about finding the one. And she was singing that to me, as if I was her one.

A sob tore from my throat. I couldn't believe what I was hearing. Emma was on a stage, in front of a room full of people, singing to me...*to me*. I know I've said it before, but to hear her... God. I was paralysed. My eyes swam with tears unshed, not sad ones, but tears of absolute joy.

She stepped off the stage, her eyes fixed on mine, singing the last stanza as she walked toward me, her hand outstretched in an invitation for me to join her.

I don't remember getting up and walking toward her, but I did. Suddenly I was standing there in front of her, as she told me how she had always known that I was the one.

She stopped singing and lowered the microphone. Aflame with emotion, her eyes looked deeply into mine. She whispered again, "And I knew it was always you."

I kissed her fully on the mouth, my lips open, inviting her tongue inside.

She didn't hesitate, devoured all that I offered, all that I promised. The microphone dropped to the floor, and she crushed me to her as our kiss became frantic. My hands roamed over her back, and then up and down her arms, wanting to possess her, wanting her to possess me.

A loud cheer erupted in the room, accompanied by applause. We reluctantly drew apart and gazed into each other's eyes. I don't know how I could ever have missed seeing the love that I saw there now.

A slow, sexy smile curved her lips. "I love you, Laura Stewart. Always have, always will."

I kissed her again, hard, and then pulled away. "Laura Stewart loves Emma Jenkins. I have done since the first moment I saw you thirteen years ago."

She kissed me with such fervour, I thought my heart was going to combust.

"Let's blow this joint." She grabbed my hand and led me to the table to get our things.

The whole bar cheered as we made our way to the door, but not as loudly as my heart did, or my soul, for that matter.

Emma Jenkins loved me...*loved* me. Understand? Emma Jenkins loved me.

And God, did I love her.

We were back at my place as quickly as we could get there—through the door, coats thrown on the floor, arms and legs wrapping around each other, tongues dancing. Next thing, we were on the sofa, her hands inside my top and grasping at my breast, her dulcet voice muttering words of love and longing.

She was grinding herself into me, and I was pushing back with the same enthusiasm, panting out staccato phrases that rang with my need. "God, Emma...oh God... Emma...yes...that's it...just there."

That spurred her on. She shoved my top up and plunged her face between my breasts.

"Fuck yes!"

Her hot mouth closed over one nipple whilst her hand clutched at the other. One of my hands slipped down the back of her jeans, pushing her into me, whilst the other one was around the front trying to open the buttons of her pants.

"Laura... God, Laura... I want you so...so much. God, I love you...love you." She was thrusting into me.

I nipped at her neck.

"Fuck me...yeeeesssss," she hissed.

My hand reached inside her jeans and slipped effortlessly into her panties. The downy hairs tickled my hand. She gasped and thrust herself forward, trying to get more pressure from my fingers. I could feel the heat of her arousal. I held my breath, waiting for the ultimate contact, waiting to touch the slick folds.

She sprang off me like she had been burned. "We can't do this. Not now!"

What the fuck?

"No. It has to be right, has to be special, not some quickie on the sofa. You mean more to me than that, Laura." She sat back on her haunches, balancing precariously on her heels. Her face was twisted with desire and dismay.

I stroked her face to ease her mind. I could tell that she was worried about my reaction. It came in the form of a small laugh escaping my lips.

She looked startled.

"Sshhh, honey. I wouldn't have it any other way." I gently stroked her cheek. "I've waited too long for you to mess this up now." My fingers settled underneath her chin, and I gently eased her face closer to mine to place a tender kiss on her swollen lips. "When we're ready, when the time's right, and only then."

She leaned forward into my arms, and I wrapped myself around her, protecting her from the world like a warm piece of bubble wrap. Her head nestled underneath my chin, and I rubbed circular patterns on her back whilst listening to her heartbeat slow to normal.

When I told her I would wait, I meant it without reservation. You might think that all I wanted was sex, but I didn't. Sex was not what I wanted with Emma. Oh no. I wanted to make love with her, and that's a big difference.

## Chapter Thirty-One

We didn't go any further that night, just sat on the sofa, arms around one another, and talked for hours. Of course, there was more kissing—long, sensual kisses that blew me away and made me both happy and sad at the same time. Happy, because we had finally overcome our fear of each other, sad, because we had wasted ten years.

Emma's voice broke through my thoughts. "I know what you are thinking."

I turned to look into her eyes, a smile creeping onto my lips.

"You're thinking that we have wasted ten years, aren't you?"

I must have looked startled, because she laughed.

"I know what you mean. But we have to live for the now. I doubt that we would have survived if we had gotten together at eighteen."

I nodded weakly. Deep down, I knew she was right.

"When Jack first spotted the picture of you and told me you were his Ms Stewart, I was nearly beside myself. I wanted to rush to the school, sweep you up and carry you away, like in that movie with Richard Gere. I couldn't think straight. Work was a nightmare. All I wanted to do was see you again and tell you how I felt."

"I thought you said you had watched me over the years?"

"I did, when you lived at Sarah's, but when you moved out, it was like you dropped off the face of the earth."

"Well, in a way, I did. I moved into uni lodgings for my last two years, and you know that is unlike anything the normal world has ever seen."

We laughed and snuggled up to each other. I could hear her heart beating strongly inside her chest. I could smell her essence. My fingers traced the contours of her collarbone, etching every nuance into my memory.

"So," I kissed her collarbone, "why didn't you come and sweep me off my feet?"

She sighed softly. "Because I didn't know if it would be the same. It had been ten years since I had even spoken to you, let alone shared anything else. What if we were completely different people now? I had this image of you in my head. What if you weren't like that anymore, if you had changed? I also worried that you might tell me to sling my hook. By not exposing my feelings, at least I still had the dream of you. For all I knew, you might even be straight."

I glared up at her.

"You never know."

"How long did you wait before making the appointment to see me using Jack as an excuse?"

"Five months."

"Five months? Five friggin' months?" I couldn't believe it,

as you might have guessed from my reaction. Emma had known where I was for five months and hadn't come to see me. I sat up brusquely, wrenching myself out of her arms. "Why on earth did you wait so long? Why didn't you come and speak to me?"

"I couldn't. I didn't know what to say. Poor Jack. I pumped him for information about you—what you liked, where you lived, whether you were seeing anyone." She slipped her hand up and down my back in soothing strokes. Her other hand made its way to my hair. "Look, honey, I was scared. I didn't know what you would say. The last time we had spoken…well…let's just say it was a little tense."

I exhaled the breath I had been holding.

"I wanted so badly to speak to you. You looked the same and—"

"Wait a minute." When I turned to look at her, her face was crimson. "I *looked* the same? But, that means…"

I noted that her face was becoming more flushed, and I could actually feel the heat of embarrassment simmering off of her.

"You watched me," I said matter-of-factly.

Her eyes looked anywhere but into mine.

"Emma. Look at me, Emma."

A shy smile played at the corners of her mouth. "I'm so sorry. I just…I just… Well, you were there and I… It didn't seem as if it would hurt just to look."

"How many times?"

She wriggled uncomfortably.

"Emma. How. Many. Times?"

"Can't remember," she answered, childlike.

I glared at her.

"Okay, okay." She held up her hands in supplication. "I don't know how many *exactly*—a couple of times a week, maybe more." She shrugged. "Sometimes every day."

I sat open mouthed. She had watched me every day for five

months and I hadn't even known it. How could I walk around so oblivious to everything about me? It's a wonder I didn't get run over.

"What made you finally decide to come and see me? What changed your mind?"

"I couldn't stand it any longer. I had to speak with you. God, I was so nervous. And then when you passed out…twice…" She raised an eyebrow.

It was my turn to blush in embarrassment.

"I thought I'd done the wrong thing, that I should have kept away."

"But look at us now," I said smugly.

We were back in position—me sprawled all over her, my arms around her waist, my head pillowed on her breast. "You would have missed this."

"Oh, but I have missed this." She leaned down and kissed me. "So much."

Ditto.

The guestroom stood empty that night. Although Emma had said it would be wiser if we slept separately, as she didn't know if she could keep her hands off me, I wouldn't hear of it. I asked her, in no uncertain terms, if she didn't think I had waited long enough for her to be next to me, snuggling.

I slept like a log. I don't think I even had a dream. Not surprising, really, as all I had ever dreamed of was actually snuggled up next to me. I was in heaven. I was in bed, burrowed into Emma Jenkins, and she loved me.

She loved me!

I wanted to shout it out to the world, but thought better of it, as the suddenly bellowing would probably have scared the shit out of her.

My life was wonderful. It seemed like I had been given back everything that I had lost, and then a little bit extra for good measure. I felt good. She felt good. Nothing could dampen my mood.

I promised myself that I would be a better person from then on. No more swearing, no more getting pissed senseless, no more ripping heads off kids who had not done their homework. I was going to be a role model for all future generations of students. People would think of me and nod their heads approvingly and say, "Laura Stewart was all that was good and perfect." God, I felt smug. I felt supreme.

So that was what it was like to be totally and utterly in love.

Thinking back to how I had felt when I was a teenager, I realised that my feelings for Emma were not a patch on what I was feeling now. I recalled what she had said earlier. Would we have made it? That's a question that could never be answered.

The biggie was "*Can* we make it?"

Morning crept into my bedroom and threw her light over the bed like an old friend. She trailed her fingers down Emma's face, caressing every gradation of her chiselled features. For a moment I was jealous. I wanted to be the only one to touch her. Lost in my musings, I was unaware that blue eyes were taking me in, waiting for my eyes to reach hers.

"Morning."

I loved her voice. It rippled in places inside me that I didn't know existed and set fire to my dormant libido.

"Hiya, sexy." I leaned in for a kiss that started gently but soon became hot and demanding. I didn't care that I had kitten breath; I just wanted to suck her right inside me. Eager hands traced the hems of tops, knees parted luscious thighs, and a rhythm moved hips that had been waiting all their lives to be in this situation.

As the tempo of my hips increased, I could feel the dampness seeping through my pyjama bottoms, hear my breathing becoming ragged with expectation.

Emma's hands drifted to my hair, gripping and tugging, stoking and pulling. Then she began to slow it down, lazily stroking down my spine, her hips withdrawing, her kisses becoming more chaste.

I needed more, but I knew that we also needed time to rediscover each other. I didn't want to just jump into bed with her and have wild, unadulterated, fantastic, ravenous— *God...calm down.*

Let's start that thought again. I didn't want things to get out of control before we had time to adjust to our relationship.

Our relationship. Oh, how I'd wanted to use those two words about Emma and me for so long...too long. I wasn't going to let my feverish libido ruin it now. We had to do it right.

She was looking at me with the same apprehension I'd seen on her face the night before. I had to make her know that I was okay about it.

"Hey," I kissed her, "we've got all the time in the world for that, Emma. It has to be right." I indulged in another kiss. "I want it to be as special as you do."

Her face relaxed and she pulled me to her, wrapping me in her strong arms so I was nestled into her breast.

I was in heaven.

Two hours later, we were showered, dressed, and eating breakfast. We hadn't showered together, although that would have been a good idea—save water, and all that.

We had a fantastic weekend, lazy, in a loved up kind of way. I was euphoric, and I think she was pretty chuffed too. It was funny to watch her expression change from stoic to puppy dog as quick as a flash. All it would take was a touch on her hand, a kiss on her cheek, a soft word murmured into her ear, and she was a ball of mush.

And I loved it.

Monday I was practically skipping down the corridors at school, students staring at me, wondering if I had finally lost my marbles. I had lost something, but definitely not my marbles.

I was the picture of restraint and grace. I responded to excuses about missing homework with, "Ah, well. Life's too short to worry about that. Soon as you can, okay?" I think this unnerved them more than if I had ripped off their heads and spat down their necks, like I would usually have done.

Period five, Jack watched me intently all through his lesson. I could tell that he wanted to ask me something, but he didn't know how to broach it.

After the lesson was over, and the kids had all piled out muttering about "bloody love poems," I could sense someone was behind me.

"Miss?"

There was that question in his voice again.

"Yes?"

Bored shitless teacher response.

"May I ask you a question?"

"You just have," I said.

I stared at him, and he didn't know what to do. When I let a smile slide onto my face, I got an all out grin in response.

God. How had I not seen it? He was the absolute spitting image of his sister, especially when he smiled.

Although I had tried to break the ice, I could tell that Jack was nervous.

"I…just…er…wonderedhowyouwere." The last bit came out in a rush, and he looked everywhere but at me.

I waited patiently for him to work up the nerve to finish whatever he was trying to get out.

"I…erm…just wanted to say," he drew a deep breath, "that I am really glad that you and Emma are friends again."

Did he know the nature of Emma's and my relationship?

"I think she's been the happiest I've ever seen her. I know that something happened between you years ago…but…erm… I'm pleased that you two have sorted it out."

I smiled at him.

"Sorry that I didn't tell you about Emma, that I deceived you for so long, but she asked and…well, you know…" He was shuffling his feet, and gripping and releasing the handle of his bag. "I was so worried about her, Miss."

I looked at him intently.

"She was wasting her life. First she married that dickhead— Excuse me." He blushed, and I gave him a smile that said it was okay. "Then she would just sleep with women left, right, and centre."

"*Excuse* me? What was that?" My voice sounded a little shrill to my own ears.

Jack looked like he wanted the ground to swallow him up.

"She slept with whom?"

"But I thought…"

"She slept with *women*?"

Poor lad. His face was the colour of plaster cast, and a line of sweat was forming on his top lip.

"Well … yeah," was followed by a deep gulp.

I stared at him.

"Emma's…you know… Well, she's…"

I said it for him, as I think it would have choked him to say the word in front of me. "Gay?"

He nodded, eyes fixed on mine, waiting for a reaction.

I laughed.

He stared harder. "Miss?"

"Yes, yes, of course she is. Don't worry about it, Jack. It just came as a surprise, that's all."

Bloody hell. Even though I had kissed, slept in the same bed as, kissed again, fumbled and nearly had sizzling scx with Emma, I hadn't even considered the fact that she might be gay. Stupid, I know, but I had arrogantly assumed I was to be her first. "You were saying?"

He studied me, almost expecting me to laugh again. Shaking his head, he continued. "Well, as I said, I was worried about her. She seemed so unhappy, like she couldn't be bothered with anything. And then I spotted that picture of you and her on the mantelpiece. When I said you were my teacher, I couldn't believe her response."

He raised his eyebrows in the "embarrassed teenage boy" kind of way and grimaced.

After an eternal pause, I prompted him.

He cleared his throat and tried to maintain eye contact, although the subject matter must have been making him nearly die from embarrassment.

"She seemed almost possessed. She grabbed my shoulders and said was I sure, not just the once, but three times." He rubbed his shoulder as if remembering Emma's iron grasp. "Then she wanted to meet you, and then she didn't. She kept on saying she was going to see you, and then she'd chicken out at the last minute."

Reminded me of someone else I knew.

"When I made the appointment, she was so happy. Then she kept on changing her mind every time I spoke to her—one minute she was coming, the next, she couldn't face it. But I'm glad that she did." He smiled broadly. "She's a different person now,

Miss. I just wanted to tell you that, and thank you."

I know I shouldn't have done it, rules and all that, but I grabbed that wonderful young man and nearly squeezed the life out of him. "No, Jack, thank *you*."

And thanks to your wonderful sister, too.

# Chapter Thirty-Two

Tuesday and Wednesday swept past in a wonderful haze. I saw Emma both evenings. I wouldn't have thought it possible, but we were growing closer and closer. I was so at peace.

I actually asked Emma about her past relationships. I knew I should have left it where it belonged, in the past, but I had to know the details.

She didn't bat an eyelid when I told her what Jack had said. Actually, she chuckled rather endearingly and told me that she had always had her suspicions about her sexuality—especially after she got to know me at school. She had married David in an attempt to fit into the narrow mould of what society deemed "normal." She freely admitted that it had been a big mistake.

I was intrigued by her reference to the bit about me and high school, but she was having none of it. Every time I broached the subject, she deftly avoided it.

Still a voice inside my head insisted, *I'll get you in the end, Emma Jenkins. And in more ways than one.*

When Emma turned up on Thursday evening, she looked beautiful. Her hair was still damp, and I could detect her signature scent, *Eternity*. I stood in the open door and waited for her to come in, but she kept hovering on the doorstep, almost as if she was shy.

"What's the matter with you? Are you coming in or what?"

She just stood there looking bashful, and beautiful, one hand hidden behind her back.

"Come on. Dinner is nearly ready."

But no, she just stood there.

"What've you got behind your back?"

"It's about time," she said with a feigned pout. "I thought you teachers didn't miss a trick." The hand she drew from behind her back held a dozen, vibrant red roses on long stalks, within a mass of greenery. "A rose for my rose." Her crooked smile was entrancing.

I brushed the bouquet aside so that I could pull her in for a deep kiss. I felt our connection click into place just before I reluctantly drew back to examine my gift. "They're beautiful, just like you."

I kissed her again, and then plucked one perfect flower from the bunch. I captured her gaze and riveted her to the spot as I held the vivid bloom out to her and softly quoted, "'My lurve is like a red red rose that sweetly sprung in June. My lurve is like a melody—'"

I didn't get to finish. She scooped me into her arms and laid one on me. I wasn't concerned about the neighbours. They could get their own woman.

My woman. *My* woman. Mine. *All* mine.

Dinner was perfect. Emma was perfect. The evening was perfect. All in all, everything was—as you might guess   flawless.

"How would you like to go somewhere special for the weekend? My treat." Blue eyes waited patiently for me to answer.

I was deliberating over the word "special." Did she mean special as in "go somewhere and do different things for a treat" special, or special as in "it has to be right, has to be special" special. My heart longed for the latter, but I would also be content with the first option.

"I'd love to."

Emma's face lit up. "Leave the arrangements to me. I'll pick you up at six-thirty tomorrow. Can you stay until Monday? I know it's a bank holiday, but you might already have made other arrangements." Eager eyes waited for my answer.

"I'm all yours."

And I was, too.

## Chapter Thirty-Three

Funny how time drags when you are anticipating something. If I was going into one of those situations where I was bricking myself, like at the dentist's or waiting for my phone bill to arrive, then time would race ahead, sticking two fingers up and shouting, "Kiss my arse," and then stop just as I was entering the testing time. Stop, and then…hold, leaving me dangling there until the will to live had been sapped out of me.

But if you are looking forward to something, time becomes Super Bitch and changes all of the rules. Each second seems like someone scraping their nails down a blackboard; each minute is a bloke fart in a lift stuck between floors and not being able to escape for what seems like forever. And every hour, God, every hour is like listening to Michael Jackson singing.

You get the drift.

Kids have a knack for recognising a weakness and pressing against it with all their might, and my students were a bloody nightmare. But they didn't stand a chance. I had more experience being a pain in the arse than they had. Believe me, I was the nightmare. Their graceful and peaceful Ms Stewart became Ms Obstinate, Ms Angry, and Ms If-You-Piss-Me-Off-Again-You're-Going-To-Regret-It. Do you remember when I said that future generations would think of me and believe I epitomised "all that was good and perfect"? Well, I would now be remembered as The Evil One.

The day was filled with childish mutterings of "how unfair," "should just grow up," "what's the point." And that was just me. The kids weren't as forgiving, and I'm certain I heard the words "tight," "arsed," and "cow" floating my way.

Bless. You've got to love them.

I was showered, packed, and pacing by five-fifteen. Eventually, six-thirty crawled around to stop languidly at my door. I was jittery, expectant, and sweating profusely. Why, I didn't know. I had been for a wee four times in fifteen minutes, that's how wired I was.

When the bell rang, my heart stopped…listened…took note, and then started again. I was like a bloody teenager.

"Hi, Emma." My voice was totally under control. The simile "as cool as a cucumber" could have been written in reference to me. "Don't tell me its six-thirty already." I had tried to sound incredulous, but it came out sounding as if I was a simpleton.

She didn't notice, and the reason she didn't notice was because she was as nervous as I was. I could see her swallowing rapidly, as if her throat was attached to her eyes, which were blinking like she'd a bit of dirt in there.

Emma cleared her throat. "You set?"

Woman of few words, that's my girl. Her body language and the lack of dialogue made me believe that maybe this was "the" special that I wanted, but I wasn't going to set my heart on it. I had done that before, and I wasn't ready to feel that devastation again. We had all the time in the world, and I wasn't going to risk that for anything. As long as we were together, that suited me down to the ground.

We packed the car and both visited the toilet again, so it was nearly seven before we set off. Emma put a classical CD in the player and turned to look into my eyes. "If I were you, I'd get some sleep. We'll be on the road for about three and a half hours."

"Are you going to tell me where we're going?" I wasn't actually too concerned about the location, but my brain was trying to digest why she wanted me to get some rest.

"It's a surprise."

She turned away. Discussion over.

I thought I should do what the lady wanted. I didn't want to be tired, for whatever the evening might bring. I pushed my seat back and inclined it.

After a couple of hours, we stopped to get something to eat at a lovely little pub in the middle of nowhere. Though it was May, it was still nippy in the evenings, and we were welcomed by a roaring fire. The blaze lured us to set up home, so we did. We ate homemade country vegetable soup and warm rolls. Emma sat with her back against the wall, facing the door. I was totally at peace as I sat opposite her, engraving every detail of her and our surroundings into my memory.

The flickering light of the fire made her features ethereal, and the setting seemed like a dreamscape. The amber glow softened her face and made it look as if she was totally relaxed, but I knew there was a tension trickling through her. I could see the slight stiffness in her body. What I didn't know was why she should be tense. It was only me and her there. She had to know I wouldn't hurt her.

We sat in silence, expectation thick in the air. The local beer slipped down our throats a little too easily.

"Another?" I asked, hoping she'd say no. She did.

"We'd better make tracks." She leaned forward and tapped my hand, and I felt the charge buzz through my arm and right through my body. "I'd like to get there as soon as possible." There was that crooked smile again, and I felt another buzz. "We don't want to be sleeping under the stars, do we?"

I wouldn't have minded, as long as I was with her.

The remainder of the journey was uneventful. I tried to guess where we were going, but as soon as the headlights lit up a road sign, it was behind us.

It was just after eleven when I woke to the low tones of Emma's voice blending perfectly with Faure's *Requiem: In Paradisum.* I think it was the closest to heaven I had ever been. And her eyes. God, those eyes. They glowed in the darkness of the car like chips of sapphire. It was then I realised we were parked.

"Laura? Laura, are you okay? Honey?"

I could hear the concern in her voice, but it took me a couple of seconds to respond; I was mesmerised. She was so beautiful, so beautiful.

"Never been better." My voice cracked a little. To cover it up, I leaned forward and captured her lips, savouring the moment, as if I was deliciously feeding from her. I drew back and looked into her eyes. "I love you so, so much."

An all out grin burst onto her face. "Good job, too, or else I would have to punish you *severely.*" She growled and lunged at my ribs, where she tickled mercilessly.

After a spontaneous tickle-come-snogging session, we exited the car. I couldn't see a thing, just the silhouette of Emma grabbing our bags. I grabbed hold of the bottom of her shirt and allowed her to lead me around to the front of the hotel. I froze when I saw the illuminated sign outside.

The Whitby Lodge.

We were in Whitby. I didn't understand.

"Ta da!" She looked apprehensive, like she was waiting for a response, any response other than my exquisite impression of a statue.

I just stared at the guesthouse. It was the same one we had gone to on our school trip thirteen years ago. Granted, the paint-work was a different colour, but all in all, it was the same place.

She set the bags on the ground and watched me intently.

"But…" I tried to scramble inside my head for something to say.

"We don't have to, Laura. We can stay somewhere else. I just thought…" Her face was falling; she looked crushed.

'No…no…it's perfect. It's just a shock. I didn't think you would remember, that's all."

"How could I forget." It wasn't a question; it was a statement.

She stared into my eyes, and I could see her eyes misting up and becoming distant as she stepped back into the memory.

"This has been engraved in here," she tapped the side of her head, "…for thirteen years. I wanted us to see it again." A long arm stretched out to me, a slender hand open in invitation. "Come on, baby. Let's check out those memories and see if we can add a few."

Her fingers curled around mine, and she pulled me close to place the softest of kisses on my forehead.

After checking in, we climbed eight flights of stairs—the ones designed for hump-backed dwarfs with extremely small feet and nerves of steel—to our old room.

My heart fell into my shoes when she opened the door to reveal two single beds, but she didn't seem at all fazed by this development. Actually, she seemed pretty happy. I felt like a twat—for want of a better word. I know I said "whatever will be, will be," but I was hoping that this would be that special time.

A sigh escaped me as my expectations went tumbling back down the stairs.

Emma closed the door behind us and then went over and turned on the lamp beside her old bed. Her attention shifted back to me. I stood rooted to the spot, trying to look nonchalant. She watched me intently, as if trying to understand what I was thinking. And there was something else. I had no idea what it was, just that there was something.

"Well, this is a surprise. Those stairs nearly killed me when I was sixteen, I think you'll have to get the Fire Service to get me down them again." An attempt at humour, but the tightening of my throat gave me away as the words had seemed to squeak out through the constricted gap.

Emma turned from me and went to the sink to get a glass of water.

I stood there, just stood there.

What was the matter with me? *"Snap out of it, girl. You're here, with Emma Jenkins, and she loves you. Loves you!"*

Lost in my mental pep talk, I failed to see Emma standing directly in front of me, her leg touching the bed that had been mine. She was waiting for me to focus on her and the water in her hand.

"Laura." Her voice was so quiet. "Laura, I… I need to tell you something."

I was focused on how close she was to me.

Her face was earnest. "Do you remember the last time we

were here?"

How could I forget? It had been the living embodiment of the pleasure and pain theory— having the woman of my dreams here with me, but knowing that she would never be mine. I nodded, still unable to speak.

"Well, I have a confession to make." Shaking fingers nervously played with her hair. "Remember how we blamed Justine Russell for absolutely everything?"

I nodded, though I didn't really want to hear Justine's name at that moment.

"Well—"

My interest was piqued. "Well what?"

She raised the glass of water and, with a quick movement, poured the contents all over what had been my bed on that long ago outing.

"I don't understand." And I didn't.

"It was me."

I looked at her.

"I poured water on your bed that last night, not Justine."

My mouth fell open. I was speechless—a very unusual condition for me, believe me. "You! You poured the water…" I gawked at her.

She nodded.

"Why on earth!"

"I wanted to see what it would be like to share my bed with someone that I…loved."

"Loved?" I was astonished. "But you didn't even know me."

"You're wrong. I first noticed you at the end of Year Ten. The image of you is still so clear in my mind. You stopped my heart that day."

I stopped her heart? Mine was now racing. I swallowed nervously, trying to calm myself down, trying to stop me making a fool of myself. "What happened?"

"Well…" She hesitated, then resumed. "I was walking down the corridor on my way to Maths, completely oblivious to school and listening to the near conquests of Maria and her cronies." She swallowed hard.

I remembered all too well that Maria was one of the Bitches.

"Then suddenly, like a vision, you were there, standing to the side with an otherworldly look on your face. I thought you were something out of my imagination."

My eyes were filling with tears. She was describing the exact same moment that I had seen her.

"When I saw you, I felt something click, like I had known you all my life, even longer. I didn't know what to do. I had never felt that way about anyone, never mind another girl." Her feet shifted nervously, and her fingers gripped the empty glass so tightly that her knuckles went white. "I felt scared and elated, both at the same time."

My heart soared and I rushed into her arms, knocking the glass from her hand. We clutched each other tight, like we were balancing on a precipice and were each other's salvation. I tilted my head back and looked into her eyes. The room seemed to fade away, and the world narrowed down to only us. I could feel her heart next to my chest, thumping out an incessant rhythm that matched my own.

"Do you know how long I have waited for you? Do you know how much I want you, need you, love you?" I watched her tongue graze over her lips. It seemed like an invitation.

The distance between us was agony. Slowly, I rose until soft lips caressed mine, making gentle circles so light, it seemed as if it was a dream. Our lips became more insistent. Repressed emotions came alive and surged to the surface. Lips parted to allow tongues to pass between and stroke until the sensation became delectably unbearable. Hands roamed, needing no guidance to direct them, their journey etched in memory from eons of travels.

As my fingers fumbled with the buttons of Emma's shirt, I resisted the urge to tear it from her torso like a mad woman and expose her body to my ravenous eyes. Slipping her shirt from her toned shoulders disclosed a delicate bra that scarcely covered her breasts, and my mouth longed for just one taste of her. I slipped down first one strap, and then the other, revelling in the unwrapping of this precious gift whilst she nuzzled my hair. I could feel her breathing me in.

Her hands had worked their way to the front of my blouse. She was dextrous and gentle, my own hands redundant in my disrobing. The cool air touched my exposed skin just a moment before her warm lips. I sighed. My hands crept around her waist to draw her pelvis to mine, pulling her hard against my body. Her lips gently sucked the pulse point on my neck until seemed as if my heart was in her mouth. The rhythm of our hips began an ancient dance, swaying seductively against one another, seeking the ultimate connection of our bodies, hearts, and souls.

The button of my jeans was prised open. Avid hands dipped inside and slowly pushed the cloth downward. I toyed with the button, flicking and stroking the cool metal until the temptation of her flesh made me succumb to my desires, and I released it.

We stood in front of each other, naked for the first time. My need for her almost choking me, my breath caught in my throat. My feasting eyes roamed over the curves and swells that underscored her beauty, her femininity, her raw carnal appeal. Random thoughts skipped through my mind, eventually settling on the phrase that I was sure I would be using like a canto: "My woman...all mine." The words sang to me, promised me life. They swore undying love and devotion.

In a blessing granted to me from a lifetime of praying for this moment, we merged together like a jigsaw puzzle of two pieces. Her softness greeted me like a memory. It was the reuniting of souls.

I moved downwards, my tongue and lips tracing taut flesh. Her breathing was erratic, soft moans issuing from her throat in a continuous murmur. My hands caressed her skin, skin like silk, yet with firm muscle beneath. I wanted to throw her down and show her how much I desired her, needed her, yearned for her touch. I wanted to love her, make love to her, show her how much I loved…

But I couldn't, even though my need was consuming me. I craved the sound of her voice crying my name in ecstasy, hungered for her hands in my hair, pushing me away only to pull me back. My hand gently cupped Emma's right breast whilst my tongue teased the pebbled flesh around her nipple of the left.

I guided her backwards until I could feel the resistance of the bed against her legs. Then I lowered her down, so carefully, as if she could break and melt away, taking my soul with her. Our breathing, our scent filled my senses. The feel of her was an addiction that subverted all rational thought.

She was on her back, and I slipped above her like her shadow. I wanted to crawl inside her, become part of her. I couldn't get close enough, couldn't satisfy the longing that was burning inside me.

The sensation of full body contact was like a balm, soothing me with her love. Her hands trickled down my spine, and then strong fingers dug into my behind, pulling my need against hers. It felt so right, so true. I don't know how anyone can say that love can be wrong, no matter who it is with.

The rhythm of our hips began again. My hands went lower, my lips on their trail. I could feel her fingers tightening in my hair, harder, more insistent. I was impelled to sink lower, licking and stroking her abdomen. My tongue delved into her navel. It felt like a connection. My fingers greedily grasped and caressed her skin—gasoline on flames of passion that were already out of control.

I reached the apex of her core, wanting to sample the fruits that would taste sweet upon my tongue and ruin me for anybody else. Soft hairs tickled my chin as I settled between her legs, preparing to enter her secret place. A gentle breath escaped my lips. She moaned, and I moved lower to kiss her parted thighs.

She thrust herself into me, wanting more, trying to rush me, but I had waited too long for this moment. I would take my time with her, taste every part of her, touch every hidden place.

I could feel my own excitement growing, but I delayed quenching it. I would wait, forever, if need be.

My tongue eased along the slick folds, lightly, as if it didn't want to be intrusive, slight licks, just to taste. My hand came up and separated the flesh that covered her innocence, allowing me access to her femininity, her essence. When my tongue plunged inside her, it was like dipping into a honey pot made just for me. She tasted as I had imagined heaven might taste, but sweeter. I nearly came then.

Her body was throbbing; so was my need. I stoked her more quickly, wanting her to feel the escalation but not yet reach the precipice of orgasm. She was gripping the back of my head, grinding her centre against my mouth. I was loving it, loving her.

I could feel my own orgasm forming, and I had to purchase my need against her thigh, her hip, her hand. I didn't care where, as long as she was there with me when I came.

My index finger stopped at her opening as I toyed with the idea of entering her. When I looked into hooded violet eyes, they were pleading with me to fill her.

Slowly, gently, I entered her, my tongue still working on her nub. I pulled out, then filled her with two fingers, gently pumping my arm in the same rhythm as her hips. I reached deep inside her, curling my fingers against the spot and then stroking in and out.

I pulled my fingers from her, and she gasped at the sudden absence of contact. My mouth sucked each lip in turn, twirling and nipping as my mouth brushed against her clit. I went lower and eased my tongue deep inside her. She was grinding against my face at an almost frantic pace. I could feel her insides tensing around my tongue.

It was exquisite torture.

I wrapped my arm around her hip, never missing a stroke. The beat pulsing from our bodies was a metronome of need, of desire, of love.

Tighter. Tighter. Her walls were imprisoning my tongue in their depths, drawing me in.

The vibrations inside her inflamed me. My hips were thrusting themselves against the bed, trying to achieve my release. And then, like a fantasy, over she went, pushing herself into me, crying out my name over and over again, which sent me crashing into orgasm with her.

Searing white light blinded me, yet I could see more clearly than I had for years. Our hips were moving, my arm trying to control her loss of control. Little jolts of pleasure still stayed around for the duration, pockets of pleasure for Emma and me alone until her hips gradually stopped moving.

I still hadn't had my fill of her. She dragged me up her body and pounded her hips against mine, and the sensations began all over again, like we hadn't just made love.

Emma effortlessly flipped me onto my back and straddled me, her lips possessing mine, frenzy on her features. She looked as if she was in a trance, but my name spilling from her lips told me she knew whom she was with.

Wild and passionate, she pushed herself between my legs and began thrusting hard. Her teeth grazed each nipple in turn, undecided about which she should possess. Disregarding the exquisite orgasm of minutes before, I wanted a second, a third. I wanted it all.

"FFFFFFuuuccccccccckkkkkkkkk… EEmmmmmaaaaa!" I crashed over the edge, Emma there to save me as I fell.

She held me, comforted me, owned me from that moment on.

Tears blinded me. Gentle fingers brushed them away, capturing some of their essence to taste. Comforting words poured from her as concerned eyes took in my state.

I stroked her cheek. "I just love you so much," I whispered.

She pulled me up into a sitting position, kissing me wetly, tongues sliding over swollen lips, hands frantic. We adjusted our position so that we each had a leg wrapped around the other's waist. We were lost in each other as our tender centres rubbed against slick thighs, easing the ache that was still there.

We each slipped a hand between clenched thighs and nurtured the bud there to flowering. Rhythms became erratic, breathing laboured, arms aching, thighs crushing.

"Llllaaauuuraaaa… Llllaaaurrra… God… God… I love… you…love you."

We came together, whispering words of love and devotion with swollen tongues into tired ears. When at last we lay down, we were exhausted, but temporarily satiated.

It seemed as if the dam I had erected to hold back my emotions before she came back into my life had burst, and I was forever lost in her.

Despite our exhaustion, we woke up throughout the night to make love again and again, each time as amazing as the first. One time, I woke with Emma between my legs, loving me with her mouth. The sight of her raven locks buried there nearly tossed me over the edge. Blue eyes glanced up from their task to capture my gaze—the swirling of her tongue incessant, fine hair tickling my thighs and stomach, her eyes never leaving mine. I could feel the orgasm building, and my eyes drifted closed.

"I want to see you. I want to watch your eyes as you cum."

I opened my eyes and focused them unwaveringly on hers, digesting all that was her as

gentle fingers stroked my stomach. I leaned forward and cupped her face, bestowing a kiss on each eyelid, each cheek, her nose, and eventually, her lips. "I love you, Emma Jenkins."

That elicited her crooked smile. "I love you, too." She climbed up my body and slipped beside me. I nestled in the crook of her arm, my head on her breast, my arm around her waist. "Sleep now. You need to rest."

I don't think I have ever felt so contented or relaxed, or so loved. She made my life complete, and I was deliriously happy.

Utterly, deliriously happy.

# Chapter Thirty-Four

Sunlight sifted in through the small space between the floral curtains. I could feel its warmth on my fingers. My right side was wedged firmly against Emma, heat from her naked body insulating me from the chill of the room. My left leg was between her thighs, and I withdrew it slowly so as not to waken her.

"Good to see you're finally awake."

My green eyes shot to twinkling blue eyes that held glints of amusement. "How long have you been awake?"

"Oohh…about…let me think, about an hour." Emma flashed me a smile. "But you were wrapped so tightly around me, I couldn't move."

"You should have just pushed me out of the way." Belying my words, I snuggled closer, embracing her, taking in the mingled scent of our bodies.

"I'll rephrase that—I didn't want to move. Though Nature is

calling."

We got up and used the facilities, then clambered back into bed and resumed our positions. Relishing the contact as we lay in each other's arms, we chatted about anything and everything. Eventually, inevitably, the subject of our last visit to Whitby Lodge cropped up.

"God but it was a nightmare being in bed with you, feeling as I did, especially when Ms Davies and Ms Wilkins started to have sex."

She laughed. "Yeah, that was a nightmare."

I stared at her. "You heard them?" My voice reflected my shock.

"Who didn't? Now, they were loud." A smile crept onto Emma's face. "But not as loud as you." She kissed me gently. "I thought I would ravish you then and there. I was so turned on—having you so close to me, being able to smell you..." she sniffed my hair, "...touch you..." she trailed her fingers down my arm, "...and have my leg between your thighs." She looked down at my thigh that was firmly planted between her own. "I honestly don't know how I managed, especially when you moaned."

My face blushed beet red. I was incredulous, and embarrassed to boot. "But you were flat out, dead to the world!"

"I don't think I slept more than twenty minutes that night. I kept watching you. I couldn't believe that I was in bed with Laura Stewart." She stroked my face with the tips of her fingers. "When they started, *really* started, my body betrayed me. I had to get as close to you as I could, as close as I dared to. It was only the horror of being caught that stopped me from trying for more."

"But you knew I was gay, right?"

She nodded.

"Then why didn't you do something? You knew I was turned

on."

"Yes, I knew you were turned on. Those little mewling noises you were making made sure of that." Her fingers cupped my chin and tilted my face up for a kiss. "What I didn't want was for us to…you know…do it,' she blushed, "just because they were doing it. I wanted you to be with me for the right reasons. I couldn't have survived it if the next day you said that it was just a one time, spur of the moment thing."

I understood what she meant, and it made sense. I would have felt exactly the same way. I hugged her to me. "Okay. But if you fancied me so much, why didn't you pin a move on me?"

"Many reasons. I tried to get you to go for me. Remember *Silence of the Lambs*?"

I nodded.

"Do you really think I was that scared?"

I nodded again.

"Cheeky bugger."

I grinned.

"No. I had seen it before, but I thought it would make a great reason to grip hold of you."

"You'd seen it before?"

She nodded shyly.

"What would you have done if I'd picked F*ried Green Tomatoes*?"

Emma grinned. "Easy. I would have been inconsolable and fallen into your arms to weep out my grief."

"Why you sly—"

She kissed me, and I felt the yearning inside me rising again, but neither of us had the strength to pursue it right then.

"What else?" I needed to know.

"Let me see."

Blue eyes became distant in thought. I actually saw her return to the present as those gorgeous eyes filled with light again.

"I know. Remember that first Christmas?"

I nodded. "The disco at the Youth Centre."

"Well, that night I was going to kiss you."

I began to interrupt, but she put her hand over my mouth. I could still smell myself on her fingers, along with the soft scent of soap.

"Yes, I was going to kiss you and then tell you how I felt. I'd spent so long plucking up the courage, and when I caught that same look in your eyes, I decided to make my move."

"And that bastard Rob Evans stopped you!"

"Laura."

"What?"

"Let me finish."

I nodded, feeling sheepish.

"As I was saying, I walked across the dance floor, and yes, Rob intercepted me."

I made a harrumphing noise, still wanting to twat that fucker. She gave my arm a little squeeze, and my anger seeped away.

"I laughed at everything he said and agreed with all his ideas about how stuffy it was in there, and then escaped. You were gone."

Shit. I knew what she was going to say next.

"I looked for you everywhere and eventually asked Justine, of all people, if she'd seen you. She told me you had gone to the ladies, and she *also* told me, and I quote, 'Keep your fucking hands off Laura, she's mine.' I couldn't believe the sight that greeted me in the loos."

"I'm so sorry," I wailed. "I thought I didn't have a chance with you. I was so upset. Cassie was trying to calm me down."

"That's not what it looked like to me."

I tried to protest, but she hushed my lips. "It's in the past. Forget it."

"Why did you get off with Evans?"

She looked pained. "I was so angry and hurt, I… I overreacted. I saw you leave and wanted to chase after you, beg you to forgive me and…and…tell you how sorry I was that I had read you wrong."

"Read me wrong? How so?"

"It was obvious that you weren't interested in me that way, and I didn't want to jeopardise our friendship. You meant so much to me. Still do."

"Why on earth did you think I wasn't interested in you? I was like your shadow. If you said jump, I'd ask, 'How high?'"

"Lots of reasons. The main one was how you would avoid touching me."

Startled, I sat up.

"You wouldn't even let me hug you. You always seemed embarrassed by it." Sadness paled the intensely blue eyes.

"It's only because I couldn't trust myself not to molest you on the spot," I protested. "My hormones went into overdrive every time you were near. I thought you would be disgusted and tell me to fuck off. I didn't want to risk our friendship either."

Strong arms pulled me back into her embrace and loving kisses were scattered all over, ending on waiting lips. Her eyes pinned me to the spot with a look that was dead sombre.

"Another reason was Justine Russell." Her eyes clouded over, and I was sure I saw hate flicker there, fleetingly, but still there. "She was forever having digs at me, saying that you and her were… You know. It made me feel sick to think of her touching you. You deserved so much more than that *bitch*." The last word erupted from her mouth like a curse.

"But we didn't… I never…well not until…"

"That's all in the past. We have our future to consider. And if you're a good girl, I'll tell you what gave me the courage to try again."

Her face lit up. She looked liberated, free of the memories

that had haunted her.

I was intrigued about that night, but mainly I was elated at the prospect that Emma Jenkins had spoken of our future. Not *the* future, but ours.

Life was good.

By twelve o'clock, we were showered, dressed, and fed. We decided to take in the sights of Whitby, as it had become quite the cultural place to visit over the years, esoteric in its own charming way. Cafés lined the streets, and books lined the cafés. It was relaxing.

We visited Whitby Literary & Philosophical Society, a charming Edwardian museum, where I was the boring one and bought a teacher's pack. How anyone can visit Whitby and not be fascinated by Bram Stoker's Dracula is beyond me. The atmosphere of the place screamed gothic, and the vision of a man in a black cape played in my imagination.

As well as the educational side to the museum, I found the toilets to be perfectly glorious. Funny expression for a public convenience, I know, but it wasn't any run of the mill visit. Emma and I went in there to freshen up and ended up in the end cubicle, clothes barely covering our bodies and deeply entangled in a passionate tryst. God. She was hot, and I was horny.

I had most of my hand inside her, pushing into her with a ferocious need that bordered on frightening. She was grunting and pushing back, her juices slicking my fingers and wrist.

The outer door to the loos creaked open, and at the sound of voices, I stilled my hand and waited.

Emma kept up a slow, rhythmic movement, her hooded eyes boring into my own. "Don't stop."

She had spoken so softly, I had to keen my ears to catch it.

She continued to grind herself onto my fingers, the tip of her tongue sweeping along her bottom lip, her perfect white teeth biting into red lips. She moaned again.

"Are you all right, luv?" came a concerned elderly voice from outside.

"Never better." My eyes never leaving Emma's, I leaned in for a kiss, and she returned it with abandon. I kept thrusting, impaling her on four fingers.

Her hands tightened in my hair as she leaned down to bite my neck.

"Oh yeah!"

"Are you sure you're all right?" The voice was closer to the door this time.

"Oh God…yeah…oh yeah."

For a long moment, there was utter silence on the other side of the door. A toilet flushed, then the hand dryer burred, and eventually the outer door opened and closed.

Alone again. Thank the Lord.

I teased her, played with her want. I wanted it all. I wanted her so much, I was blind to everything else around us.

"Please don't stop…*please*…"

And I couldn't. The rhythm of my hand was beyond my control, and breathing had become secondary to my need to please her.

Her orgasm ripped through her, from her, and the roar of it ricocheted around the empty room. Her legs gave way almost immediately and she slipped down the wall, taking me with her. We were tangled in a cocoon of limbs, my head nestled on her quivering stomach, my hands still underneath her, clinging to warm, sticky flesh. A slow kiss ensued, our mingled breathing rough.

Not the most romantic of places, the loos. But it didn't matter where we were as long as I could be with Emma, in any way.

My own gratification was achieved through her satisfaction. I was content to give.

And I wanted to give her everything.

Outside the toilets, we were greeted by some amused looks and some not so amused glares. Bugger. Everyone must have heard what we had been up to. It was definitely a situation for what is commonly known as a "Sharp Exit" manoeuvre. We scuttled to the door and ran outside, laughing and hugging each other.

I had never done anything like that before. Well, teenage fumblings, but never anything like that, never anything so overwhelmingly powerful that it robbed me of reason and propriety. It a long while before the euphoria ebbed.

From the history museum, we went to a local historic site. The Abbey was an old ruin that exhibited the ruthlessness of mankind, its decimated walls showing the destruction imposed upon it during Henry VIII's dissolution of the monasteries all those centuries ago. It was also a reminder of the cruelty inflicted in the name of religion, especially when Henry decided papal rule was a thing of the past, and money collected should go to the kingdom and not Rome. Of course it also gave him the all clear to divorce and marry again.

Visiting the remnants sobered us both up. It felt pretty creepy, too, especially with all the Goths roaming the place, their whitened faces and black hair creating a tableau like that of a black and white horror film. I was one never to pass up an opportunity to get a grip on my girl, so I clutched at Emma's arm.

It was an exhausting day—physically, mentally, and emotionally.

That evening, we sat eating fish and chips out of the paper while watching the ships enter the harbour, like an old married couple. I was contented. There I was, with the one person I loved above all others, and she loved me in return. Tranquil.

Idyllic. Perfect.

The weekend flew by in a blur of activity, Emma and I exploring Whitby by day, and exploring each other in ardent lovemaking at night. The landlady of the guesthouse gave us curious looks whenever we collected our key. She would study us intently, as if hoping that whatever she was searching for would spring out and bite her on the ass.

It wasn't until we were checking out that Emma whispered in my ear, "I wonder if she has had complaints about the noise."

"What noise? Shit…no!" My face turned crimson, then paled. "You don't really think she… Oh no! I'm so embarrassed." I hid my head inside Emma's jacket, and I could feel her giggling in the rippling movements of her chest.

I think Emma felt a little unnerved too, but was trying to pretend that she didn't care. I didn't want to face the woman, but Emma persuaded me to go with her.

The landlady stood behind her desk—fag hanging from her lips, reading the local newspaper. A cat that had seen younger days was trying to get her attention, as cats tend to do, by pawing at the open paper.

"Pack that in, Fudge. Go and kill a mouse or summat."

Emma cleared her throat. "Erm…excuse me."

Aged grey eyes looked up.

"We'd like to pay the bill, please."

She shuffled some papers and gave Emma a grim look as she passed the bill over.

Emma swiftly produced her Visa card. "It's my treat," Emma insisted, refusing my offer to share the cost.

I chucked the cat under the chin, then sniffed my fingers. Fuck, that cat stank to high heaven. I furtively wiped my hand down the side of my jeans.

Emma signed the credit slip and handed it back to the proprietor, who was still glaring at us.

I'd had enough. "Is there a problem?"

Her eyes looked everywhere but at us. "No."

"Then why do you keep staring at us?" There was definitely unsuppressed annoyance in my tone. I stood directly in front of her, my body language saying I wasn't going anywhere until she told me what her problem was. "Is it because we're gay?"

Her eyes flicked to mine and I saw a hint of hatred there, just a hint, but it was present all the same.

Emma tried to defuse the situation, and my anger. "Come on, Laura. Leave it."

"Why should I leave it? It's her problem that she can't accept that not everybody's the same."

In her mumbled reply, I distinctly heard "unnatural."

My anger flared up and out before the woman knew what hit her. "It's people like you who are unnatural." I yanked my arm out of Emma's restraining grasp. "Let go, Em!" I redirected my words to the proprietor. "You live in hatred and ignorance, and can't accept that some people are different from you."

Emma whispered, "Leave it, she isn't worth it."

But I was so angry, so fed up with people's uninformed assumptions about who I was. "What is so wrong with people being in love? What's so wrong about love, eh?"

"You're perverts, corrupting everyone with your filth."

Honestly, if Emma hadn't been there, I would have jumped over the counter and knocked ten tons of shit out of her. Fuck the fact she was getting on in years. People like her turned my stomach—so pious, so bigoted. The scary thing was, we were surrounded by people who believed as she did. And there was no way I could beat them all into a pulp, could I?

"Come on, baby. Leave it."

I allowed Emma to lead me to the door, knowing that if she let go of my arm for a second, I would be back at the counter, ready for more than just arguing.

Emma knew it, too. I'm sure that's why she didn't let go until we reached the car.

Still, I wasn't going to let the opinions of people in this world ruin what I had just because they couldn't accept others for who or what they are.

This was right. This was the truth…my truth.

My anger having completely dissipated, the ride home in the car was quiet yet comfortable. We didn't need to talk to communicate.

The car pulled up outside my house just before eight in the evening. I turned to ask if she wanted to come inside for a while, but the question died on my lips as her sigh answered before I had chance to speak.

"Sorry, I can't stay. I've got to go to the office tomorrow and pick up some information about the new clients. I haven't done the groundwork for the account yet."

It was a reasonable excuse, although I hated to admit it. I didn't know when we would see each other again, and I so wanted, no, needed to see her soon, needed to see her constantly.

I tried to hide my disappointment. "Don't worry, love. I know you're busy. Don't stress about me. I'm free for most of this week. Whenever you can make it will be great."

"Tomorrow night—you, me, a nice bottle of wine. I'll even throw in some nibbles." Her eyebrow rose saucily and lodged underneath her hair.

"I wish I could, but I've got dinner arrangements," I said with genuine regret.

I had promised Sarah, Elaine, and Harry that I would go to see them as soon as I got back. Harry wanted to introduce me to his new girlfriend, and I couldn't disappoint him. I think he wanted my approval of his choice.

"Really?"

I could hear the hurt in her voice, so I tried to smooth it over. "Why don't you come?"

She looked pensive.

"It's with my family—you know, Sarah, Elaine, Harry."

Her smile beamed.

"They would love to see you. You'll be surprised at how much Harry has grown."

"I'd be more surprised if he hadn't. I'd love to see them." She leaned forward and placed a tantalising kiss on my lips.

I wanted to drag her inside and ravish her until she begged for mercy, but I knew she had to be somewhere else, so I dragged my not-as-understanding lips away.

She helped me to my door, declaring, "I'm sure you need help with your bag, on account of you're vertically challenged."

Her dig earned her a dig in the ribs. We shared soft, lingering kisses at the door, and then she was gone.

"Well, Harry won't be the only one to bring home a girlfriend tomorrow night," I sniggered to myself. All of the people I love most would be under the same roof.

I was sure that life couldn't get any better.

# Chapter Thirty-Five

Sarah was intrigued when I said that I wanted to bring some-one over for dinner, especially when I wouldn't tell her who. She even tried to pump me for information. I couldn't believe she didn't guess who it was straight away.

I was a bit nervous about how the evening would pan out. Elaine had a habit of interrogating anyone I took round, almost like a father looking out for his daughter's well-being. It was equivalent to "What are your intentions toward my little girl." She was a little more subtle, but not by much.

It was uncommon for me to take anybody around to "Meet the Family." I had only done so maybe once or twice before. It wasn't actually because of the mini Spanish Inquisition imposed on them by Elaine, but because I had not really thought enough of anyone that I allowed them into my fold, hadn't ever stayed in a relationship long enough to even consider introducing them to that part of my life.

Emma was different.

I picked her up at her place just after seven. She looked stunning, per usual. I wanted to skip dinner and go straight for dessert, but she eventually prised me off her and gave me that look.

"Come on, Laura. We don't want to be late."

My mind wanted to object that we were thirteen years late as it was, and what would another hour matter, but she was right. I didn't want to turn up bedraggled and smelling of sex; at least not the first time that my family was to get properly introduced to Emma.

I didn't want to steal the limelight from Harry's new relationship, either.

Harry was a bundle of nervous energy as he opened the door. He nearly knocked me backwards with the enthusiasm of his greeting. Emma was welcomed as if she had never been away, and I could see knowing nods and smiles passing among Sarah, Elaine, and even Harry—whenever he could tear his eyes from his girl.

Susan was all that he had described: blonde, brown eyed and beautiful. She was also hopelessly smitten with my kid brother. Every time she looked at him, I could see her utter adoration on her face. I felt a sense of peace, as I knew Harry had found his special someone, the one that would complete his life.

Funny thing was—she had been a student of mine. Small world, eh?

Dinner flew by with constant rib tickling and general taking the piss. Nobody seemed surprised that Emma was my "date," and they treated her to the same piss taking as I was getting—which was always a good sign.

The evening was nearly over when Harry took me to one side. I thought he was going to interrogate me about what Susan had been like at school, but he didn't.

He opened with, "Guess who I saw yesterday staggering out of the pub."

"Father Christmas?" Sarcasm was always my forte.

"Well, he was there, but guess who else."

I could tell he felt uncomfortable about broaching the subject, so it wasn't going to be anything good. Like a true Northerner, I looked at him with my "I don't give a shit" expression. That was the usual way that I dealt with problems I didn't, or couldn't, handle.

His eyes never left mine. "None other than Daddy dearest."

"And?" I turned to go. In my book the conversation was over.

Harry grabbed my arm. "Look, Laurie, I know you don't give a rat's ass about him, but I thought I'd warn you."

I glared at him.

"He seems intent on looking you up, said something about apologising."

"He can go *fuck* himself!" It came out a little too loudly, and I could sense Emma making her way over from where she had been chatting with Elaine.

"Laurie—"

"No, Harry. End of discussion. I have avoided that bastard for thirteen years, and I'll be buggered if I am going to talk about him now."

Now at my side, Emma reached out and put a hand on my arm. "What's the matter, Laura? Are you okay?"

And I'd be buggered if I was going to discuss him, and what he had done, or tried to do, in front of Emma. She didn't need to know.

"What bastard?" she persisted

I turned to look into troubled eyes. "Nothing, honey, no one."

Emma knew I was lying, but she also realised I didn't want to talk about whomever it was Harry and I had been discussing.

Not long after, I feigned a headache and we left. I felt totally deflated. The evening had started out wonderfully, and with just the mention of that twat's name, everything had folded in. I couldn't understand why that would happen. It wasn't as if I had thought about him at all, or about what had almost happened that night. It was just… I didn't know, just something.

On the drive to her house, Emma tried to start a conversation and I tried to pick it up, but I couldn't concentrate. My mind was decidedly elsewhere. She finally gave up and stared out of the window, and now the car was silent.

I pulled up outside her place and turned off the engine.

"Are you up for a nightcap?" Blue eyes looked at me hopefully.

"Not really." I just stared ahead. "Maybe tomorrow? Sorry, I'm quite tired." The last part was an obvious lie, and my heart hurt with the telling of it, but what could I have said? 'Sorry. Just thinking about the time my father tried to fuck me.'

I didn't think so.

"Okay." Her voice was so quiet. Was there a hint of hurt, too? "See you tomorrow. You know where I am…" She left the unspoken offer hanging in the air. "Whatever it is, I'm here, and I love you. Night."

I heard her open the car door, and I reached out and grabbed her arm, pulling her back into the seat. The door closed behind her. I tried to turn her around, but she kept her back toward me.

"I just… I… I need to sort through some things. Please understand. I love you, Emma. Nothing can change that."

She turned to face me, and I could see the tears shimmering in her eyes.

"Hey, baby, come here."

She fell into my arms, her body wracked with the force of

her sobs.

"Ssshhhh. Hey… I'm sorry. It's not you. God, no."

She was trying to control her breathing, and watery eyes shot up to peer into my own. I thought my heart was going to break.

"I thought I had done something, said something to hurt you." She began to cry again. "I don't know what I'd do without you, Laura. I love you so much."

I clutched her to me, and it felt almost like a nurturing. I felt protective. Funny thing was, what she needed protecting from was me—from all the crap from my past, from all the hang-ups I carried with me.

Her lips searched out reassurance from mine. Hands gripped my hair as she fell forward into me. I returned her embrace, relishing the contact, knowing that this was what mattered—the here and now. A hot tongue trailed over my jaw and descended to my throat. Her hands slipped down to my breasts, and I arched into her touch, needing to feel her hands on my skin.

My wish was granted as her fingers slipped inside my top, pushed past the filmy material of my bra, and caressed my pliant breasts. My breathing became laboured, and I was moaning. She pulled the nipple to full attention and pinched the sensitive nub, eliciting another moan. My body was pressing her back against the door, and I scrambled over my seat, paying no heed to the steering wheel or the handbrake.

Pinning her against the door, I became frenzied in the restricted space that we had. I pulled her t-shirt up and plunged into her breasts, taking as much of the soft flesh into my mouth as possible. I could feel my jeans being pulled over my hips and down, the cool evening air chilling my overheated skin. Grinding my mound on her hip, my need for her swelled. My hands were tugging at her top, my fingers desperate for uninhibited contact. Her arms raised to release the bit of cloth, and her hands came to rest against the interior roof.

I pulled her down onto the seat and pressed the lever to tilt the back to give us more room. She slipped backwards, taking me with her. Another press, and the seat back dropped down almost flat, taking Emma with it. My left knee braced against the central console as I straddled her, stripping off my top.

My hands tugged at her jeans, undoing the buttons. I gripped the waistband and tugged her pants down her thighs, then used my knee to push them down to her ankles. She kicked them free. My hands ripped at her underwear. Nothing would stop me from touching her, loving her.

Carnal sounds rose from deep within us—guttural, animal, primitive. Fingernails scraped flesh, marking ownership. Sweat slicked our bodies; our need coated our thighs, thighs that were clenching, clasping, smearing slippery juices like a balm.

Sensations pulsed through me, every nerve ending on alert, every noise, every movement adding to the rising fire that was likely to consume us both. Her deft fingers chafed my bud, and I positioned myself over her hand and speared myself onto her fingers, pushing them deep inside, my own three fingers buried deep within her.

She filled me. I filled her. For an agonising moment, we both froze—enjoying the delicious sensation of penetration.

The rhythm of our hips began, not slowly but with a haste born of desire. Grunts were followed by moans of expectation. Her name fell from my lips like a mantra.

I could feel her juices running down my hand. Her walls were tightening, her hips frenetic in her need. Moans came from below me, and I searched them out to quell them with my mouth. Teeth nipped hard into swollen flesh, drawing just a hint of blood, followed by soothing licks. I poised my thumb atop her engorged clit, hovering over the spot like a prize to be claimed. And I did.

Her cry reverberated around the car until I captured it within my mouth.

A scream bellowed from my lungs and into her mouth as my orgasm ripped through me.

We continued to thrash against each other, unrelenting in our fevered coupling. Tears flowed freely as our lips murmured against each other's necks and faces, kissing and calming. Convulsions jolted throughout our bodies.

Slow and sensuous dancing of hips and mouths, as lips sought lips.

Hips began to slow.

Urges began to ebb.

Desire was slaked. For now.

Violet eyes rose to mine. Swollen eyes, swollen lips, and a tear-stained face.

"I love you, Emma," I whispered, and punctuated my declaration with a gentle kiss.

"I love you so much," she sniffled out.

I was sprawled half on, half off her on the reclined seat.

"I hope your neighbours are the understanding sort," I said, looking pointedly at our nearly naked bodies lying flat on the front seat of my car, a car that was parked on the street directly outside her house.

Her eyes followed mine and then rose to meet my gaze. "Gives them something to moan about." Embarrassed chuckles relieved the tension.

I lay beside her, snuggling close and inhaling the scent that was purely her. "Emma."

"Mmhm?"

"I'll have that nightcap now."

She scooped me into her arms and clasped me so close to her that I couldn't breathe. But—who needs to breathe when, right there and then, you could die a happy woman?

That was a rhetorical question, in case you were wondering.

Inside her house, our lovemaking resumed. Not the hurried carnal coupling we had experienced outside in my car, no. It was gentle, tender, beautiful. Hands that had seemed almost violent with possession now seemed reverent, worshipping each other, stroking every curve and swell, every dip and line. Hips that had been frantic in their search for satisfaction, now became temperate—the rhythm slow and sensuous, the speed increasing only as the crescendo approached. Hours passed. Words of eternal love whispered into fevered ears; promises of forever etched into skin.

We lying in each other's arms, me half across her breast, her arm secured around me, I felt at peace. For the first time in my life, I felt truly protected and content. Happiness seeped through me. There was only one last thing for me to do, one last secret demon that I had to exorcise. I had to tell her about my past.

"Emma?" My voice cracked, so I cleared my throat and spoke again. "Emma?"

"Mmm hmm." She sounded like a cat, purring in pleasure.

"We need to talk."

Her body stiffened.

I couldn't believe that after what we had just shared, she would still be anxious about my feelings for her.

"I need to get a drink. Want one?" And she was gone without even waiting for my answer.

It seemed like an age before she came back carrying two glasses of juice. She handed me one, climbed carefully back onto the bed, and propped herself up on her pillows. She sipped her drink, trying to appear calm, in control, but I could see every emotion, every uncertainty on her face.

I gulped my own drink, and then gently eased her glass from

her grip. After placing the glasses on the side table, I snaked my arm around her waist and pulled her down beside me. She was tense initially, but soon relaxed into my arms. I nuzzled her neck, placing gentle kisses on her collarbone.

"I need to tell you something, something about my past." She stiffened. "Don't worry, love, it doesn't affect us." I gave her a little kiss of reassurance, then propped my head up on my hand and looked into her eyes. "It happened years ago. It's...about my parents."

I could see the concern in her eyes, but I also saw relief, relief that she tried to cover.

I lay in her arms and told her the story of my miserable child-hood—the beatings, the arguments, the insecurity. Memories washed through me and out of my mouth: Harry losing his front tooth to a drunken father with ready fists, lecherous stares and gropings that no child should have to endure. Black eyes, frac-tured arms, threats—all were revealed.

I couldn't look at Emma. Periodically, I stopped to get my bearings and try to control the emotions that welled up along with my exposé.

I told her of how my mother had turned a blind eye to the hor-rors our father had inflicted on Harry and on me, how I hated her for her lack of support and for her inability to stand up to him, how I hated her even more than I hated him. "She was just glad when he left her alone, didn't give a shit about what we were going through."

Emma pulled me closer, embracing me soundlessly, soothing me with love, understanding, and a promise of protection. She held me in her arms as I got my anger under control, her soft, caring strokes easing the ache deep within and healing my soul.

"I need to finish."

"It can wait, Laura. You need to shut down for a while."

"No. I have to tell you all of it before I lose my nerve." Being wrapped up in Emma's arms was the only thing giving me the courage to go on. I took a deep breath and began again.

"He was always a dirty fucker." I couldn't even look at her, but her arms held me tighter. "He'd been put in the slammer for beating the crap out of Mum one too many times. All he got was three lousy days, then he came back."

The memory was so strong. It wrapped itself around me and began to choke.

Emma made soothing noises.

"When the bastard came at me, I told Harry to get out of there." I hastily wiped away the salty wetness of the thick tears that smeared my face. "I knew it was my turn, and I knew it wouldn't be just a slap this time." The room seemed so big, so quiet, that I had to turn and look to see if she was still awake. "I was so scared. I'd never…you know… Still haven't.'

I swallowed nervously and snuggled deeper into her. "He slapped me so hard my teeth rattled. The next thing I knew, I was flat on my back with him on top of me. All I could smell was beer and sweat—I can still smell it." My stomach roiled at the memories: his words, the wild look in his eyes, the feel of his fat fingers clawing down my legs, my feeling of helplessness. "Harry saved me. Whacked him over the head with a glass ash-tray and knocked the fucker out. He saved me from him—saved me…when for years I had been powerless to keep him from hitting Harry."

The pain tore me open, exposed my vulnerability to both Emma and myself.

She folded me inside her, taking great care not to make me feel smothered or trapped, holding me against her with one hand whilst the other soothingly stroked my back and my hair.

After thirteen years of being held inside, the tears I hadn't shed that night flowed with cleansing abandon as I faced the fear and the shame of my life, and my lack of courage in failing to look after my little brother.

We lay like that for an age—her soothing, me crying.

Finally I plucked up the courage to look into her eyes, dreading what I might see. I flinched at the anger that blazed there, anger that I thought was aimed at me.

"That fucking bastard! I'll…I'll…fucking kill him…*fucking…kill him*!" Teeth clenched around every word, her features became a macabre mask. She looked primal, savage, and just a little insane.

Our roles changed as I soothed her, trickling words of comfort and calming on sensitive nerves.

When she began to cool off, her pale eyes caught mine, concern and love regaining the upper hand. "You will never have to worry about him again. Got that? As long as I live, he will never hurt you again." She pulled me into her arms to nuzzle my hair and whisper words of love and security into my ears. "It's not yours or Harry's fault that those bastards couldn't see what perfection they had."

I was flooded with relief. I thought it was my fault, that I was abnormal in some way, because all parents love their kids. Right?

I didn't tell her about what Harry had told me earlier about my dad looking for me. There didn't seem to be any point.

L.T. SMITH

Chapter Thirty-Six

The weeks flew by in a blur. I was blissfully happy now that I had gotten that burden off my chest and Emma hadn't left me in disgust. She was the most important person in my life, and we spent every possible minute together.

Beginning to know each other as the women we had become instead of the teenagers we had been all those years ago, I loved Emma even more than I'd have ever thought possible. Although we had always had a connection, now we were totally as one.

When Emma had to go away on her business trips, I could feel the pain inside as if I actually had a wound. The aching for her was incessant; nothing could numb it. On the evenings before her trip, the atmosphere would be strained, mainly because we loathed being apart. Her trips were getting less regular, and shorter too, but even that didn't stop me aching for her when she was gone. When she returned, we were nearly frantic with need. Nothing seemed to satiate our desire to be with each other. It wasn't the sex—not for me at any rate. It was the feeling of connecting with her again, and having her close to me was all that really mattered.

On her return from her latest trip, she barely made it through my front door before I was on her, tearing at her clothes. I heard the pop of her buttons and the plink plink plink as they scattered down the wooden floor of the hallway. My hands delved inside her underwear, and hot wet juices welcomed me.

She was just as desperate. I didn't make note of her undressing me. No. All I knew was that I was whole again because she was with me.

Frenzied, we tried to get closer, to reconnect, as if the closeness would show how much we loved each other. Declarations of love mingled with expressions of need. Cries broke from deep within and reverberated off the walls, only to be recaptured inside trembling bodies and full hearts. Our breathing erratic, we found ourselves slumped on the floor, half undressed, and clasping at each other.

Gazing into the glistening eyes that radiated love, I delivered a soft kiss on Emma's cheek. "Welcome home, love."

"I think we should go on into the bedroom."

Her voice was thick with need, and I felt my arousal surge again.

She stood over me, then, as if I was made of air, she scooped me into her arms and carried me towards my room.

## Chapter Thirty-Seven

Year 11 had finished classes the previous month, and those students were only coming in for exams. As the school year drew to a close, relief spread throughout the school, as the teachers were allowed a little down time. This was the perfect opportunity to get lessons planned for the following year so that the summer could be free to do whatever Emma and I wanted.

Jack had been one of the leavers, and I was sorry to see him go, although I did get to see him occasionally when he visited his sister. He was preparing himself for college in the autumn and occasionally wanted my advice on courses. I didn't mind, and not because I was desperately in love with his sister, either. He was a good kid.

Emma had arranged a holiday cottage for us in the Lake District, a little place near Eskdale, really out of the way. I couldn't wait. Two weeks in the middle of nowhere with Emma Jenkins—just what the doctor ordered.

I loved the Lakes Region. The beauty and tranquillity bordered on the sublime. On the previous visits I had made there, though none of them would be as perfect as this, I had found that the tranquil setting allowed me to take stock of my life.

The cottage was incredible. A huge open fireplace dominated the room, although we probably wouldn't light it, considering it was the beginning of summer, but the good old British weather made a person very aware of the capriciousness of nature. In other words, it usually pissed it down.

The master bedroom was breathtaking. A magnificent four-poster bed stood in the centre of a rustic room with oak beams across the ceiling and down the walls. Throw rugs were scattered across the floor, and most of the furniture was stripped wood that had been waxed. Though the place was wonderful, I wouldn't have cared if I were stuck in a tent with her. Just being with Emma was all it took for the holiday to be idyllic for me.

The first three days were spent languishing in lovemaking, eating unhealthy foods, and getting a feel for the place. On the fourth day, we actually ventured outside to take in the lay of the land.

Our first port of call was Wastwater. The atmosphere of this lake was one that couldn't be replicated anywhere else in the world. Its ethereal beauty captivated the soul, as the lake lay alongside Scafell Pike, the largest mountain that England has to offer. However many people came to Wastwater, it never lost the feeling of solitude. It was like you were completely on your own, you and the power of nature. It made me consider the arrogance of man at thinking he could control nature, thinking he had a chance of being superior when all we have to do is look about us at the sheer magnificence of nature. In the grand scheme of things, our existence is transitory. It made me reflective and very aware of my own mortality. The knowledge that

I was insignificant in this scheme—well, not insignificant, but aware of my life and how short it was going to be in the natural order of things—also allowed me to let go of a few more of the restraints I felt had shaped my life.

As I said…reflective…and bloody morbid. I'd better move on.

We took a packed lunch and our bathing gear, as the day promised sunshine. Lying flat on our backs against the shoreline at Wastwater, we immersed ourselves in each other's company, the hazy sun beating down on us and drying our water-flecked skin. I don't know how long we had been napping, but the sound of frantic shouting pulled me out of Morpheus' realm.

"Ernie! Ernie! Come on, fella! Come on!"

The shouting was getting closer, and the voice was sounding more desperate.

I shot to my feet, Emma close behind me.

A tall, dark haired woman came over the edge of the bank carrying what looked to be a ball of black hair, a wriggling ball of black hair at that. She looked frantic, her face a dark crimson and her long hair stuck to her sweaty face. She caught my eye.

"You wouldn't happen to have seen a dog running this way, would you?" Hope was apparent in her voice. The bundle of hair in her arms began to whine and wiggle, exposing the most adorable dark brown eyes and shaggy head. "Now, Bert, stay still."

"Sorry, I…" I looked at Emma, who shook her head, "we haven't seen anything."

Her eyes were casting about wildly.

"Do you need any help?"

"Thank you so much," she gushed, her relief evident. A smile broke through for a moment, until "Bert" started to squirm in her arms. "I haven't got his lead with me. Ernie, his brother, has run off after some bloody sheep, and I just left everything where it was and chased him. My partner is well up the road trying to hunt him down. She has the lead."

"Do you want me to look after this little man while you go and find the other one?"

She flashed another smile, and I was handed the bundle of living, breathing, licking flesh. Interested eyes appeared in front of my own, and I was hooked. The dog was the epitome of lovability. Shaggy hair bunched over sparkling eyes, a shiny nose pressed itself against the exposed flesh of my arms, and a tickly tongue wanted to wash my face clean. I was so mesmerised that I failed to notice when the young woman and Emma left to look for Ernie.

I nestled my face into Bert's fur and breathed deeply. He smelled of open air, the lake, and fun. I tickled his stomach, and he emitted a contented whimper and stretched himself back into my arms to expose the underside of his belly.

"Ah, you want to be tickled, do you?"

Twenty minutes passed quickly, as I was having the time of my life. Bert was so much fun. I had found a stick for him to fetch, and he obediently brought it back every time, then sat in front of me waiting for me to pitch it again. It took me a moment to realize that Emma and the young woman had returned, along with another woman with blond hair and a stubby dog on a lead.

"Ah, this must be the infamous Ernie," I said.

Big brown eyes landed on me, eyes full of expression and... guilt, I suspect.

The blonde laughed. "Yes. The fastest Border Terrier in the Lakes."

After introductions, we chatted about the dogs and Ernie's impression of a speeding bullet, all the while stroking the dogs behind the ears. Ernie fell asleep, the events of the chase having tuckered him out.

The dark-haired woman, Annie, said, "Bert & Ernie have never chased sheep before, but then again, they have never been so close to sheep before."

It looked to me like the rest of the boys' holiday was going to be spent on the end of their leads. Bless them.

After profuse thanks and the promise of a drink one night, Annie and Helen and Bert and Ernie were gone.

I missed the dogs immediately, and I couldn't help sighing. "What a lovely pair of dogs." An image of Bert fetching his stick made me grin like an idiot. And then I thought about what I had said. "Erm...the owners were nice, too." I did feel a prat, but I also felt loved up, thinking of Bert's adorable brown eyes.

The add-on didn't escape Emma's notice. "Funny how you commented on the dogs first." She laughed and slapped me on the shoulder. "Border Terriers, weren't they?"

I nodded, still looking at the stick that Bert had repeatedly brought back to me just a short while before. I sighed again. I had always loved dogs, but as I've said before—it's too cruel to leave them cooped up all day on their own. "Ah well, maybe I can get a dog when I retire, eh?" The mumbled words were no sooner out of my mouth than they disappeared into the wind.

We packed away the remains of our picnic and headed off to Ennerdale for another bout of sunbathing and relaxation. Emma seemed lost in thought, so I let my mind drift to my four-legged friends once again.

I was smitten.

L.T. SMITH

Chapter
Thirty-Eight

The Lakes were all that was promised and more. The sheer beauty of the place left me breathless and feeling insignificant. The only thing that surpassed that beauty was Emma.

Buttermere was more commercialised than both Wastwater and Ennerdale and hosted a myriad of different nationalities that all converged there to bask in the serenity it offered. Because so many people visited there, it had lost some of its mystery. All the same, a good, long walk around the lake was still a lovely way to spend a few hours and enjoy a picnic.

We were sitting on the shoreline, just about to start our lunch, when the sounds of shouting reached us. The familiar voices were not frantic this time, just alerting the pair of fluffballs as to where their owners were.

We heard pounding feet racing towards us, but we couldn't

see anything. Then they were there.

Bert offered me a red rubber ball covered in spit, his eyes sparkling and begging for a game of fetch. Ernie had Emma pinned on her back and was giving her face a thorough washing.

"There you two are... Oh. Sorry." Annie blushed as she tried to pull Ernie off Emma. He wasn't having any of it and pounced back with even more determination.

Bert was whimpering at my feet, a look of desperation flitting over his shaggy face, the ball resting against my foot.

I tickled his head, loving the feel of his fur.

When Helen appeared, both Emma and I stood up in greeting. The boys sat next to our feet, looking back and forth from us to their mums.

"So, here we are again." Emma laughed. "Fancy stopping by for a while? We were just about to have some lunch."

Ernie yapped at the word "lunch."

"You are welcome to join us." And although this was meant for the humans in their foursome, Emma directed it to the panting dog who lay down at her feet.

"Great. We were just about to do the same." Annie said.

Helen swung the bag off her back, nearly wiping out her partner in the process.

"Hey... watch it," Annie said as she ducked.

Helen grinned as she dropped the bag on the ground with a clank. They unloaded the rucksack that contained the boys' packed lunch and water, as well as their own lunch.

It was fun. We chatted about the Lakes, our lives, and the boys. Bert and Ernie played in and out of the water, fetching sticks and the red ball until they slumped down, exhausted from their exertions.

I chatted with Helen, finding her easy to talk to.

"Annie and I love it here. We try to come every year if we can." She was collecting the plates and packing leftover sandwiches back into containers whilst I helped.

"Did you come far? You sound local."

Helen laughed and nodded, before scrunching up her face. "I did, well didn't. I'm from Manchester originally, but we both live in Norfolk now."

"Oh. I thought Annie sounded more southern."

"She is, kind of. South East coast, actually. Annie is proud of her Gorleston on Sea roots." A soft laugh escaped her as she zipped up the top of the rucksack and moved it off to one side. "I moved there when I was seventeen. It took me years to admit I quite liked it there."

"Would you ever move back to Manchester?"

Helen shook her head and looked over at her partner. My eyes followed her gaze and landed on Emma, who was engrossed in conversation with Annie. They were having an animated discussion, about what, I didn't know.

"How long have you two been together?" I think the question was spurred by a grain of jealousy as I watched my lover chatting easily with someone else.

A soft smile graced Helen's face. She was totally in love with Annie; that was obvious. "Eleven years. What about you and Emma?"

"Two and a half months." A contented sigh escaped me. Two and a half months of being alive.

"Is that all! You two seem like you've been together for ever."

"It's a long story."

Helen smiled encouragement.

"Well, it all started thirteen years ago…"

I gave a brief account of the events that had led up to that moment. Not all the happenings, especially not the Justine Russell fiasco, but the bare bones of our saga.

After a couple of hours and lots of play fights with the Terrible Twosome, as they were dubbed, we said our goodbyes and went our separate ways. It had been a lovely afternoon and made me feel contented, though I wasn't sure why.

"Good to see relationships getting stronger over the years instead of breaking apart." Emma's rich timbre trickled into my ears.

That was it. Seeing and chatting with two people who were so obviously in love had given me hope for the future. My hope was that in eleven years, our relationship would still be as strong as Annie and Helen's.

The rest of the holiday sped by, leaving us breathless by how rapidly the time flew, yet totally at peace with the world and each other. It was like a dream come true to be spending all day and every night with Emma, and I didn't want it to end.

We spent our last evening on the patio, sharing a bottle of chilled wine, watching the sun dip down below the hills, and witnessing the appearance of the stars. Emma's face was obscured by shadows that danced and played with her features, making my eyes strain to capture her fascinating blue orbs.

"Why did you finally make a move on me?" I had to know. What had been the difference between the earlier years and now? "You haven't told me yet."

She smiled that crooked smile, and my heart began to race. "Can't we just say that I couldn't resist you any longer?"

"We could, but I really need to know. What made you make a pass at me after college, and then again years later, after all that had happened? You said that you knew that I wasn't interested. What changed your mind?"

It was so quiet. I could hear her breathing.

"Well," she looked sheepish, "at college I had all these emotions racing around inside me that I couldn't deal with. You were

a constant in my life, someone I had come to love so much…"
Her voice faded into the night.

"And?" I prompted.

"You always seemed so content with your lot. You dated on and off, and then there was Justine Russell, who was always ready with some sarcastic comment about how you wouldn't give me a second look."

"But we didn't see Justine all the way through college."

"I know, but it used to prey on my mind, especially after the Youth Centre debacle." She looked wistful, staring out at the darkened horizon.

I fiddled with my wine glass and waited.

"I dated a great deal through the college—"

"I know," I interrupted.

She laughed at the feigned expression of hurt on my face. "It was my way of dealing with things. I tried to block my feelings for you, thinking they were a crush, a phase, a *something* that I shouldn't be feeling for my best friend."

I entwined my fingers with hers and gave her hand a reassuring squeeze.

"Then, when we went to the Gay Village and I saw everyone else making out, my reason kind of took a holiday. You looked so beautiful, I thought my heart would burst out of my chest and declare its love for you." She took a sip from her glass and licked the excess from the rim.

A flame kickstarted inside me.

"I was arguing with myself—should I…shouldn't I? You were oblivious. I watched you laughing and chatting with everyone. Women were flocking around you, wanting your attention, wanting to claim you, and I was jealous."

"You? Jealous?" I was stunned.

"Yes, me, jealous." She leaned forward and placed a kiss on my lips.

The flame inside began to venture south.

"Then you looked at me." A sigh escaped her lips, and she turned and caught my gaze. "I could see myself reflected in your eyes. Just a glimpse. I had to know once and for all if what I had discerned was true…that you wanted me, too."

"Oh God, yes."

"That's when I asked you to dance. Holding you in my arms was like coming home. I couldn't think straight. The scent of you, the feel of you, they smothered my senses. I couldn't stop myself, and when you responded to my kiss… God." Her eyes went glassy at the memory.

I lifted her hand and kissed each knuckle. "Why did you ask me to forgive you?"

Confusion was clear on her face.

"Just before you kissed me, you asked me to forgive you. Why?"

A slow smile appeared as the memory came back in more detail. "It was in case you didn't feel the same way. I was covering all my bases."

"But I did."

"Yes, you did." Her kiss was a little longer this time. "The rest is, as they say, history."

We were quiet again. I knew she was lost in thought about how that evening had played out, how it broke our lives apart. I didn't want to ask her again about why she'd decided I was worth the effort, so we just sat there, lost in the memories of days long gone and revelling in the closeness we shared now. Fate was a fickle player, I knew that, and I didn't want anything to get in the way of my feelings for Emma. I couldn't survive losing her again.

"I am so happy."

Her almost reverent whisper broke through my reverie. I thought it had seeped from my head until I was ensnared in eyes turned pale grey in the growing darkness, eyes that bored into my own.

A ghost of a smile turned up the corners of her perfect lips as she looked at me for a response. When I smiled, her hand came out and grasped mine, her thumb rubbing soft, small circles on my palm.

"It's hard to believe that we will be back in the city this time tomorrow." I sighed, deliberately ignoring the fact that I was most concerned about having to sleep alone in my overly large bed.

She stood up, and although we hadn't been snuggling, I missed the warmth of her skin. Stretching a long toned arm towards me, she smiled, a hint of sadness playing along her mouth.

I felt a spark of nervousness at not knowing why she would look sad. I didn't want to know.

"Well then, let's make the most of our time here."

I allowed her to lead me to the bedroom, anticipation fluttering in my stomach like a captive butterfly.

She slowly drew me towards her and inhaled my hair, then my neck. "You smell wonderful."

Her breath caressed my skin, leaving it tingling. Sure hands trailed down the front of my shirt, fingering the buttons until I could feel the pop as they were released from their buttonholes.

The cool evening breeze embraced my exposed skin, and I closed my eyes in expectation. Delicate kisses flickered on my chest, then moved steadily downwards to waiting breasts. Her hands gently pushed my cargo shorts away from my hips and down into a cotton pool around my feet. All I had between immodesty and me was a thin piece of material that would have been a minimalist's idea of underwear.

My hands set out on their own quest. Firstly, they stroked her hair, trailing through long dark strands that felt like freshly spun silk under my touch. They rested for a moment on her cheeks, cupping the supple flesh and allowing my fingers just a hint of a caress. They told her without words that I was hers and I always would be, then they ventured to her collarbone to lightly stroke the protruding bump.

All the while she was circling my breasts, tantalising them with the promise of attention only to pull away at point of contact. Her head lowered, and moist lips opened and then closed around a waiting nipple that was rigid with longing, the puckering flesh around it demanding attention.

My breasts ached with the need for her touch, and as the wetness of her mouth enveloped me, I moaned. I felt her lips smile against my skin and her hand came into play, flicking the other nipple and rolling it gently between her finger and thumb. Her palm rubbed directly over the stub, and I moaned again, deeper, more guttural.

Her fingers captured the nipple between them and set up a coaxing rhythm. The stroking and her possessive suckling shot desire straight to my core, and I wanted to throw her on the floor and take her hard.

But not this time. This time was meant to be slow. It was meant to be a joining, a gentle coupling, an affirmation of our love.

I desperately wanted to kiss her. Her mouth snaked its way back up to my waiting lips and took them firmly. I moaned deeply within her mouth, felt her moans enter me, and the wetness pooled between my legs.

I don't know how we got to the bed, I can't even remember undressing her, but the feel of her skin on mine made me want her over and over again. It felt like the first time...again. Every time with her felt like the first time.

She came hard, quivering underneath me, breathing out my name in throaty moans, her nails trailing down my back. I nearly tipped over the edge at just the sight of her. She was absolutely beautiful—her face flushed, her eyes hooded, a fleshy tongue sweeping over plump lips. I licked her neck, tasting her—the taste that was purely Emma.

My beautiful girl flipped us over and straddled me, her eyes burning with desire. "What do you want?" Her voice was sultry and breathless. "Tell me. What would you like me to do?" Hungry kisses peppered my throat, her tongue intermittently swiping and licking. "Tell me." She captured my breast in her mouth and feasted.

"Touch me... I need... God... I need to you to touch me."

My breast hindering her speech, she mumbled, "How?"

Her hips were rocking against me, and desire coated my thighs. I was becoming desperate. I needed to feel her in me, against me...anywhere. "Fingers...tongue...wherever. Just touch me."

She pulled away, breaking the contact of skin and tongue and lips. "Tell me what you want me to do." Her voice held an air of command.

Her thigh came between my legs and began to press against me. I wrapped my thighs around her legs and pulled myself into her, baring my want against firm muscles. My hands gripped her hips, steadying me as I ground myself into her.

She pulled away, leaving me gasping.

"Please, Emma!" My voice held a note of entreaty, my fingers clutched at her hips, trying to pull her to me.

"Please what?" With a playful smile, she reached between my legs and slipped her fingers along swollen lips, sending shuddering jolts through my body.

My eyes fluttered closed. When I opened them again, she was staring at me, the curve of her lips obvious. Probing fingers came to rest outside of my opening with just a gentle pressure to announce their location.

"What do you want, Laura?"

"To feel you inside me," I panted.

"And? What do you want me to do then?" Her thumb grazed my clit, and my body arched off the bed.

"Fuck me, just fuck me!"

Strong fingers entered me, pushing inside until I was filled. I nearly came right then. She thrust in and out, the rhythm frantic. Her tempo became quicker, the strokes deeper, her thumb more insistent. I could feel the orgasm building as she took me, her free hand pinning me in place, her legs straddling my thigh. She ground herself onto my knee, short grunts emanating from deep within her, her passion slicking my thigh, her fingers still deep inside me.

I could feel her tensing, and I knew we were both close. "Harder, Em, harder!"

And she did as I asked.

We burst into climax together, unintelligible sounds escaping from deep within us as we each rode our passion, drawing out every shudder, quiver, and tremor, little jolts searing through our bodies. Hot, wet lips found each other, and I was surprised to find tears on her face. I was even more surprised to find them on my own.

"I love you" tumbled from our lips like a catechism.

Sated for the moment, we folded into each other and drifted into slumber.

# Chapter Thirty-Nine

It had been nearly a week since our return from the Lakes. Emma had been busy catching up with work, and we hadn't seen each other very often. I spent my time preparing for the return to school in a few weeks, wanting to be ready well beforehand, as that would leave me more time to spend with my girl once it started up again.

Friday night, I left Sarah and Elaine's and was on my way to meet Emma at the Red Lion. I was so engrossed with seeing her again, that it had gotten quite dark before I noticed. I checked my watch, sighing when I realised I was running late. The pub was still some distance away, and I fumbled around in my hand-bag for my mobile to call Emma and tell her I was nearly there. Like usual, I couldn't find it right away.

If I hadn't been waxing lyrical about the love of my life, I might have seen it coming.

"Hello, luv."

I would have recognised that voice anywhere.

"What the fuck do you want?" I spun around, and there he stood—my father. Older, dirtier, but him all the same.

"That's no way to talk to your old man, is it?"

I turned to go, but a grimy hand landed on my upper arm. I tried to shake it off, but his grip became tighter, more insistent.

"I've nothing to say to you."

"Look, luv," his strong hand pulled me around to face him, "I just wanted to chat, catch up. Your old man's missed you."

His leer threw me back to a time when his face was poised above me, fat hands between my legs. Fear seeped into my stomach, and a cool sheen of sweat covered my body. I felt my face draining of all colour.

"I've... I've...got nothing to say to you."

"Pity." Greedy eyes trailed down my torso, his focus settling on my heaving chest as he licked his lips.

"Look, I'm meeting someone and...and I'm already late. They'll come looking for me soon."

I had consciously avoided indicating gender, hoping he would think it was a male, or even a group of people.

"Yeah, I know, that big leggy dyke you're hooked up with."

I couldn't keep my surprise from my face.

"Your old man doesn't miss much. Bet she's a goer."

"Fucking leave her out of this!" I spat, anger roaring up from somewhere deep within me, anger I had swallowed back for years. I couldn't stand the thought of him even thinking about Emma, never mind anything else.

"A little touchy, aren't we?" he sneered. "Maybe I'll pay her a visit next." He licked his lips again, leaving them wet and sticky.

"If you go near her, I'll—"

"What? You'll do what? Get someone to hit me over the head

again?"

"Just fuck off and leave me alone." I tried to jerk my arm free from his grip.

The pressure behind his hand increased abruptly, and I found myself slammed against the wall with his forearm across my throat.

"Play nice, or you'll be sorry," he snarled.

I was finding it increasingly difficult to breathe as his arm steadily increased the pressure. His body was crushing into me. I tried to shout out, but he applied more force, making it impossible.

"I'd like to carry on where we left off," he growled as he nuzzled my hair. His leg pushed between my thighs, parting them.

I closed my eyes, and the bile rose in my throat. I knew that this time, Harry wasn't there to save me. There was no one there to stop him.

"You need to feel what a man could do, then you'll realise what you've been missing, what you can't get fucking a woman." He pressed closer. "Although I'd like to watch," he snarled into my ear.

One hand slid underneath my top, and I was paralysed by fear. I was helpless—alone and helpless. A voice inside my head screamed, "Why doesn't someone stop him?" But I knew that no one was there. It was nearly nine o'clock on a Friday night, and everyone would be either in the pub or at home.

His hand grabbed my tit, and I could feel its calluses and roughness even through my shirt. He kneaded it painfully whilst still holding me secure by my throat. His hips were striking up a rhythm, and I could feel his erection begin to rise against my pelvis.

*God no!* I couldn't bear the thought of him taking me. My inner voice was screaming loudly, but my anger was aimed at myself. *Why didn't I come in the car? Why did I think I would be okay walking to the pub? Emma offered to pick me up, but no, I had to be Miss Independent.*

His groping hand left my breast and fumbled its way down to my zipper. The weight of him was heavy against my small frame. I could feel him tugging, but was helpless to stop him. I resigned myself to what he was going to do.

"Come on, sweetheart, show your daddy how much you love—" He whimpered as his body was physically hoisted away from me.

My hands went instinctively to my neck as I cringed away from him. I couldn't digest what had happened. One minute he was there, the next…

He was slumped against the wall, fear in his eyes.

Six feet of anger towered above him, dark hair flying about, blue eyes mere slits. Lips were parted in a grimace that oozed fury. Emma's hands balled into fists as she struggled to control the anger radiating from her.

To me, she looked like an avenging angel sent to earth to save me.

She didn't even blink as she faced him down. "What the *fuck* is your game?" Her voice was ice.

"So, the dyke appears," he spat.

Although Emma exuded power, he apparently believed that she was still only a woman. His big mistake.

He struggled to his feet, trying to regain control of the situation. "What you gonna do, try to stop me?"

He was a large man, but Emma made him seem tiny, insignificant. As she stepped closer to him, I could only watch from the sidelines; I still felt faint. My whole body was shaking, and I couldn't really wrap my mind around what was going on. Finally, my legs gave way and I slumped down the wall. I fumbled in my bag for my mobile so that I could ring the police.

My old man puffed himself up and adopted an air of confidence. I could tell that he didn't want to appear weak in front of a woman, a dyke at that.

"You fuckers are all the same. Just 'cos you fuck like a man, you think you are one." He laughed, albeit shakily.

"And *you're* a man? Attacking a woman…your own daughter."

"She's no daughter of mine. She's nothing but a bastard. I took on that whore of a mother of hers when her real father didn't want anything to do with them." He laughed that manic laugh again.

I was stunned. He wasn't my father? His name was on my birth certificate. A jolt of relief began to mix with anger. Why hadn't anyone told me? Sarah must have known. Wait. She said something about my mother settling for second best.

"Hello? … Madam? … Could you please state your location? … Hello? … Are you—"

The operator's voice broke through my shock, and I quickly passed on the details whilst avidly watching the scene in front of me.

"Feels good, doesn't she? Firm tits." He was taunting Emma. "But I liked 'em better when she was younger." He smacked his lips like he had just enjoyed a tasty treat. "Her pussy was all wet for—"

Emma's fist struck him so quickly that we were all surprised.

He rubbed the side of his face. "Not bad." Blood trickled from his mouth, and he swiped at it with the back of his hand then inspected the red smear. "I knew she wanted it. She was gagging—"

Emma hit him harder this time, and the bastard reeled back, dazed.

I could see that Emma was controlling her fury with difficulty. Her chest was heaving, her posture rigid.

"Tell me, is she still limp in the sack?"

In an instant, her hands were clutching his shirt and she slammed him against the wall. "You dirty fucker, dirty…fucking bastard!" she screamed into his face, slamming him harder and harder into the brick with each epithet.

His feet were not touching the ground; his teeth were clacking together.

One of Emma's hand left his shirt as she backhanded him across the face until his eyes bugged out. "How do you like to be on the receiving end, huh? Huh?"

The scene was actually playing out in front of me, but it seemed surreal. I struggled to my feet and moved toward them. "Em." I gently laid a hand on her shoulder, and could feel the tension emanating from within her. "Come on, love. Leave it. The police are on their way."

I felt her relax under my touch. Her fingers slackened, and she pushed him back against the wall, like she was dismissing him.

He slumped to the ground, keeling forward so his face was nearly touching the asphalt. I thought he had passed out.

I turned her around to face me, and her face instantly lost the darkness it had harboured. A look of concern gathered around her eyes and mouth.

"Oh, honey!" She scooped me into her, cloaking me with love. "My poor baby," she mumbled into my neck.

"My hero."

She tensed and pushed me away, then delivered a roundhouse kick to my stepfather's gut.

The breath left his body in an agonised gasp, and he flew into the wall with a sickening thud. I knew he wouldn't be getting up from that anytime soon.

She turned and took me into her arms again, holding me safe. "Don't worry. I'm here."

When the police arrived a couple of minutes later, I was enveloped in Emma's arms and the bastard I'd thought was my dad lay slumped unconscious on the pavement. She and I went to the station to give our statements, and the pervert was taken to the local medical centre to get checked over before being taken to the police station.

Feigning fatigue, I refused counselling from the police. I promised I would return to see them, or find someone else to talk through my ordeal. The reason I actually did not want to talk to a counsellor was that I felt like a fool. Not only had I almost been raped by that sick pervert, but I had also found out that I had spent the better part of my life living in ignorance about my parentage. I couldn't sit and tell someone I didn't know how stupid I felt. No. I had to get on with my life, push this mess behind me and carry on.

Three hours later Emma and I were curled up on my sofa, softly stroking each other's back. I felt safe in her arms.

"You won't have to worry about that jerk anymore. You've got me now."

"Thank you, Emma. You honestly don't know how much I needed to hear that."

Emma stayed with me for the weekend, comforting me when my emotions became overwhelming. But deep inside, something was niggling at me. Not anything I could put into words… just something. A seed had been planted after the attack; what it was going to grow into was yet to be seen.

It's funny how things can come back to haunt you.

The next morning, a Saturday, I had a tearful conversation with Sarah. Livid wasn't the word sufficient to describe her re-action. She told me that what he had said was true—he wasn't my father. I became angry at that point

"Why didn't anybody think to share that nugget of information with me, especially back when Harry and I had moved in with you?" I demanded.

Sarah seemed uncomfortable with the question. "Well… see…Elaine wanted to—"

"Elaine knows, and I didn't?" The words spat out from between my clenched teeth, sounding harsh and accusatory, even to myself.

"Look… Laura, honey, we thought you were beating yourself up about no one loving you enough to give a damn. We were afraid that if you were to find out the truth about…you know… your real father walking out, well…" She blew out a deep sigh.

The fight left me. What could I say? It was true. That was the key thing about my teenage years, all I rattled on about. I always felt I wasn't wanted—Mum… Dad… Emma. I could understand why they hadn't told me. What good would it have done?

The conversation ended on a happier note than it had begun. The bastard was looking at five to seven years, and it was only later that we found out he was wanted for other things too, mainly petty theft, and would be serving a long stretch at Her Majesty's pleasure.

Good riddance.

It should have made me happy, but no. It didn't change anything.

# Chapter Forty

Until the night of the attack, I had no idea that Emma had studied martial arts. She nonchalantly informed me that she had taken it up in Cambridge as a way of relieving tension. I could have done with a little stress relief myself—especially after losing her. It might have diminished the number of one-night stands and mentally beating myself up over the years. I had to laugh when Emma said she thought she was getting rusty.

Good job, really. I doubt that the bastard would have gotten up from the pummelling if she hadn't been.

Funny thing was, he tried to press charges against her. Can you believe the gall of that man? The police laughed at him and put it down as self-defence. Thankfully, they didn't check Emma's record, and so they didn't find out about her attack on Justine all those years ago. I don't think they would have been able to brush it away as easily if they had decided to dig into her past. Her name change might have helped too, as her last name was now Sanders.

It was also a good job the bastard—can't call him Dad any-more—didn't know, as he would have trotted it out to save his own neck.

Don't want to write about him anymore. He is dead to me.

Probably because I didn't want it to end, the summer flew by. I couldn't see Emma as much as I wanted to—like twenty-four/seven. She was busy with some large project she had to get finished before the end of September.

The school year rolled around and delivered another set of rookie high school kids who were visibly shaking on their first day, wide-eyed and innocent and immaculately dressed in their new school uniforms. I knew it would be only a matter of weeks before that all went out of the window. They were so impressionable, and the upper school kids would have a whale of a time getting them into the school routine.

As all teachers are, I was really busy for the first couple of weeks. The word "frantic" sums it up nicely. I had assessments to do, national testing, rearrangement of set lists, and a GCSE analysis to write.

As I said…really busy. So busy I didn't really notice that Emma wasn't coming around as often as I would have liked. Well, I did notice, and I did feel put out, but…but I was up to the eyes in paperwork. You know how it goes. I didn't give myself time to think.

After the first couple of weeks, when things had started to settle down at school, it hit me. When we spoke on the phone, Emma seemed a little edgy, like she had something else going on and she couldn't concentrate fully on what we were talking about.

Don't get me wrong. When we did see each other, our bond was still as strong as ever. But something was niggling at the back of my mind, something I didn't really want to think about, just in case that by talking about it, I might make it happen.

Three weeks into term, Emma turned up late for our date. I hadn't seen her for two days and was feeling vulnerable. I missed sleeping with her, holding her close, feeling her next to me as I spooned against her. It wasn't sex; it was so much more than that. I just missed her, you know?

Although Emma was only fifteen minutes late, we missed the beginning of the film. I was not pleased. I didn't give a flying fuck about the film, I just felt that she was slipping away from me and there was nothing I could do about it. I began to think she was losing interest, that she had come to realise what we had when we were nineteen was infatuation; and now that she had sated her desire, she could move on, but didn't know how to tell me. And I was hurting. As I said, it wasn't just sex, she was my best friend, and I didn't know how I would cope with not having her in my life again.

After the film, we ended up going for a coffee at the local book café. She seemed totally relaxed as she spoke about what she had been up to since I'd last seen her. I just listened and answered her questions as economically as I could without seeming rude.

The evening went downhill from there. Every time she received another curt response, her brow would crinkle just that little bit more. And every time I did it, I wanted to throw myself at her feet and beg her to love me. Or if she couldn't love me, just to let me be near her, look at her, live in her shadow. The more I thought about it, the more depressed I became.

Concerned blue eyes gazed into my own, and she leaned across the table and took my hand in hers. "Laura, baby, are you okay?"

The cool smoothness of her fingers made my heart ache. I would miss those hands, those eyes, that voice, so, so much.

"Just a headache. I think I need to sleep it off."

Now she looked even more concerned. "Do you want to go home, get in bed? I'll look after you." She squeezed my hand.

It was as if I could actually hear a tiny crack coming from my chest. I felt faint, as if the blood was seeping out of my heart and drowning me in anguish. "I'll be fine. It would be better if I just get into bed and sleep. We can do this another time."

"But I don't mind. I'd like to—"

"I wouldn't hear of it. It's better if I'm on my own."

Never had a truer word been spoken. I believed I'd definitely be better on my own. Full stop. End of.

Hurt flashed across her face like she had been slapped, and then she looked concerned again. Her hand grasped my own, tightly. She looked down at our hands and a small sigh escaped her lips. "Come on then, let's get you to bed." Nervous eyes looked into my own.

She dropped me off outside my door, again offering to take care of me.

Once again I turned her down.

She leaned forward for a goodnight kiss, and I turned my face away so she only brushed the side of my mouth. I scrambled out of the car.

"Laura?"

I turned and nearly looked into her eyes. If I had looked into those blue depths, my resolve would have turned to water and I would have begged her to come inside so I could memorize the feel of her, the scent of her, the sound of her, the taste of her skin, the taste of her love. Commit to memory the way she looked when she was in the throes of passion, the way she looked at me as she made love to me, as if she loved me.

Commit to memory the essence of my one true friend.

"I love you." Her voice was gentle, and for a split second I wanted to believe her.

"I love you too, Emma, so much."

I leaned back into the car and claimed her lips. They were soft, inviting. My tongue slid inside her mouth and she drew it in, a little groan escaping her.

I pulled away, leaving her reeling at the abrupt loss of contact. "Goodnight, Em." And I fled inside, not turning around to see if she was still there. I felt like Orpheus, wondering if his beloved Eurydice was behind him, but knowing if he turned around, he would lose her forever.

Unlike Orpheus, I stood my ground, although I was losing Emma anyway.

I entered my house, went straight to the side window, and peeked outside. She was sitting there in her car, illuminated by the interior light. She didn't move, just stared at my front door with a pained look on her face. The flooding in my chest was heaving its way to my throat, and I choked back the tears that had been threatening all evening. Emma stayed for fifteen minutes longer before she started her car and pulled away from the kerb.

The dam inside my chest collapsed, and the sobs tore free. I was crumbling. I knew I had to let her go. I didn't deserve her. I was utterly devastated and doubted I would survive losing her again. Once again I thought, *Harry can't save me this time.*

I fell to my knees, tears cascading down my face unchecked. I was finding it increasingly difficult to breathe. A low-pitched keening was emanating from deep within my soul, gradually escalating into something bordering on a wail. Gripping my hair and pulling, I rocked myself back and forth.

I was dying inside.

The next morning I found myself in the same spot in the hallway, bundled up into a ball, clothes crumpled and eyes burning. I dragged myself up and staggered upstairs to hide underneath the duvet until I couldn't feel the pain anymore.

That would be a long time coming.

I know what you are thinking. You're thinking, "Why don't you just ask her?" I would be thinking the same thing if I were in your position. I hate it when I read something that sounds similar to this, and the person doesn't do anything about it. So, why didn't I ask her?

Simple.

All my life I'd had people rejecting me. I'd always stuck around and waited for the inevitable outcome, and look where that had gotten me. I just couldn't face Emma telling me she didn't feel we were going anywhere, that it would be for the best if...

I can't even finish that sentence. I couldn't face looking into her beautiful face and listening to the reasons she didn't think our relationship was working out.

Yes. I'm a coward. But unless someone has been through the same thing, they can't possibly know how they will react. And I hope they never have to find out.

Funny thing was, everything was going great between us until the night of the attack. It seemed me as if it that was the turning point. I figured she must have been sickened by what she saw. She probably got a really good look at what she was getting into and decided that she should get the hell away. I didn't blame her, really.

I just loved her so much.

And it was agony being away from her.

The phone was ringing constantly. I knew it was Emma trying to talk to me, but like the coward that I was, I let it ring. The doorbell rang numerous times. I ignored it and pulled the pillow more firmly over my head to try to block out the sound.

A couple of times I could hear her shouting my name below my window, and like the weakling I am, I closed my eyes and let the tears trickle down my face.

Two days, I spent like that. I didn't have the energy or the motivation to get up, go to work, eat, wash...anything. The only thing I did was break my heart over and over again. That took up all my time.

On the third day, I heard my front door open and close, then soft footsteps roaming around downstairs. I hoped it was a burglar who would find me and suffocate me with the pillow.

The footsteps made their way up the stairs, across the landing, and stopped at my bedroom door. A gentle tapping followed. I snuggled deeper under the bedclothes that smelled of stale sweat.

"Laura? Are you in there, love?"

Sarah.

I ignored the question, but my ears picked up the sound of the door opening and the heavy sigh that escaped the woman who I had come to regard more as a sister than an aunt.

"Oh, honey, what's up?"

The sound of her voice, so full of concern, made my heart break all over again. I was buried beneath the covers, and all she could have seen was the shaking movement as the pain pulsed through me. Every part of my body hurt. My eyes were so swollen, I could barely see.

The covers were lifted away from me, allowing the light of the room to flood through my self-imposed darkness.

"What on earth?" Sarah's voice held a hint of panic. "Laura, honey, what's happened?"

Her arms circled my shoulders and lifted me up into an embrace. I was like a rag doll, completely without purpose, just a pile of disused cloths to be thrown out with the rest of the trash.

My sobs sounded louder now that the muffling effect of the duvet was gone.

Gentle hands stroked my back, and Sarah rocked me from side to side whilst making shushing noises into my ear. "What on God's earth has happened?"

I couldn't answer. My throat was blocked; I'd lost the ability of speech.

"Is it about your father?"

I shook my head, the tears coming faster now as the memory of that night mixed with the loss of the light of my life.

"What is it? Come on, baby, tell me. We are all so worried about you. Emma came around to our place three times today, saying she couldn't get any answer."

I lifted my head. Why would she care?

"She is so worried about you. Has been since the night of... You know."

I started to cry again.

Sarah held me for over an hour. Kind words of comfort accompanied by gentle strokes alleviated the crying, until I was just lying still in her arms, completely numb.

"She doesn't want me." My voice was barely audible.

Sarah stopped her rocking, but her hand still rubbed my back. "Who doesn't want you, honey?"

"Emma." Her name was like honey on my lips. I loved the feel of it as it trailed off my tongue and ventured out into the world on its own.

"You are joking, right?" Sarah's tone was clearly one of disbelief.

I shook my head.

"Laura, look at me." I hesitantly met her worried green eyes. "Emma is completely head over heels in love with you. What on earth gave you the idea that she isn't?"

I shrugged. I didn't want to go into detail; it was too painful.

"She is beside herself with worry. We had to stop her from breaking down your door this afternoon."

I stared challengingly into Sarah's eyes. "If she's so worried, why isn't she here with you now?"

"She wanted to come, but I said that I would feel the way for her first. She kind of has the impression that you want to break it off with her and don't know how to tell her."

"Me!" I shot up straight, knocking Sarah's hands away. "I want to break up with her! That's a laugh. More like the other way around!" I was shouting.

She looked incredulous. "What on earth gave you that idea?"

"She's always making excuses why she can't see me. Turning up late…looking harassed, like she's got better things to do with her time," I shot out. "Are there enough reasons there?" My tone was cutting. Why I wanted to be spiteful to Sarah, God only knew.

"Have you ever asked her why?"

Such a simple solution. But what was the point of asking when I already knew the answer?

I felt the fight leave me. "I need to sleep. I'm so tired." I was lowering myself to the bed when Sarah's tone changed dramatically.

"Get your sorry arse out of that bed, Stewart. Stop playing the martyr and get the fuck up."

My eyes grew huge. I had never heard her come out with such language, and now those words were being directed at me.

"Don't feel so goddamn sorry for yourself. If she's going to leave you, get it over, but don't make decisions for her." She grabbed my arm and yanked me off the bed, then grabbed my shoulder and shook me. "Christ's sake! Don't just curl up and die. Sort this fucking mess out before you fuck it up big time."

I didn't resist her shaking me, but my eyes beseeched her to stop.

Her grip loosened, and her eyes dropped. She swallowed rapidly, trying to control her emotions. When she had composed herself, her voice returned to its soothing tone. "Come on, sweetheart, she loves you. I can feel it in my gut. Don't lose what you have together over some silly hunch."

I fell forward into her arms and began to cry. "I'm so sorry… so…so sorry," I sobbed, whilst she shushed me, and once again became my saviour.

# Chapter Forty-One

As I showered and ate the meal Sarah had left for me, I came to a decision. I was going to call Emma and talk it through. We both deserved to be in the picture, not one on the outside making all the arrangements whilst the other was standing centre stage, waiting to be told where to stand.

I picked up the phone and dialled her mobile number.

"Hello!" Was that panic or relief in her voice? "Laura? Is that you?"

"Yes, it's me." I spoke softly, my throat still raw from all of the crying I had put myself through. "We need to talk."

"Oh." I heard the hitch in her voice. "Yeah, sure. When do you want to see me?"

Bile rose in my throat. "Can you come over now?"

"Erm…"

My reaction to the hesitation was instantaneous. I was crushed. "Look, forget it. Some other time." She couldn't even be bothered to come straight away and tell me to my face.

"Laura... I... Can I come over later, say about nine?"

Her voice held something. I couldn't tell what, just...*something*.

"Suit yourself." I slammed the phone down, then picked it up and lay it off the hook. She had put me off again. Anger flooded through me. "How dare she? How fucking *dare* she piss me about? Fuck her! That was it!"

I paced around the house like a caged animal, occasionally picking things up and throwing them against the wall. Curses spewed from my mouth as if I was possessed by some demon. Adrenaline raced through me, making me buzz, my senses razor sharp.

By the time nine o'clock arrived, I was a boiling pot of anger. I couldn't wait to let fly at Emma. I would make her sorry that she ever walked into my life again.

At the chiming of the doorbell, I jumped, spun around, and charged at the door. I wasted no time in nearly yanking it off its hinges to get at my target.

There she stood, a couple of steps back from the doorway, hands hanging limply at her sides, her head slightly bowed, blue eyes peering into my anger filled ones.

"How dare you fucking fuck me about!" I screamed at her. "How dare you waltz up here like there's nothing wrong!"

I had started to close the door in her face when she lurched forward and grabbed the edge to stop it from closing.

"Laura, please, let me explain."

"Explain what? That you want out? That you don't give two shits about me? What?" I pulled the door open and stood my ground.

"Can we go inside?"

Her voice was calm, but I could hear the note of anxiety ringing out as clear as day.

"Why? Don't you want the neighbours to hear you breaking up with me?"

"Breaking— What on earth are you talking about?"

She pushed her way into the house and strode into the front room, leaving me standing at the open doorway feeling like a complete dick. She stood with her back to me, her shoulders slumped.

I slammed the door shut with all the strength I could muster. The sound thundered through the house. "The way you've been acting, like you don't give a shit, that's what I'm talking about."

She turned to face me, her face crumpling.

Even though she had broken my heart, I couldn't bear to see her upset. I fought the urge to pull her into my arms and tell her it didn't matter, not to worry.

"But I love you, Laura," she croaked out, tears pooling in her beautiful eyes. "What did I do?"

Anger surged up inside me. It was so unlike me. I usually wasn't an unreasonable person, but my judgment was way off kilter at this point. I had spent three days as a hermit under my duvet, gradually disintegrating, and I needed to know—one way or the other. "If you love me so much, why have you been avoiding me?"

She tried to answer, but I cut her off. "Why have you been so distant when we have been together, huh? Don't feed me any crap, Emma. I know a knock back when I see one. I've had enough of them in my life."

She stepped forward, tears running down her cheeks, hands reaching out to me.

I stepped away from her.

She stopped and dropped her hands to her sides, then lifted one to swipe away the wetness on her cheeks. I could hear her snuffling, trying to regain control.

Why couldn't she just say it, and then go and leave me to my sad little life?

"But…I love you…always have…always will."

Her voice was a whimper, a cry in the night. She was beginning to shake, and my resolve wavered.

I don't know how I got to her, couldn't remember moving, but I felt her in my arms, so fragile, so vulnerable. Her body was heaving with the force of her tears, and she was clutching me like I was *her* salvation, instead of the other way around.

"Don't leave me, Laura. Don't leave us. I don't think I could survive it a second time."

I couldn't process what I was hearing. Was she worried that I'd leave her? But…

I cupped her chin and tipped her head back. I had to look into her eyes; they allowed me to see deep within her. See her, really see her.

My stomach flipped at the heartache I saw in those blue depths, heartache that I was responsible for. "Em, I'll never leave you. God, I love you so, so much. I just thought—"

Her kiss was passionate, demanding. She was reclaiming me, reaffirming our love for one another. I felt weightless, elated.

The kiss became more frantic in our need for each other. Our hands were everywhere— pulling and tugging at clothes, seeking fevered flesh.

I pulled away and looked at her. "Em, do you still want to be with me?"

"God, yes!" She leaned in for another kiss.

I pulled away, and her expression turned to confusion.

"Tell me, was it my imagination, or were you distant with me?"

She just stared at me.

"After the attack, you seemed to change. You always seemed

harassed and were forever arriving late. I thought that you wanted to finish it. You know, didn't want to be involved with my problems."

A smile spread over her face.

It was my turn to look confused. Why was she smiling?

"Laura, I didn't lose interest." She laughed aloud. "God, how could you think that? I didn't see you for nearly ten years, and still I never lost interest."

"That was before you really knew me."

"I know you like I know the back of my hand," she lifted it up in front of me, "like I know myself. God, even better than I know myself." Emma scooped me into her arms and nuzzled my neck. "I love every part of you *and* your life. I love the changing colours of your eyes, the pout of your lips," she gently kissed them to punctuate her point, "the way your nose wrinkles when you smile." She rubbed my nose with hers. "The smell of you drives me insane. Your kisses sustain me. Your hands... God, your hands."

"Enough already." I laughed, mainly out of relief, then turned serious again. "What about my life?"

"What about it? You're an English teacher, but I'll get over it." She smiled a full out smile.

"What about...you know...the...the incident and all." I couldn't even bear to think about it, never mind verbalize it.

"That was no reflection on you." She pulled me to her again. "The blame rests solely on his shoulders."

I laid my head on her chest.

A kiss landed on top of my head. "You were the victim, love, but we have to move beyond that now and carry on with our lives."

Anger at the perpetrator welled up inside me. "Why did he have to try it again!"

Emma made shushing noises into my hair as the tears flowed

freely down my face. "I don't know, honey, but we need to get this sorted out. You can't live the rest of your life under any shadow of doubt that you might have somehow been responsible for anything that he did."

I nodded against her chest, and she stroked my back in leisurely circles.

We stood there for a long while, each soaking in comfort from the other and revelling in our reaffirmed bond. Eventually I suggested we should sit down, as my legs felt as if they had just completed a mini marathon.

We curled up on the sofa together, so close I doubt a human hair could have wedged between us. I felt her inhale a deep breath and hold it before she released it back into the air.

"Laura?"

"Mhm?"

"There are a couple of reasons why I've seemed harassed lately."

I looked up to face worried blue eyes. "What is it…or they?" My voice wavered right at the end.

"Well…number one, I was thinking about selling my place and…" She stopped.

"And?"

"I was worried about asking you…"

"What?"

"Wouldyouliketomoveinwithme?"

"What!"

She blew out a breath and sat up straight, then she plucked my hand from her shirt and held it between both of her own. "I said, would you consider buying a house together, moving in together?"

I was stunned, but three seconds later my mouth was on hers, drinking her in.

When she eventually escaped, she laughed. "Shall I take that as a yes, then?"

I kissed her again. Hard.

After a couple of minutes, she pulled away again. "That was the first thing. The second thing was a little harder to arrange."

I looked at her expectantly.

She stood up and offered me her hand, and then pulled me to my feet. "Follow me." She led me outside to her car.

"Where are we going?"

"Nowhere." She fumbled with her car keys as she unlocked the door, then leaned in to unlock the back. "Come here." Her voice was muted.

I walked towards her hesitantly, my eyes flickering from her face to the open door. I could hear a scrabbling noise coming from within. My interest was definitely piqued.

The inside of the car was dark. An orange box rested on the back seat. Inside it was an old blanket that was thoroughly tangled up.

I shrugged. "What am I looking for?"

"Look closer."

Twinkling brown eyes peered over the top of the box. There was a little whine and a pant, followed by a yap.

"A puppy? What's a puppy doing in the back of your car?"

"Probably becoming a little annoyed at having to wait to meet his new mum."

The automatic protest rose to my lips. "But I can't have a puppy. It would be cruel to leave him all day." Even as I was demurring, my hands were reaching for him, wanting to feel that chubby ball of roundness and hug it to me.

"But he won't be left all day. I'll be there to keep him company, won't I?"

I didn't know what to do—put the puppy down and hug and kiss her senseless, or hug the puppy tighter, so I did them both. Puppy firmly entrenched in my arm, his head resting across my chest, I gripped Emma and laid a soul-satisfying kiss on her lips.

"Careful. You'll do a Lennie on him in a minute."

I laughed out loud, then kissed her soundly again.

I drew back and lifted the puppy up to look into his eyes, his little body hanging limply below him. His pink tongue lolled out of his mouth, and he panted contentedly. His stubby black nose glistened.

"What's his name?" I asked Emma without breaking eye contact with my new friend. "Ouch! He just nipped my nose."

"I don't know his name, you haven't told me yet."

"What about Buster? Chester... Shakey... Brian?"

"Brian?" A hoot of laughter burst from Emma.

"Okay. I get the message. What about Stumpy? Stubby? Bruce?"

Emma raised an eyebrow. "Bruce? What on earth possessed you to suggest Bruce?"

"Look at his little overhanging jaw and his straight teeth—looks like Springsteen to me." I rubbed the pup's nose against my own, and he bit it again. "Ouch!"

"What about Nipper?"

I heard the amusement in her voice, but I gave the suggestion brief consideration.

"Maybe. Oh, he's so cute. Did you see that little yawn he just did? How adorable."

"I always knew there was a maternal instinct in there some-where. Come on, let's get him settled, he's had a long day." Emma gathered his belongings from her car and locked up.

The puppy lay contentedly in my arms as we walked back into the house like a new family.

It was amazing to think how dramatically the course of my life could change in one day. If it hadn't been for Sarah, the day would have undoubtedly panned out differently. As usual, I will be forever in her debt.

I filled a box with old jumpers and a blanket, and put it in my bedroom, then settled the puppy inside. He had warm milk and puppy food, and was looking contented and sleepy. His brown eyes fluttered closed as a tiny yawping yawn escaped his mouth.

I lay on the floor next to him and petted his head, staring in amazement at the little ball of wonder that had entered my life.

Fresh from her shower, Emma came into the room and settled down on the floor next to me, pulling me into her arms.

I sighed. I felt like a mother watching over her child, both of us surrounded by the protection of daddy bear. Sickly sweet—I know, but hey—all through our lives, that is the one thing that we search for—the ultimate feeling of belonging.

"Are you coming to bed?"

Her voice was husky, and I could hear the promise lingering behind the question. I doubted sleep was on her mind.

I turned and placed a gentle kiss on her lips, my eyes captured by her intense gaze. "I love you, Em. I'm sorry…about… I don't know what came over me."

"Shush…don't worry about it. You've been under a lot of pressure lately, and we need to get that sorted, right?"

I nodded and snuggled closer to her chest.

"Come on, baby…up." And she lifted me into the air and carried me, giggling, to the bed.

Good job I'd changed the sheets.

She laid me down, then leaned over me and captured my lips with her own. "Now, we have some serious making up to do."

I squealed with delight. Her fingers trailed down my blouse, fiddling with the buttons in a tantalising manner. I started to unbutton them myself, but she slapped my hands away.

"Patience." Her eyebrow lifted, as if daring me to object.

As Emma slowly undressed me, I felt myself getting wetter. Every movement was punctuated with a kiss, a lick, or a stroke. I reached out and brushed her hair away from her face, loving the feel of her under my fingers. Before long, I lay naked underneath her gaze with her straddling me.

"You are so beautiful," she murmured, her fingers tracing a circle around my breast.

My nipples strained into her hand, eager for attention. They didn't have to wait long, as a warm wet mouth captured one and gently sucked, grazing strong teeth up the sides. I moaned as I pushed into her face, needing to feel the pressure of her.

"I want to feel you," I panted, tugging on her sleepshirt.

Emma grabbed the back of the shirt and pulled it over her head with one swift movement, revealing perfect full breasts to my eager eyes. My hand floated towards her as if captured in a gravitational pull. I was mesmerised by her beauty, her slick form, her silky skin.

I drew my finger in lazy circles around each breast in turn, watching her tilt her head back and close her eyes in response. She moaned. I moaned. I rubbed the underside of her breast, and leaned forward to capture the waiting bud in my mouth. Her gasp stoked the fire between my legs. It was beginning to rage out of control. I could feel her rhythm beginning and her hips trying to purchase themselves onto my thigh.

"Off!"

I tugged at her shorts and she lifted herself up so I could pull them down to her knees, and, with a quick movement, they were gone. There was nothing between us anymore, and I don't just mean clothes. We were fully exposed to one another, our emotions on display, without reservation.

I pulled her down towards me and pressed my lips against her neck, loving the feel of her pulse racing at my touch. I loved the sensation of sucking on the part of her neck where it meets the shoulder—the slight dip, the sensuous taste. Her hands pressed me closer, seeking closer contact. I could hear her breath catch as I stroked her breast.

The weight of her body was pressing into mine as she lowered me to the bed and covered my body with her own. She positioned herself between my thighs, pushing her mound into mine. I could feel the connection, the sensation of our wetness mingling as the rhythm became more intense. Her hands snaked themselves underneath me and gripped, pulling me deeper within her. My hands went to her hair and latched on to the nape of her neck, fingering the short hairs there, only to pull her in for a searing kiss.

Faster and faster, we ground together as the kisses becoming more intense. I wanted to open my mouth and swallow her whole, savour the taste of her for eternity. I could feel her body tensing; I knew she was going to cum. So was I. I felt her stiffen, and hold, and then release her climax into the night. White flashes appeared in front of my eyes as I followed her.

We folded ourselves around one another and just lay in each other's arms for a while, steeped in our love. Again and again, we resumed our lovemaking, thinking each time that perhaps this time would quench our desire, only to start again as soon as we got our breath back. We made love through the night until exhaustion stopped us; otherwise I might have died making love to her. And done so gladly.

Sometime the next morning, we awoke to the feeling of the duvet being tugged from our languid bodies.

Small growling sounds emanated from somewhere near the floor, and when I peeked over the edge, I was greeted by sparkling brown eyes and a wagging tail.

"Wap grr wap!" Excited panting accompanied the oral dissertation, his whole body swaying with the force of the tail. "Wap!"

"Hello there, little chap."

He got even more excited at hearing my voice.

"Do you want to get up here with me and mummy?"

"Wap wap!"

"I'll take that as a yes, then." I leaned over and scooped the bundle of wriggling flesh into my arms and placed him between Emma and me.

He was excited to be on the bed and clambered all over the both of us before lying flat on Emma's chest.

"My dog, eh? Seems he thinks differently." I tickled him behind the ears and he let out a contented little whine.

Emma laughed.

I looked into her mischievous eyes and smiled a full-toothed smile. "What's so funny?"

"Well, he may think he's my dog, but he takes after you."

I looked at the comfortable puppy, who was stretched out along Emma, whuffling at all the attention being bestowed on him.

"What can I say? My dog's got great taste." I leaned over and kissed her. "Just like me," I whispered, my eyes not leaving hers.

"Wap grr!"

"Ahh…he's jealous, bless," I cooed to the dog. "It's all right, little chap. We have enough to share."

More than enough.

# Epilogue

That was three years ago. Where has the time gone?

Eight months after that episode, Emma and I moved into a detached house with a huge garden, and I have been living on Cloud Nine every day since. Sometimes, I even pinch myself to see if I am dreaming. I know—how stupid can I get?

Emma started her own business, working from home so she didn't need to travel, and that suits me down to the ground. It is still in its baby stages, but we are both optimistic. I still teach, although I have drawn a definite line between school time and home time. You have to, or else when would you ever get any work done with that tall, dark haired beauty around?

I met with a counsellor for quite a few sessions to work through all the anger I held for my parents, and for what the man I thought was my father had done to me. I have put that all behind me. All my energy is focused on my own family.

Talking of which, the puppy is not so puppyish anymore. He has grown into a bigger ball of fur, with the classic otter-shaped head of the Border Terrier. Although we think of him as our baby, he thinks of himself as the pack leader, but lets us get on with all the details of feeding and walking him.

He's snuggled up to me now as I write this, his head planted on my knee, making snoring sounds as if he is asleep. He's waiting for the jingle of his lead to alert him to a day at Lyme Park—lots of leaves to chase and birds to yap at. A much-loved pooch, and he knows it.

Well, I have come to the end of my tale of love and loss—love and near loss—and love. I hope my messages are clear to you all.

Don't ever take life for granted. You are only here once, so don't waste it like I nearly did. If you want something, or someone, go for it. It may be that the person you are longing for feels the same way as you. One of you needs to make the move, or else you will be back to wasting life again.

Also, never be contented with your lot. Whether it is a job you hate or a person you don't love, second best is never enough, believe me. My mother opted for that, and look what life gave her—an abusive man who could never get over the fact he wasn't her number one. I still think that was the catalyst for their abusive behaviour. I mean, what else did my mother ever have? I know she treated Harry and me badly, but it seems as if she just shut down. To her, love had definitely flown out the window leaving her existing instead of living. Funnily enough, I pity her more than I hate her now.

Another one—honestly, I'm nearly done preaching—talk about how you are feeling, don't keep it locked away. I nearly lost Emma, nearly lost my mind. All that pent up anger almost kept me from being blissfully happy with the woman I have loved ever since I was sixteen. It stopped us being together for ten years because I didn't have the gumption to knock on a door and ask what was going on instead of assuming the worst.

But mainly—never let the actions of others make you think less of yourself. Life is what you make of it, and my life is bordered by hearts and flowers.

LAURA STEWART
*Loves*
EMMA JENKINS
WHO BOTH
*love*
LENNIE

# About L.T. Smith

L.T. is a late bloomer when it comes to writing and didn't begin until 2005 with her first novel *Hearts and Flowers Border* (first published in 2006).

She soon caught the bug and has written numerous tales, usually with a comical slant to reflect, as she calls it, "My warped view of the dramatic."

Although she loves to write, L.T. loves to read, too—being an English teacher seems to demand it. Most of her free time is spent with her furry little men—two fluffy balls of trouble who keep her active and her apologies flowing.

E-mail her at fingersmith@hotmail.co.uk

# Other books from Ylva Publishing

http://www.ylva-publishing.com

# See Right Through Me

L.T. Smith

ISBN: 978-3-95533-068-2
Length: 295 pages

Trust, respect, and love. Three little words—that's all. But these words are powerful, and if we ignore any one of them, then three other little words take their place: jealousy, insecurity, and heartbreak.

Schoolteacher Gemma Hughes is an ordinary woman living an ordinary life. Disorganised and clumsy, she soon finds herself in the capable hands of the beautiful Dr Maria Moran. Everything goes wonderfully until Gemma starts doubting Maria's intentions and begins listening to the wrong people.

But has Maria something to hide, or is it a case of swapping trust for insecurity, respect for jealousy and finishing with a world of heartbreak and deceit? Can Gemma stop her actions before it's too late? Or will she ruin the best thing to happen in her life?

Given her track record, anything is possible…

# Puppy Love

L.T. Smith

ISBN: 978-3-95533-144-3
Length: 158 pages

Ellie Anderson has given up on love. Her philosophy is "Why let someone in when all they do is leave?" So instead, she fills her life with work and dodges her sister's matchmaking.

Then she meets Charlie—a gorgeous, brown-eyed Border Terrier. Charlie is in need of love and a home, prompting Ellie to open the doors to feeling once again.

However, she isn't the only one who is falling for the pup's charms.

Emily Carson is her rival for Charlie's affection, thus starting what can only be classed as a working relationship.

By allowing herself to love Charlie, can Ellie open her heart to anyone else?

# Hot Line

Alison Grey

ISBN: 978-3-95533-048-4
Length: 114 pages

Two women from different worlds.

Linda, a successful psychologist, uses her work to distance herself from her own loneliness.

Christina works for a sex hotline to make ends meet.

Their worlds collide when Linda calls Christina's sex line. Christina quickly realizes Linda is not her usual customer. Instead of wanting phone sex, Linda makes an unexpected proposition. Does Christina dare accept the offer that will change both their lives?

# L.A. Metro
(second edition)

RJ Nolan

ISBN: 978-3-95533-041-5
Length: 349 pages

Dr. Kimberly Donovan's life is in shambles. After her medical ethics are questioned, first her family, then her closeted lover, the Chief of the ER, betray her. Determined to make a fresh start, she flees to California and L.A. Metropolitan Hospital.

Dr. Jess McKenna, L.A. Metro's Chief of the ER, gives new meaning to the phrase emotionally guarded, but she has her reasons.

When Kim and Jess meet, the attraction is immediate. Emotions Jess has tried to repress for years surface. But her interest in Kim also stirs dark memories. They settle for friendship, determined not to repeat past mistakes, but secretly they both wish things could be different.

Will the demons from Jess's past destroy their future before it can even get started? Or will L.A. Metro be a place to not only heal the sick, but to mend wounded hearts?

# Broken Faith
(revised edition)

Lois Cloarec Hart

ISBN: 978-3-95533-056-9
Length: 415 pages

Emotional wounds aren't always apparent, and those that haunt Marika and Rhiannon are deep and lasting.

On the surface, Marika appears to be a wealthy, successful lawyer, while Rhiannon is a reclusive, maladjusted loner. But Marika, in her own way, is as damaged as the younger Rhiannon. When circumstances throw them together one summer, they begin to reach out, each finding unexpected strengths in the other.

However, even as inner demons are gradually vanquished and old hurts begin to heal, evil in human form reappears. The cruelly enigmatic Cass has used and controlled Marika in the past, and she aims to do so again.

Can Marika find it within herself to break free? Can she save her young friend from Cass' malevolent web? With the support of remarkable friends, the pair fights to break free—of their crippling pasts and the woman who will own them or kill them.

# Coming Home
(revised edition)

Lois Cloarec Hart

ISBN: 978-3-95533-064-4
Length: approx. 440 pages

A triangle with a twist, Coming Home is the story of three good people caught up in an impossible situation.

Rob, a charismatic ex-fighter pilot severely disabled with MS, has been steadfastly cared for by his wife, Jan, for many years. Quite by accident one day, Terry, a young writer/postal carrier, enters their life and turns it upside down.

Injecting joy and turbulence into their quiet existence, Terry draws Rob and Jan into her lively circle of family and friends until the growing attachment between the two women begins to strain the bonds of love and loyalty, to Rob and each other.

# COMING FROM
# YLVA PUBLISHING

http://www.ylva-publishing.com

# Conflict of Interest
(revised edition)

Jae

Workaholic Detective Aiden Carlisle isn't looking for love—and certainly not at the law enforcement seminar she reluctantly agreed to attend. But the first lecturer is not at all what she expected.

Psychologist Dawn Kinsley has just found her place in life. After a failed relationship with a police officer, she has sworn never to get involved with another cop again, but she feels a connection to Aiden from the very first moment.

Can Aiden keep from crossing the line when a brutal crime threatens to keep them apart before they've even gotten together?

# In a Heartbeat
RJ Nolan

Veteran police officer Sam McKenna has no trouble facing down criminals on a daily basis but breaks out in a sweat at the mere mention of commitment. A recent failed relationship strengthens her resolve to stick with her trademark no-strings-attached affairs.

Dr. Riley Connolly, a successful trauma surgeon, has spent her whole life trying to measure up to her family's expectations. And that includes hiding her sexuality from them.

When a routine call sends Sam to the hospital where Riley works, the two women are hurtled into a life-and-death situation. The incident binds them together. But can there be any future for a commitment-phobic cop and a closeted, workaholic doctor?

# Still Life
L.T. Smith

After breaking off her relationship with a female lothario, Jess Taylor decides she doesn't want to expose herself to another cheating partner. Staying at home, alone, suits her just fine. Her idea of a good night is an early one—preferably with a good book. Well, until her best friend, Sophie Harrison, decides it's time Jess rejoined the human race.

Trying to pull Jess from her self-imposed prison, Sophie signs them both up for a Still Life art class at the local college. Sophie knows the beautiful art teacher, Diana Sullivan, could be the woman her best friend needs to move on with her life.

But, in reality, could art bring these two women together? Could it be strong enough to make a masterpiece in just twelve sessions? And, more importantly, can Jess overcome her fear of being used once again?

Only time will tell.

**Hearts and Flowers Border**
© by L.T. Smith

ISBN 978-3-95533-179-5

Also available as e-book.


Published by Ylva Publishing, legal entity of Ylva Verlag, e.Kfr.

Ylva Verlag, e.Kfr.
Owner: Astrid Ohletz
Am Kirschgarten 2
65830 Kriftel
Germany

http://www.ylva-publishing.com

First Edition: 2006 by PD Publishing
Revised second edition: March 2014

Credits:
Edited by Day Petersen
Cover Design by Amanda Chron

65908696R00191

Made in the USA
Lexington, KY
28 July 2017